# The Yellowstone Faithful

It's bad enough when a VIP's daughter is killed by a grizzly in Yellowstone National Park. But when the park's most famous feature stops working, people start to listen seriously to a crafty and radical environmentalist who says the park should be closed to the public for good.

In this fast-paced adventure, two rangers are left to fight a steamroller of interests determined to chain the gates of the world's oldest and best national park.

*"Kyle Hannon hits the nail on the head when he writes about the conflicting philosophies of preservation and use in the National Park Service. The conflict between those who want to 'use' the parks and those who would prefer to restrict human use goes back over 150 years in this country. Leaders such as John Muir leaned towards a more preservationist philosophy whereas Gifford Pinchot, considered the father of the U.S. Forest Service and a close associate of Teddy Roosevelt, was more inclined to permit 'wise use.'"*

James M. Ridenour

Director, National Park Service, 1989-1993

Author, *The National Parks Compromised: Pork Barrel Politics and America's Treasures*

And the debate continues...

# The Yellowstone Faithful

### by Kyle Hannon

*Nancy,*

*Thanks for all your input.*

**Filibuster Press, Elkhart, Indiana**

# The Yellowstone Faithful
## by Kyle Hannon

Published by:
Filibuster Press
55836 Riverdale Drive
Elkhart, Indiana 46514

0987654321

Cover Design by Gregory R. Miller, Indianapolis, Indiana

*To my wonderful family*
*and to the Lake Lodge crew of '84- '86*

# *ONE*

"Please, God, don't let that be a bear."

Jennifer Patrick trembled, alone, inside her tent. Outside she could hear snorting, grunting and tearing. The thin nylon walls of her only shelter did nothing to keep every detail of sound away from her. She was awakened when the whatever-it-was ripped her properly hung backpack from its hiding place 50 yards away. Now she listened, horrified, as her pack was being destroyed so the offending animal could get tomorrow's breakfast and lunch.

Moose don't do that. Elk don't do that. Even pesky marmots don't do that.

Trying not to do anything to draw attention to herself, Jennifer surveyed her belongings. With quivering hands she carefully and quietly felt around her sleeping bag, inside and out. No food in her tent. That's good. What else might attract a bear? She had changed from the clothes she cooked in before she came to bed. She wasn't menstruating.

*There can be no reason that bear will come over here. He'll eat his fill from my pack and go on his way,* she told herself, not convincingly.

She focused every sense in the direction of the noise, trying to see what could not be seen through the flimsy tent wall. Inside her small dome-shaped shelter, she certainly felt her rapidly pounding heart. Could she hear it? No matter. The thumping in her chest couldn't drown out the sounds of tearing, eating, digging and snorting outside.

After minutes that seemed like days, the heavy sounds of the creature moved toward the tent. Not fast. Not slow. But steady. And direct.

Jennifer looked around for a fast escape but the dull walls of the tent provided no insight. If she could unzip the door flap quickly, which was unlikely, where would she go? She whimpered and tried to remember the campsite. Her tent was between three or four lodgepole pines, the tall, straight trees used to make utility poles. Could she climb any of them? Should she stay put and see if the bear would leave her alone?

Now the heavy footsteps were right next to her. She could hear the bear, smell the bear and -- following a quick tearing of the flimsy tent fabric -- see the bear.

****************

"Now's your chance, Eva," said park ranger Dusty Steward into his phone.

"Already?" responded the groggy, just-went-to-bed voice of Eva Lacy, a ranger from another part of the park.

Earlier that evening, Steward and Lacy had been talking over drinks at Lake Lodge. The two knew *of* each other before then but had never worked together. Steward, a

District Ranger, lived near Yellowstone Lake. Lacy, a geyser expert, was based across the park at Old Faithful. She had been complaining to him that ever since she switched from being a Visitor Protection Ranger to a Ranger Naturalist, she never got to go on any ranger adventures. Steward had promised to oblige her.

"Sorry," he sighed into the phone. "Adventure never sleeps. But you get this night at least. Meet me at the Turbid Lake trail head at sunup, if you still want to do this."

"Oh, I'll be there," she said with agitation at the challenge. "What's going on?"

"A young lady was camping by herself and didn't show up when she was supposed to. I've gotta go check it out, but we don't go before morning."

"Are you getting a search team ready?" she asked.

"It's in the works, but I'm supposed to do it quietly, almost secretly."

"Huh?" her voice was much more alert now.

"I guess Marks doesn't want to draw any attention to this. He wants me to go in first, in case she's just loafing or something." He frowned. Lacy sounded puzzled by the clandestine technique, and it didn't seem quite right to him either. But Bobby Marks was the park's Chief Ranger, Steward's boss. If Marks said to go quietly, he'd go quietly.

"Anyway," he continued, "I'm supposed to pick someone to go with me. Marks approved you. A few hours ago you said you wanted to go on a back-country adventure with me some time. This may not be anything, but are you still interested?"

"It sounds kind of weird. All the secrecy, I mean. But I'll be there," she said. "Thanks for thinking of me."

After they hung up, Steward stared at the phone.

"After a couple beers you said my job sounded exciting," he said to the phone. "Let me know what you think tomorrow."

*And after a couple beers I thought she looked pretty good*, he thought. *I hope I didn't just drag her into something awful. Not a very good first date.*

With a humph, he flopped into bed and waited for a fitful sleep to take over.


As morning sunlight leaked over the Absaroka Mountains, the two rangers met at the trail head. They checked their packs for their short hike to Turbid Lake. The sky was the kind of clear blue that one can only see in the Rocky Mountains. And the air was incredibly fresh, except for the faint hint of sulfur from an unseen hot spring. This promised to be a beautiful July morning, and Steward cursed to himself that he had to spend it looking for a girl who had probably made a stupid mistake. He hated this part of his job.

"So what's the deal? You didn't tell me much on the phone last night." Lacy was looking around, taking in the scenery, but evidently trying to look focused.

Steward sized her up in the light of a new day, trying to decide if she was ready to tromp around in this part of his world. Fairly tall for a woman, with a strong build and shoulder-length brown hair pulled into a pony tail that hung below the back of her ranger hat. Her blue eyes were serious and intent. Among the rangers she had a reputation as a hard worker, though not many slackers worked in Yellowstone. He knew he cut a pretty imposing figure himself. Over six feet tall, unusually broad, strong shoulders, able to out-hike and out-climb most of the other rangers. But she looked like she would keep up okay. Besides, she bragged last night that she put in the time and training to keep her law enforcement commission active.

"A group of park employees called the ranger station in a panic last night because one of their friends didn't return from a camping trip," he started. "Now we get to go in to try and bring the camper back to safety. It's not so unusual. A lot of hikers underestimate the length of hikes or they don't count on the fatigue factor. You and me and every other ranger is prepared to handle missing hiker situations."

"Dusty, you don't have to shield me from the details. This isn't the usual case, is it? That's why you were called in." Her eyes were probing. "The missing girl and her friends were camping at Turbid Lake which has been closed to hikers and campers for the last three seasons because it's a notorious bear area."

"Right. Of course, some of the college kids who work here think we close areas to give them a challenge," he said with a sour tone.

Hoisting their packs, the rangers started the trail, boots crunching on small rocks and dry dirt. The activity of hiking, with its surrounding sights and sounds of nature, lifted his spirits. It always did.

"You know, this really is a beautiful place," he offered. The cool air. The blue sky. The mountains and scented pine trees. Every step was a step into a postcard.

"Never get used to it, do you?" she responded cheerily, obviously feeling the same natural lift he was experiencing. "I don't know how many times I've seen Old Faithful erupt, but it is still great every time. We're lucky to work here."

He nodded. The millions of tourists who came and went each summer only got a taste of what he and Lacy lived. For most visitors, the typical visit to Yellowstone followed relatively safe boardwalks and roads. A visit along these thoroughfares rewarded the traveler with beautiful and fantastic scenery. But such a visit covered less than 1 percent of the park. Park employees, who spent the entire summer in Yellowstone, had more time, opportunity and temptation to venture into the back country. Early on, this was not a problem as employees were somewhat cautious. But continued hikes bred imprudent confidence. Steward's thoughts darkened.

"A couple weeks in the wild and they think they're damned Jim Bridger," he added, referring to a famous fur trapper from before the park was a park. Bridger was the kind of early adventurer that now had things named after him.

"Dusty, people around here think *you're* damned Jim Bridger. I've had to find my share of people who wandered too far, or suffered heat exhaustion waiting for Old Faithful to erupt. But I wanted to tag along with you once, because you get all the assignments that are ..." She hesitated. "Um, a little tricky."

Steward grimaced. He must have talked too much at the bar last night. Or his friends did. The truth was that most hikes were more beautiful than dangerous. And most cases with missing hikers had happy endings. However, when circumstances hinted that the hiker or hikers may not be coming back in one piece, Steward was usually called into action. He wasn't sure how he had become known as a specialist in unpleasant search missions. A few years back, during his first search assignment, he found the body of a hiker who had fallen off a cliff and broken his neck. Steward climbed up a treacherous cliff and brought the body down, nearly breaking his own neck several times. His supervisors were impressed with the heroic retrieval. And when the parents came to claim the remains, they were so grateful for his effort that they sent a commendation letter all the way to the Secretary of the Interior in Washington, D.C.

Since then, every time a climber was missing and probably dead, or someone had not returned from an illegal soaking journey to one of the park's many hot springs, Steward was called to try and find the victim, alive or otherwise. It wasn't a job he asked for, but he was willing to tolerate the unpleasantness if it meant his job was secure in Yellowstone, the world's oldest and best national park.

He looked at Lacy again. Even with long sleeves and slacks she revealed a strong, fit body. The help would be appreciated. Besides, she was kind of pretty. He stopped to take a swig of water. Normally he wouldn't be thirsty already, but he needed to stop and refocus his thoughts. He looked around to take in the refreshing scenery of tall trees and blue sky. Momentarily rejuvenated, he started down the trail again, delivering a briefing over his shoulder as he walked.

"The employees, including the missing girl, work at

Canyon Lodge. They sneaked into the closed Turbid Lake campsites three nights ago. They said the first night went by without incident and all the campers had a good time. Their original plan was to camp for only one night, but one camper, Jenny Patrick, decided to stay another night by herself."

"There's some good thinking," Lacy added sarcastically.

He continued. "She didn't return the next morning. She wasn't expected at work until late afternoon so nobody thought much about it. When the sun set and she was four hours late for work her friends started to worry."

"Why did it take them so long?"

Steward shrugged. "I guess she had a lot of friends, but they said she was basically a loner, if that makes sense. It was like her to extend her stay as long as possible and barely make it back in time to work. They admitted she had done at least one solo camping trip before with no problems. This time they thought she was late because she had trouble finding a ride back."

"Didn't she have a car?"

"None of them did. If they parked at the trail head, we would have seen their cars and caught them."

"And they get such crappy pay they couldn't afford a fine."

"Yeah, they don't get the huge salaries we do," he said cynically. "Anyway, they arranged to have friends drop them off and pick them up at the trail head. Jenny planned to hitchhike back after camping one more night."

Lacy said nothing for a moment, boots crunching

along the dry dirt trail. Finally she said, "So when she didn't make it back in time for work they began to panic. Despite the risk of a fine, they called the rangers at Canyon, confessed their illegal adventure, and begged for a search party to locate Jenny."

"Right, and they were told we couldn't initiate a search until daybreak. It's not like the park is lighted for nighttime activities. To ease the kids' panic the Canyon rangers suggested that Jenny was probably taking one more unauthorized night under the stars."

"Of course, the rangers didn't believe that garbage themselves. Hitchhiking is pretty safe in the park, compared to bedding down with bears at Turbid Lake. So they called you and told you to be ready first thing in the morning," she added.

"That's me. Death scout," Steward brooded.

Lacy didn't reply and the two walked on quietly. Finally, she spoke up.

"It still seems weird that they want to keep it quiet. I mean, if she's lost they should have a mob of us out looking. If she's dead, well, I guess they don't need that many. But still …"

"Nevertheless, here we go." He was already beginning to regret having chosen Lacy to tag along. It wasn't that he didn't think she could handle it, but there was something odd about their entire mission. His tasks tended to be unpredictable anyway, and this one was shaping up to be even more so. Here he was, taking a stranger into a strange situation. Not the safest thing to do. He had worked with a handful of other rangers before, knew what to expect from them. Why didn't he choose one of them? On the other hand, she seemed sharp enough. And they were keeping up a good pace. He breathed deeply.

Once again the trail, trees and air worked their magic. He felt better already.

"Eva, thanks for coming along."

"No problem," she murmured. Embarrassed perhaps.

The two walked silently for some time, each in their own thoughts. The trail shrunk in front of them and lengthened behind them.

After a while Lacy spoke up in a cheery voice. "Maybe she really is just lost."

Steward gave her a skeptical glance. Turbid Lake was only about two miles off the road, along a well-marked trail. In fact, they were approaching the campsite already and they had been hiking less than an hour.

"But if she went exploring deeper into the back country, then she might have merely gotten turned around and spent a chilly night or two under a pine tree."

"But why here?" snorted Steward. "Why do we even bother to close areas because of bear activity? It's like begging some of these people to come here. We do it for the safety of the bears and for the safety of the people, but it's so damned important for some people to see a bear before the summer's over. Well, this girl might have gotten a closer look than she wanted."

He continued to sulk about his role as the messenger of death.

"But to hear you talk last night, you think the park is better off with people scrambling over the trails," she taunted.

He actually smiled. "Yeah, I did kind of go on about that, especially after a couple Watneys. But it's true. As goofy as some people may be, the bad mistakes some of them make, the park is a lot better off if the visitors keep coming."

"I think they damage the place," she said.

If she was egging him on, it wasn't going to work. "Sometimes the place damages them. And that's when we have to be careful."

"You know, Dusty, we're jumping the gun here. I mean, lots of people camp in bear areas without any problems. You and I have each been out to find lost hikers before. It's no big deal. Just because the bears have been active doesn't mean this is any different. I bet she's just wandering around, looking–"

Steward had stopped suddenly and raised his hand to get her to do the same. They both stood motionless, as Steward sniffed the air. He looked a little like a dog, but Lacy didn't laugh at him. In the cool, clean air of Yellowstone, it is possible for humans to be more sensitive to scents than when they are in a city. Certainly, a human nose is no match for other snouts in the animal kingdom, but once a person got used to filtering out the sulfur smells from the park's thermal features, he could quickly notice the scent of anything unusual. Lacy raised her head slightly and joined in the sniffing.

Bears smell very well, but they don't smell very good, and both rangers caught a whiff of a strong, musty odor.

Steward glanced at Lacy who acknowledged the sign and reached over her shoulder to take her rifle off her pack. He readied his own weapon.

"Well, I guess we'll just wander into the campsite and look around!" shouted Steward.

"Yeah, I'm with you!" Lacy yelled back.

The conversation wasn't as important as the volume. Basically, bears do not like to be around people. If they hear people coming, they usually run off. Steward and Lacy had been talking the past few minutes, but maybe not loudly enough. Now they were compensating. The next to last thing they wanted to do was surprise a grizzly.

The last thing they wanted to do was have a grizzly surprise them. The bears that didn't flee might be curious. Or aggressive. If the rangers were distracted before, they were tuned in now. Steward slowed the pace, noticing the trail, the trees, the bushes. Everything.

After another 50 yards, he stopped again. "Look at this," he said as he picked up a crumpled mess of nylon and aluminum.

Lacy had an uneasy look on her face. She could recognize the debris as the remains of an overnight backpack. Steward watched her eyes hesitantly follow a trail of pots, containers and clothing that led to a lodgepole pine. From one of its straight, dark branches hung a severed piece of rope.

"At least she tried to hang her food," she said.

"You all right?" he asked with genuine concern. She looked a little shaky.

She nodded, without making eye contact.

Cautiously, Steward advanced to the next tree down the trail, where something had caught his eye. He reached up with his hand spread against vertical gashes in the bark. Bears score trees to mark their territory and to condition their claws. The sap-oozing tree marks were farther apart than Steward's hand.

"Bigger than you," Lacy said.

"Bigger than you and me together," Steward responded quietly.

He continued slowly down the trail, Lacy close behind. As he stepped through some brush he got his first view of the campsite. About 20 yards away he saw another pile of nylon, larger than the backpack, but equally mangled. Tent remnants.

Then another smell caught him. A rotten smell that burned his nose and penetrated every pore, unsettling his guts. It was an odor never forgotten and one he had smelled far too often.

"Better radio back that we've got a fatality. I'll look around and see if I can tell where the bear went," he said, proceeding cautiously.

Lacy grabbed her radio, blurted out the brief message, and ran to catch up with Steward.

They met at the former tent and began a visual sweep. Where was the body? And where would a bear hide? The smell of both were around, but not directional. The rangers were standing in a small clump of trees. Lodgepole pines are very tall and very straight, with few low branches. A large bear neither could, nor would, try to hide behind one. The trail they followed into the camp was more wooded, offering slightly more cover, but besides the claw marks they hadn't seen any sign of the animal on their way in. Then there was the lake, not far from the campsite. No place for a bear to hide there. On the other side of the lake were hills, too far away for immediate concern. That left the continuation of the trail they had followed in.

Slowly, weapons drawn, they followed the trail north. With a buzzing whoosh a black cloud rose and fell nearby. The rangers would have marched right past the spot had those flies not caught their attention.

Steward spat and kicked dust angrily. "I know what that is." He tromped toward the swarm.

Just off the trail, in a clump of tall grass, a small mound of dirt and pine needles was alive with the whirring of insects. No other life was present. Lacy began to gag as she realized what was partially buried before her.

He led her to a log to sit. *She'll be fine in a minute. I hope. I don't want to drag two bodies out of here.*

"Please be careful," he advised. "They don't usually stray too far from their stash."

She nodded without looking up.

He continued another hundred yards. Nothing. Giving up on the bear he returned to examine the campsite.

A crumpled sleeping bag pushed through a long slice in one wall of the tent, which was now lying in a heap of nylon. The shock-cord tent poles were not broken but disconnected from the tent base and unable to provide any support.

Taking it all in, Steward formed a pretty good picture of what had happened. The bear had cut open the tent and dragged her out, pulling the sleeping bag with her. The ranger frowned at the torn bag, Holofil stuffing poking out holes and tears in the outer fabric. Near the bag a large dark area in the ground betrayed where most of the bleeding took place. The bear probably began to feed right there.

From that point Steward could easily see the trail where the bear dragged her over to bury …. He finally noticed that Lacy was still hunched, hands on her knees, not saying anything.

Steward walked over to her and gently took her by the shoulders. He helped her legs over the log so she was facing away from the body and the campsite.

When her gag reflex finally subsided, she looked up. "Can you ever be fully prepared for this? I've worked some gruesome traffic fatalities in the park, but this." She gestured over her shoulder to the body. "I mean, I know how bears feed. I've seen unfinished elk carcasses dragged into shallow graves to save for later. It's just so different when it's a person."

"There's no reason for a grizzly to treat us any differently from an elk, once he decides that we're food."

"I know, but I hate being reminded of that." She shivered to try and shake off the discomfort, then stood. "What do you suppose happened?"

"It looks like our bear smelled food in her backpack," Steward said, pointing over to the first mess they discovered. "The girl hung her pack like she was supposed to, but it

wasn't high enough. Our bear must be a pretty tall one."
While they were talking they walked back along the trail
toward the demolished backpack.

He continued, "After he cleaned out all the food and
tossed things around, he followed the trail toward the
campsite." Steward stopped, turned and began walking
toward the mangled tent. Lacy was right behind him.

"Over here near the tent he dug up something. They
might have left a dirty campsite," he continued. He kicked at
the hole in the ground. "Man, you've gotta put your food
away."

"Do you suppose the girl heard him?" she asked.

"Who knows? Bears aren't exactly quiet." They
stopped at the tent. Steward bent down and ran his finger
along a large slice in the side of the tent, next to the torn
sleeping bag.

"The bear smelled something inside," he said.
"Usually, the human scent will drive a bear off, but this one
is either not afraid, or else the girl had a candy bar with her or
something else that was too tempting to resist. So he stuck out
one claw and sliced through the tent, just like a surgeon with
a knife."

"I'm sure she was awake by then," Lacy murmured.

He nodded. The thought of the terror the girl must
have felt made his skin crawl. By the look on Lacy's face, she
felt it too.

"Yeah, I expect her thrashing pissed off the bear," he
said, trying to remain professional. "It looks like he knocked
the tent around, then dragged her out of the hole he made. She

either rolled or crawled over here, and this is where the bear probably killed her."

Lacy turned away again. Steward didn't notice and continued to follow the deadly path from the feeding spot to the temporary burial ground. He looked at the body. There was a shallow layer of dirt on top, but the human form was unmistakable. And the stench of death was unrelenting.

"Poor girl. I hope she died quickly."

"Where do you suppose the bear is?" asked Lacy. Steward jumped, unaware that his partner was no longer beside him. He looked at Lacy, over by the tent, facing the other direction. Lacy seemed pretty tough, but a fatal mauling is difficult to face. Steward himself had vomited the first time he was assigned to one. This time he knew what to expect.

"He took off. I don't know if we scared him away when he heard us coming up the trail, or if he was already gone."

Again, he looked around, not quite convinced they weren't being watched.

"Usually they try to defend their kill," he said cautiously. "This bear might be out finding some other food and come back here later."

He looked at Lacy, who was also surveying their surroundings.

"Anyway," he added. "I would guess this is as good a spot as any to set a trap."

Lacy's radio cackled, startling both rangers. "Lacy, Steward, we're at the trail head with the equipment, do you read?" "Equipment" meant a body bag and other devices used to collect evidence.

Lacy took the radio off her belt and spoke into it. "Okay. Steward says we need a bear trap."

"Ten-four," replied the radio. "Can I talk to him?"

Steward unhooked his own radio. "Yeah?"

"Steward, you won't need to call the parents. Someone else is taking care of it."

"I can't say I'm disappointed, but I *am* curious. Who gets the job?"

"Hershauer."

Steward looked at Lacy. She, too, was shocked. Steward turned back to the radio, "As in Jerome Hershauer, Secretary of the Interior?"

"Affirmative." The voice on the radio was uneasy. "Look, I'd rather not talk about this over the airwaves. I'll explain when we get there. We're on ATVs so it won't take long."

Steward and Lacy sat on a log by the trail, waiting for their colleagues to come and tell them the news.

Upon hearing the details, Steward sat shocked for a moment.

"Well," he finally said. "That explains why they were trying to keep this search quiet."

# TWO

How tragic. Jenny Patrick, the only daughter of U.S. Senator Phil Patrick, was killed by a bear, in a national park, no less. Lester Crane tightened his narrow jaw and reflected.

How sad. How horrible. How ... perfect.

News of Senator Patrick's loss spread quickly. The Associated Press wire story was picked up by nearly every newspaper, radio and television station in the country. On Capitol Hill the Senator's colleagues delivered compassionate speeches on the floors of the House and Senate. And the Patricks were flooded with sympathy cards from concerned constituents and lobbying organizations.

That could have been the end of it.

Most people saw the death of Jenny Patrick as a woeful story. The unfortunate young girl should have her whole life in front of her, they thought. Cut down in her prime. Freak accident, really. Who's ever heard of a bear attack, a fatal one at that. Darned shame. On with our own lives.

Then there was the small portion of the public who felt no sadness. Most of that perpetually resentful group viewed the story with a serves-her-right-for-breaking-the-rules attitude. Girls from a privileged background usually get away with murder. Now one of them is a victim of it.

And of the remorseless segment of the population, there was an even smaller minority. They saw her death as an opportunity. Lester Crane was a proud member of that tiny minority. For him, tragedy was not to be mourned. It was to be used to advance a cause.

"Got it. Randy come here please," said Crane, sitting on the floor of his office between two stacks of newspapers, an open file in his lap, clutching a yellowed news clipping. He was only slightly yellowed himself. Years of fighting the good fight in the arena of public opinion and legislation had left a few lines around the eyes and mouth. Brown-becoming-gray hair was longer than fashionable for anyone his age, outside the movement. Currently the strands were pulled back into a ponytail that hung just below his frayed collar.

His disheveled clothes fit in well with his surroundings. The cluttered office was adorned with only plain furnishings and two posters on the wall. One poster was a boot advertisement that showed a rugged hiker on a mountain top. The other ad displayed a freestyle rock climber hanging confidently from a negative pitch. It was a great picture but Crane disapproved of a few of the company's obscure corporate policies so he had cut out all references to the product. Stacks of files, newspapers and magazines were piled around the office. To visitors it appeared haphazard but Crane swore he had a personal system of organization.

Since the announcement of Jenny Patrick's death, Crane had been scrambling through his personal system, swearing quite a bit, looking for information to support the case he was preparing to make to the American public.

"Did you find your bear, Les?"

Crane looked up to acknowledge Randy Pierce. A twenty-year-old idealist, Pierce was spending his summer break from Indiana University as an unpaid intern for Crane's organization, People for the Environmental Way.

The young man looked a little like Crane. About the same height, maybe slightly heavier. His dirty blonde hair was long, but not enough for a ponytail.

"Yeah, Randy. Could you make about ten copies of this for me?"

Pierce received the clipping as Crane hopped into a squeaky surplus office chair to face a blank computer screen. He was not intimidated by the emptiness. He knew that within a few minutes, and after furious click-click-clicking on the keyboard, the screen would be full.

"Yesterday we were pulling together information about the wastefulness of wooden chopsticks in Japan," Pierce interrupted. "Why the switch? Why the bear stuff?"

Crane looked at his watch, at the blank monitor, back to his watch, and decided he had time to answer.

"Mood rings," he said.

Pierce looked puzzled. "Huh?"

"How much do you know about mood rings?"

"I've heard of them. Not much really."

"I founded People for the Environmental Way about the same time mood rings were a hot item." Crane reached into his desk drawer and pulled out a metallic ring with a large glass oval on it. He tossed it to Pierce. "Here, put this on. That dark patch under the glass is supposed to change color to let the world know what kind of mood you're in."

The intern looked at him and the ring skeptically.

"Exactly," said Crane, answering the look. "Pretty stupid. But they were a big deal in the '70s. So was my little organization. These rings have faded into history but People for the Environmental Way is still the most confrontational and successful environmental group in America. That's because I've been able to adapt and keep from being yesterday's fad."

Crane would never admit it but in this way not-for-profit special interest groups like his were like the industries he hated. Just as businesses needed to improve and update thier products to maintain strong sales, groups like PEW had to be innovative to keep their ideas fresh. That was the key to a constant flow of donations. Crane avoided using that analogy.

Pierce tossed back the ring. Crane continued.

"I keep this around to remind myself that if I don't want PEW to go the way of the mood ring I've got to stay on the cutting edge of issues. I know you're up-to-date on our issues of the last five years but how much do you know about the first five years?"

"I've heard of the PEW stickers. And they mention you in some of my history classes but I don't know many details," Pierce said.

"When I founded the group in the early 1970s, some cynics laughed at the acronym. 'How could a group called

PEW be taken seriously,' they asked. 'Why didn't you just name yourselves YUCK or BELCH or something equally ridiculous?'

"I knew it wasn't a foolish name. It was intentional. I founded PEW around the topic of air pollution, which was the big issue of the time. I identified the nation's biggest polluters and urged the public to boycott their products. To help the public know which products to avoid, my volunteers entered stores and marked those products with a bright orange sticker bearing 'PEW' in white letters. People understand that air pollution stinks. When they drive past a smelly factory, they say, 'Pew, that stinks.' The acronym caught on."

He stood up and started gathering some of the papers on his desk. Sorting work and chatting with a young idealist at the same time was no big deal.

"The companies and the retailers were furious, but they could never catch the 'PEW Police' who were marking their products. The stickers were one of the first environmental guerilla actions in this country and I'm proud of it. News teams covered it. Most media and policymakers denounced it. But the public learned about it. By the time the three networks and the major newspapers were through criticizing me and my group, every shopper knew exactly what a PEW sticker meant. Eventually, the companies began to control their emissions."

He sat back down in his chair and began arranging news clippings and notes.

"Sure, they first tried to intimidate me," he added. "Every day, I was contacted by an attorney, issued a restraining order or otherwise threatened. But they couldn't catch us in the act. A good prosecutor could have made a solid case against me. But the bottom line was that public sentiments in the 1970s were turning toward environmental issues. No prosecutor interested in a lengthy career would have been interested in standing up *for* air pollution.

"PEW was unscathed and I'm proud to say I became a hero of the environmental movement." Crane could read the admiration in Pierce's face. "Within a few years, PEW stickers lost their novelty and I quit printing them. I moved on to other topics and tactics. TV specials that look back at the '70s inevitably mention the stickers. That's probably why you've heard of them. And even twenty years later an occasional sticker strike occurs in the middle of Missouri or someplace but I have nothing to do with those."

Pointing to the news clipping in Pierce's hand Crane added, "I think we have a winner this time. As you see in that article, I've criticized the National Park Service for its bear management policies in the past. Now, with the death of Jenny Patrick, it looks like the issue will be a good one again." He turned back to the computer and began manipulating the keyboard.

Pierce carried the clipping to the copy machine in the next room. His father was a fat-cat executive with one of the coal companies in Southern Indiana. Predictably, Pierce showed his appreciation for his privileged upbringing by rebelling against everything Big Daddy stood for. Many a dinner table conversation erupted into a heated discussion about acid rain. The week before he took the internship was a doozy.

"How can you stand yourself knowing your precious coal is killing the forests and streams in the East?" it started.

"People have got to have electricity, Randy. It's got to come from somewhere and I remember you griping about nuclear power. For me, I'm more concerned about radiation than some half-baked theory about burning coal turning into acid," Dad replied. He used to get red in the face and scream, but Randy's mother convinced him that he would burst an artery if he didn't learn to control himself.

"Besides," she had told him, "Randy's just a young man exploring his limits."

Randy felt his dad's calmer demeanor and his mom's "help" were merely acts to placate him. Besides, he was beyond exploring and was firmly committed to pushing.

"It's not either/or. There are choices besides burning filthy coal and toying with radioactivity. If it wasn't for companies like yours and their influence in Washington, our government could have promoted safe, clean alternate fuels by now."

"Yeah, right. Like what."

"Like solar power, Dad. It's clean, it's renewable, and you can get it without raping the earth with your mining equipment."

Mr. Pierce responded with a smirk. He then made a big production out of leaning back in his chair and peering over his shoulder, through the window to the gray, overcast sky. It was winter in Indiana and the sun hadn't been seen for the past three days. He turned back to Randy, still smirking.

With that, Randy threw his fork down on his plate and

stormed up to his room, slamming the door and cranking up his stereo.

The music was blaring but he was tuned into his father's voice enough to hear him say, "You're right, Honey. It *is* much more pleasant when I don't scream at him."

One argument Mr. Pierce avoided was the fact that electricity produced by coal had cooked Randy's food, warmed his house and even powered his loud stereo. Randy knew his dad was often tempted to remind him of that fact, but Mom and Dad were afraid that would sound like an invitation for him to leave home. And, to be truthful, he probably would have taken it that way. Whether he wanted to leave or not, he would have felt like his back was against the wall. Gotta stand up for principles.

He knew his parents still loved him, they just hadn't yet come around to his way of thinking. And at the end of high school, when Randy informed them he wanted to attend Indiana University's School of Public and Environmental Affairs, he could see Dad fighting the temptation to mention that coal profits were going to be paying for his education too. But Dad let it go. The saving grace that kept the tuition checks coming was his dad's misplaced hope that Randy would wise up and transfer over to IU's renowned School of Business.

But Randy didn't "wise up." He was in his second year with SPEA, and loved it. He concentrated on environmental issues. When he heard about a summer internship with PEW, he immediately applied.

Mr. Pierce wasn't too thrilled. Didn't most college kids find summer jobs that actually paid money? Leave it to his boy to find a position that would cost him money for room and board but would pay no salary. In addition, he would be working to fight an industry that fed his family and paid for his schooling.

"When you're pruning a tree, you don't cut the branch you're standing on," he told Randy.

Randy answered by launching a tirade about the evils of clear cutting in the Hoosier National Forest.

Mr. Pierce just scratched his head and didn't say any more about it.

Now, Randy had a beat-up desk in a small office at PEW's Washington, D.C., headquarters. His duties included answering phones, organizing volunteers, keeping the web page updated and running errands for Crane. He was learning everything about running the most influential environmental group in the world. He loved it.

**\*\*\*\*\*\*\*\*\*\*\*\*\*\***

"We got him!" Ranger Joe Lowry cheered to his partner as they drove their pickup toward the large, corrugated metal pipe with heavy grating on both ends. Inside, a snarling grizzly eyed them with a combination of hatred and fear.

"First trap too. We knew he'd come back here," replied the other ranger.

"Big sucker. It'll be a shame to lose him."

"Yeah, but it would be a bigger shame to let him wander around eating people all summer."

"I wish we could train him to just eat the idiots,"

laughed Lowry. His partner, Bill Kruse, laughed too. Both rangers had spent enough time trying to explain to tourists the dangers of walking up to a bison for a close-up photo. The rangers understood that most visitors to Yellowstone had no concept of the wildness of the place. They tried to be patient, but it was frustrating.

"You got the PCP ready?" asked Lowry as the two men climbed out of their truck toward the trapped bear.

"You bet," said Kruse, holding up an air gun and black medicine bag. "I don't see a tag or a collar on him. Could be our guy."

Thanks in large part to the ongoing work of Dusty Steward, the Park Service knew quite a bit about many Yellowstone bears. Monitoring tags and radio collars, plus considerable time spent on the trail gave rangers and scholars the opportunity to compile profiles of known bears. Where they liked to roam. What they liked to eat. Any cubs. And, most importantly, potential threat to humans. Steward had logged the most data and seemed to have the best instincts about each bear's patterns and quirks.

When Jenny Patrick was killed the rangers poured over the profiles. Was the culprit "Chunky," an aggressive male grizzly with a big chunk out of one ear? Was it "Suede," a light-brown female in the area with cubs to protect? Steward said no.

Based on his word – he knew bears better than anyone, after all – all the park's rangers concentrated on finding an unknown, untagged bear. Could this bear in the trap be the one?

The rangers estimated the bear's weight – just over

500 pounds – to figure the proper dosage of tranquilizer. As they approached the trap, the bear gave a half-hearted lunge toward them, but the gate held. After a night of thrashing and pounding at the ungiving steel, the bear was worn out.

Lowry walked around to the back of the cage and banged on the metal with a long stick. When the bear turned around to lunge at him, the other ranger shot a tranquilizer dart into the bear's rump. He watched the bear slowly drift off to sleep while Lowry fetched the truck and backed into place behind the wheeled trap.

The park's bear traps were equipped with wheels and trailer hitches to ease the process of placement and removal. When the traps were set, one end of the tube was opened and a slab of raw meat was rigged inside at the other end. A bear who climbed into the tunnel and tugged at the meat would cause the open gate to come crashing down, effectively trapping the bear. After Jenny Patrick's death, a dozen such traps were set within a five-mile radius of the Turbid Lake campsite. The rangers hit paydirt with the trap placed on top of the spot where her tent had been.

Ordinarily, they would have pulled the drugged bear out of the trap and conducted a series of tests on the spot. That way, the bear could return to the wild – sporting a radio collar and ear tag – as soon as he woke up. A little grumpy, but no worse for wear. If this bear had a tag, the rangers would have run a few quick tests, drawn some blood for more tests in the lab, then let the bear go.

But today's catch was not meant to be returned. He was an unknown. The bear was going to Bozeman, Montana, where his droppings would be examined for hair, bone or other evidence that he was the bear that killed Jenny. Once that was determined the grizzly would be labeled a "nuisance" and destroyed.

"You know, I still get the creeps at the thought of a bear killing someone for food," said Lowry as they drove off, cage and snoozing bear in tow. "But I can't help thinking about that one *Far Side* cartoon where the two alligators are lying on shore next to an empty canoe and bits of clothing. That one gator is commenting how their last meal was so great because it didn't have any claws or shells or horns."

The other ranger laughed. "I've seen that one. You're right. It's pretty sick. But you know, I can't figure out why there aren't more bear attacks. I mean, say you're a hungry bear and walk into a clearing and you see a hiker and an elk. You've got an elk that can run pretty damned fast, and he's got a big rack on his head that could give you grief. Then you've got some guy in shorts and a tee shirt, carrying a backpack that probably has even more food in it. You can outrun him. And his only defense is to crap his pants as soon as you charge after him. Now why would you ever go after the elk?"

"Because the hiker might have a gun," Lowry replied somberly.

"Do you really believe a bear thinks about that? There's no hunting in the park. Shooting grizzlies is illegal. How do they know what a gun is?"

"I don't know. They just seem smarter than we usually give them credit."

\*\*\*\*\*\*\*\*\*\*\*\*\*\*

"Recycle some of these damned things and save a forest or two." Crane stood just inside the office door looking at a stack of old newspapers, probably a good six-months worth. The papers were leaning precariously against a dented four-drawer file cabinet, olive green except for the rust spots that had taken control where the paint had been chipped or scratched. A similar stack of news magazines decorated another corner of the wire-service reporter's office, and several photographs of the reporter in important locations with important people decorated the walls.

Phil Grossman looked up from his laptop computer and laughed as soon as he saw Crane.

"Les, I've seen your office and I know it's not much cleaner than this one. If Congress ever passes one of those mandatory recycling laws you're always begging for, we'd both have to buy furniture to take the place of our stacks."

Grossman had worked with Lester Crane on a number of environmental stories. In fact, Grossman was the first journalist from a major news source to recognize that Crane was more than a kook. The reporter saw how Crane's shrewd and calculated political maneuvering eventually produced results. When the wire service decided that environmental issues warranted a separate beat, Grossman immediately applied for the job. His first action when he won the assignment was to contact Crane and build a working relationship.

Over the years the relationship had become quite comfortable. Grossman could always call Crane when the reporter needed a fast quote to finish a story. And Crane usually went to Grossman first when the activist had a scoop.

"Phil, my stacks of paper are *very* important," Crane said, stretching out the word "very" to make it sound like he was up to something mysterious.

The reporter was amused. "Oh, here we go," he said as he leaned back in his chair with his arms stretched out and his eyes closed. "I predict you dug through your papers and files just to find some obscure article that you will now present to me. And I predict you will have some explanation about why said article is relevant today."

Crane shook his head and chuckled as he plopped down in a chair next to Grossman. He put the folder he carried on the desk in front of him and pulled out one of the photocopied articles and a news release.

The reporter held both sheets of paper in front of him, his eyes alternating back and forth between them. Grossman was good at picking up information quickly. By essentially reading both the news release and the article at the same time, he would know enough to begin asking questions within a few seconds.

"God, it gives me the creeps when you do that." Crane had a sour look on his face.

"If you're in a room full of reporters and you can't get the gist quickly, you'll never get your questions in," Grossman replied, still reading. He finished and set down the papers. "I always get my questions in first."

"Not much competition today," Crane said while looking around the office. No one else was there.

"Exclusive tip appreciated as usual, Les. Now, let's

get to it. I see you're still insane."

"Insanely committed to a cleaner world and safer wildlife, Phil."

"Come on, Les. The only angle to this Jenny Patrick death is that it's a tragedy. We all mourn the senator's loss blah, blah, blah."

"It's a tragedy all right. But she wasn't the only victim. What about the bear? You realize the rangers are out trying to trap it so they can murder it?"

"So what. The thing's a killer." Grossman usually sympathized with PEW's positions, but he always tried to argue the other side to draw out better responses from Crane.

"The bear did what bears do. What was the bear's crime? Feeding in its own feeding area? Even the Park Service knew that campground was in bear territory That's why it was closed. How long are we going to keep trespassing on grizzly property and then killing any bear that responds the way nature intended?"

Grossman was turned back to his computer, furiously keying Crane's comments.

Crane continued. "We are all saddened that one life was lost, but we should be equally saddened that soon another life will be taken too. And the second life lost will in no way make up for the first." He paused for effect. "The real tragedy … The *real* tragedy in Yellowstone is a bear policy that can only result in the deaths of more people and more bears."

Grossman nodded as he entered the last of Crane's statement. Then he turned and looked again at the news release Crane had brought him. "So your position is to close off most, if not all, of Yellowstone?"

"At the very least, close off far more than is closed now and enforce those closed zones." He pointed to the copied article. "See, we've taken this position before and if our advice had been heeded, Jenny Patrick would be alive today."

"Yeah, and millions of people would have missed seeing Old Faithful erupt. You can't believe there is much support for this."

"Look Phil, we've got to make a commitment to preserving our country's rich wildlife. Our violent and idiotic species has managed to nearly remove grizzly bears from this planet. Now we act proud because we let a few of them continue to live in Yellowstone. Well, we are going to lose those pretty quickly if things don't change.

"In a zoo, the animals are in cages and the people roam free. Well, Yellowstone's not a damned zoo. It's a nature preserve. The animals roam free. So maybe the people who go there should be kept in cages.

"I said it eight years ago," he pointed to the article one more time, "and I'll say it again. People and bears don't mix."

Grossman pressed him. "Maybe the public isn't as committed to wildlife as you think."

Crane smiled at him. "Don't underestimate public compassion for endangered species, especially when it's man's fault the animal is endangered. Public acceptance brought the wolf back to Yellowstone. I think people want to preserve the grizzlies too.

"I'll tell you what. To sweeten the pot, let the public keep its geyser. Let the throngs come see Old Faithful spit water, and then let them leave. That's what most of the visitors do anyway."

"Well, Les, you may be onto something. Between your statements and the stuff you gave me I should be able to find a story. I'll see what I can come up with." He looked at the PEW media kit and chuckled. "Only you would try to capitalize on the death of a co-ed."

"Thanks Phil. You've got a head start, but I'm going to talk to the networks this afternoon."

Phil sneered. "I hope you have your release written in crayon for the TV guys."

Crane laughed as he left.

**************

"Joe, this is Dusty Steward," the ranger said into the phone. "Did you guys get your bear up to Bozeman all right?"

Lowry replied, "No problems. The bear is contained and the samples have been taken. We should hear something by tomorrow."

"I don't need to wait for the results. Better start planning to take your bear back where you found him."

"What?!"

"You got the wrong bear."

# THREE

Steward and Lacy surveyed the damage. The trap was sprung, but there was no bear. For that matter, there wasn't much of a trap either. The heavy, corrugated pipe was dented in several places, but most severely by the lodgepole pine tree dropped across it. Ten yards away lay the grating that was supposed to be welded to one end of the trap. One tire was punctured, probably by teeth, and the axle was bent. The bait was gone.

They were about eight miles from Turbid Lake, headed south toward the little-traveled Thorofare Region. Ordinarily, the location was beautiful. The trail which had been used by the earliest explorers in Yellowstone was bordered by Yellowstone Lake to the west and the snow-capped Absaroka Mountains to the east. A visitor to the Thorofare trail could enjoy not only the scenery but also solitude because few vacationers, or even park employees, had time to wander the long trail that could take you as far from a major roadway as any place in the lower 48 states.

Currently, the two rangers were only a mile from a road, the one leading to the east entrance of the park. They weren't in the mood to enjoy the scenery and they were more than a little uncomfortable with the solitude. It would be another day before they received official word, but Steward was certain that the bear caught at Turbid Lake was not the same one that killed Jenny Patrick.

"Okay, I'll start," said Lacy. "The bear didn't tear up the trap. Instead, this tree fell and popped off the end grate. Our bear was just lucky enough to wander by and collect the bait."

"Do you believe that?" asked Steward.

"No. But I have a hard time believing a bear could destroy a trap that's supposed to be bear proof."

Steward grunted a response, then walked around the trap, taking photos and measuring footprints.

"Here's what I think," he said after some time. "I think the furry beast sniffed out the bait from some distance off. When he got here, he also smelled a human scent. From that, he figured out this was a trap. So he didn't crawl inside. Most bears would have left, but this one wanted the food so he started knocking the trap around."

"I'll bet that's when he triggered the door," Lacy added.

"And since he was outside at the time, he wasn't trapped. Instead, it just made him madder. So he started really knocking it around, pushing it over its wheel blocks and rolling it over here where he kept flailing at it. Most of these smaller dents and the flat tire probably occurred at this time."

"What about the tree?"

"Believe it or not, I think he pushed it over on purpose."

"You're kidding," Lacy laughed.

"Well, it's an old tree and it's broken off rather than uprooted. And look. Here are claw marks on the trunk. And I'll bet …" Steward said as he walked to the part of the tree that was still in the ground, "Sure enough. Bear prints. I'm not saying he calculated that a falling tree would knock the thing open, but I bet he did it to damage the trap."

Lacy was looking at the trap. "In fact," she said, "I don't think the tree even knocked the end off. Look at these claw marks on the metal. The tree probably just broke part of the weld and he tore it open the rest of the way."

She looked over to where the grating had been thrown. Her expression revealed the mental calculations of the strength it would take to break heavy iron grating from a weld and toss it 10 yards. She whistled softly.

After a moment, she added, "Why do you suppose he took the time to climb on top and defecate?"

"I think that's for us," Steward answered.

"This doesn't make sense. Surely that bear burned more calories tearing up our trap than he got out of that chunk of meat we left for him. And any bear that suspected human activity wouldn't take the risk."

"Right. That's why I think this is the one from Turbid Lake. He's not too concerned about humans. If anything, he wants to let people know who's boss."

"No way. This may not even be the one who killed the girl."

"There's only one way to find out," Steward said as he pulled a plastic bag from his pack. Carefully, and with some disgust, he scraped the bear droppings off the top of the trap into the bag. This sample would be sent to Bozeman for analysis.

**************

"... Thanks, Janice, for that look at next spring's hottest swimsuits." The attractive, dark-haired anchor man turned to face the camera. "And next up on The Scoop ..." The screen changed to a shot of two rangers dragging a limp bear out of a trap. "The rangers are trapping a record number of bears, but the Yellowstone killer is still on the loose. We've got the tape the Park Service doesn't want you to see. Stay with us."

As the commercial came on, Lester Crane pointed the remote toward the VCR and watched the ads whiz by.

"Aren't you going to miss our spot?" asked Randy Pierce.

"We bought the spot after this story. Didn't you see it last night?"

"Uh, no. I had to get my journal caught up." Mentally, Pierce kicked himself. To get credit for this internship, he had to keep a daily journal. It was a real pain in the butt and he had fallen behind. Last night, he decided to get it up-to-date and lost track of time. He hated admitting that to his boss. "Besides, I knew we were going to watch the tape today."

"That's all right." Crane punched another button on the remote. "Okay, here we go."

The screen filled with bright colors and the words

"The Scoop" in bold letters. A catchy synthesizer tune and the unmistakable sound of a clicking computer keyboard blared out of the speaker. That dissolved into the same tape of the two rangers and the limp bear. A voice-over took the place of the music. "When a senator's daughter was killed by a vicious grizzly in Yellowstone National Park, the Park Service vowed to bring that bear to justice." A tape of rangers poking bears with tranquilizer darts took over the screen. "Many bears have been caught, but so far the killer remains at large." Cut to the anchor at his desk. "Some groups are furious about the treatment toward our nation's endangered bears. The Scoop's Mark Donahue has the story."

Donahue stood on a boardwalk with the Old Faithful geyser in the background. "Yellowstone National Park. One of our nation's treasures. It's known throughout the world for Old Faithful ... and bears. But some groups say the government's attempts to catch one killer grizzly are threatening to destroy the rest of this park's bears."

The scene changed to the Turbid Lake camping area. Donahue's voice continued. "Our story begins three weeks ago at this campsite where a lone camper, Jennifer Patrick, was mauled to death by a large grizzly. Other campers and hikers have been hurt in the past by bears, but *this* camper was the daughter of a United States Senator." Cut to a shot of Senator Patrick, with his name printed beneath him, walking in slow motion out of a Congressional committee room.

Donahue continued, "Immediately, the Park Service began setting traps to try and catch the killer." The scene changed to a picture of a bear trap. A low, ominous tone vibrated from the television speaker. "They haven't found him yet. But they *have* caught a lot of innocent bears, and some say the treatment of these bears is nothing short of harassment. We talked to Lester Crane from the People for the Environmental Way."

Suddenly, Crane's face appeared on the screen. His intense look helped drive home his words. "If these innocent bears had half the rights of people, the U.N. would send a peacekeeping force in here to stop our government."

Pierce glanced away from the television to admire his boss sitting next to him. A smirk broke out on Crane's face as he watched himself. Pierce turned back to the story.

Once again, the tape of limp bears being pulled out of traps commanded the screen. Donahue narrated. "And here is the tape your government doesn't want you to see. Volunteers for the People for the Environmental Way secretly took this footage of captured bears being drugged and submitted to invasive testing."

The screen was split. On the right, the PEW secret tape continued to run. On the left, Crane's face appeared to say, "Most of the Yellowstone bears try to stay away from people, but our government is deliberately luring them into traps, keeping them trapped overnight in their own excrement, and then shooting them up with PCP so these people can poke and prod the bears without getting hurt. It's a shameful outrage."

The story paused. Pierce looked up and noticed Crane had stopped the show to look at him. "Randy, did you notice that I kept referring to 'the government' instead of the rangers or the Park Service? Keep that in mind. Most people like rangers and they like parks. But nobody likes the government.

To win the support of the public, we need to identify a common enemy." Once again, Pierce was filled with admiration.

Crane restarted the story. The shot went back to Donahue in front of the famous geyser. "Crane warns that many bears will be hurt or killed if this aggressive trapping continues. His solution is to stop trapping, which hasn't found the killer yet anyway, and to keep people safe by restricting access to bear areas. The government has refused to comment. Reporting from Yellowstone National Park, this is Mark Donahue with The Scoop."

With remarkable timing, and most likely several takes, Old Faithful began to erupt during Donahue's closing comments.

Back to the studio anchor. "Hmm. Emotional story, Mark. Thanks." Then smiling and turning toward the camera he said, "Next up on The Scoop: She weighs nearly 400 pounds but she still has to turn men away from her bed. Her secret is next. Please stay with us."

This time Crane didn't fast forward. The screen went dark and then faded into a pan shot of beautiful Yellowstone scenery. Suddenly, and with a loud angry-sounding piano chord, a shot of an exhausted grizzly peering from a trap filled the screen. Cut back to the beautiful panorama. Bang! A shot of rangers drawing blood from an unconscious bear. Back to the lovely scenery. Bang! Rangers poking a trapped bear with a syringe on the end of a stick. More lovely scenery. Bang! A close-up of an unconscious bear, tongue hanging out of its mouth. The ear tag and radio collar made the bear appear even more pitiful. This time the scene stayed and a deep, rich, sad voice-over reached out to listeners.

"Something terrible is being hidden by the beauty of Yellowstone National Park. The few remaining grizzly bears in this country are being viciously harassed and abused by our government. These bears are one of our national treasures. Let's do something to save them. If you want to protect the American grizzly, please call People for the Environmental Way, and we'll work to put a stop to this outrage." PEW's toll-free phone number and web address appeared at the bottom of the screen. Then the screen faded back to black and Crane stopped the tape.

"Well, that explains why the phone was ringing all day," Pierce said.

As if on cue, the phone rang. Pierce looked at his boss shrugging his shoulders as if to say, "And there you go." He picked up the receiver.

"People for the Environmental Way. Randy Pierce speaking. May I help you?"

Suddenly his eyes stretched wide and his jaw dropped. "Uh, yes, Senator. He's right here." Nervously, he reached across the desk to hand the receiver to Crane. He mouthed the words "Senator Patrick."

Pierce wasn't sure what to think. He was proud, even boastful at times, of his political activism, but this was the first time he had ever actually spoken to a United States Senator, a member of the most exclusive club in the country. Secondly, he knew from Crane's briefing, that Patrick was not a friend of PEW. He wasn't considered an enemy either. But Crane's working list of Congressional members labeled

Patrick as "Moderate to Scary," meaning the man would at least consider environmental issues, but was known to launch anti-PEW tirades without warning.

The elder activist was calm as he took the phone. "Hello, Senator Patrick. What can I do for you?"

Crane stared toward the ceiling as he listened. Pierce could read nothing from the man's face.

After a couple minutes of silence Crane said, "That would not be a problem. Is Monday too late? ... Yes, I understand, but it will take us longer than that to get the enlargement made.... Oh." A few more seconds of listening. "Normally I'm not comfortable letting materials get out of this office, but ... Of course.... Exactly.... I can send it over with my intern this afternoon. He's trustworthy." Crane smiled at Pierce. "Who should he give it to? ... Tom? ... Okay. Thank you, Senator.... Any time." Calmly, he returned the receiver to its cradle.

With deliberate and patient motions, Crane walked over to one of the many piles of folders and began digging. Pierce was dying to scream, "What the hell's going on?" but didn't. Answers would come in due time. He had been working with Crane long enough to expect the man's need for drama. Surely Crane knew Pierce was chomping at the bit for details, so Crane was purposefully making the wait seem like eternity. Pierce didn't understand it, but he accepted it.

Finally, Crane pulled a color photograph out of one of the folders and dropped it into a plain envelope. On the front he wrote "Tom Herman, Staff Director, Sen. Patrick." This he handed to Pierce. "I need you to take a trip to the Hill."

# FOUR

"I suppose I've served in this chamber long enough that I know how to give a proper speech, filled with carefully planned highs and lows, praise and indignity. But today, I don't have it in me." The normal din on the Senate floor began to soften. Every senator and most gallery visitors knew what Senator Patrick was going to be talking about.

His dark, tailored suit hung gracefully on his tall, slender form. The gray highlights of age brought his neatly combed brown hair a certain dignity becoming a high-ranking senator. But today his usually powerful, chiseled facial features betrayed tremendous recent stress.

He continued. "In our debates about public policy, we like to talk about rights and wrongs, yeas and nays and blacks and whites. But we know most issues involve a lot of grays. That's why our decisions are always tough ones. But in what I'm going to say today, there are a few definites, a few undeniable truths."

Patrick paused to clear his throat and take a sip of water from the glass on the podium. *Come on, keep your composure*, he thought to himself.

"The first truth, my beautiful daughter Jennifer is dead. She's not coming back." His voice cracked. All the more evident because of the total silence in the distinguished chamber. Even long-time door keepers could not remember such quiet.

After a deep breath and another sip of water the senator continued. "Second, she was killed by a grizzly bear in Yellowstone National Park. Third, the bear is still at large. Fourth, the Park Service is going above and beyond the call of duty to capture that bear and bring it to justice. There is no argument about these facts."

He ran through those points fairly quickly, hoping the faster pace would help him get through them without breaking down.

"Now things get a little more gray." He reached down and grabbed a poster from behind the podium and placed it on an easel next to him. An enlarged copy of the drugged bear from the PEW commercial stared at the senators, its glassy eyes peering through nearly closed lids. Still, the Senate chamber was quiet, though a few members rustled in their seats.

"Men who sat in these chairs a long time before us created Yellowstone Park to protect wildlife. How can we sit in these chairs now and let *this* happen?" He paused again. His composure was intact, but he wanted the effect. "Those of you who have worked with me for some time know I'm not a champion of environmental groups. In fact, I usually don't like the way they look or act. But this issue involves me and my family."

He straightened and scanned the faces of his

colleagues. A murmur passed across the chamber. Usually, a person who loses a family member to a bear wants the rangers to go into the woods and kill all the bears. Truthfully, that was his initial reaction. But he tempered his rage when he thought about Jenny's dedication to wildlife. Her love of animals. Some of the faces in the audience, the people who never knew Jenny, seemed surprised at his acceptance of wild bears.

But shock was not the prevalent expression in the crowd. Pity was. Pity shone from the faces of friends and foes alike. Nobody likes to be an object of pity, especially lawmakers who depend on their image for influence. He felt weak. Nevertheless, he plunged ahead.

"These bears are being grossly mistreated and it's because one of them attacked a senator's daughter. The hunt would not be as intensive nor as harmful if it had been the daughter of a trash hauler. And what's especially annoying is that my daughter *was* a champion of the environmental movement. She would have been storming around the house demanding action if this kind of thing were happening when she was alive." Abruptly he stopped. It was still difficult for him to accept that Jenny was gone. He could say it when he concentrated on it, but "when she was alive" rolled off his tongue during this speech like a discussion of tax abatement. He supposed his therapist would say that was progress, but to him, it was tormenting.

He fought back tears, worked on the glass of water for a moment, and leaned closer to the microphone. "I'm asking the Park Service to call off their hunt. They can handle dangerous bears better by keeping people away from them. I'm doing this because I don't want the memory of Jennifer to be clouded by the resulting bad park policy. And I'm doing it so she can watch me from heaven and be proud."

The senator walked from the podium, not to his seat, but out of the chamber. He was openly weeping now, and did not think it was appropriate behavior on the Senate floor. A colleague called for recess and noise erupted as reporters raced to get quotes from Patrick. His aides immediately moved in to block the media onslaught and turn it away.

Standing nearby to rebound, was Lester Crane.

As Randy Pierce looked on, his adoration grew. When the reporters cleared -- their notebooks satiated with printable snippets of wisdom from America's leading environmental activist -- Crane told Pierce that they would be working late that night. The intern was bursting with pride that he was a part of this great man's organization.

"Les, that was brilliant. How did you know to be here when Patrick was done speaking? How did you know you would end up being the center of media attention? God, it's amazing," Pierce gushed.

"It's a big pain in the butt is what it is," grumbled Crane. "That weeny Patrick screwed us."

Pierce stopped short. In shock he watched his boss get further in front of him. *He's clairvoyant. He sees something I can't*, thought Pierce as he jogged to catch up.

When they were outside and away from prying eyes, Pierce finally blurted out "How did Patrick screw us? Didn't we get what we wanted?"

Crane stopped and looked at the student. "He was too early. Can't you see that?"

The shamed and frustrated look on Pierce's face answered him. He calmed down and explained. "I didn't want him to do this kind of thing for another month at least. When he called, I even wanted to hold him off until next week. But he had to go cry to his colleagues today." Crane gestured toward the Capitol with contempt.

"But we got what we wanted sooner, didn't we? Isn't that what we're after?" Pierce asked.

After a long, condescending sigh, Crane said, "Do you know how much money that commercial on The Scoop cost? Do you remember how the phone was ringing yesterday? People calling in to support us and send us money?"

Pierce nodded.

"How many calls do you think we'll get tomorrow?" the mentor asked.

"I expect we'll get a lot of calls and money. We won." Pierce answered, or did he ask?

"Phfft! This isn't a profit-sharing corporation we're working in. We don't get rewarded for a job well done." Reading the confusion on Pierce's face, he continued, "We don't get money for the battles we win. We get money for the battles we're fighting. If we lose, all the better. A few victories give us credibility, but it's the ongoing struggles that keep the donations coming in."

Crane started walking again, Pierce a half step behind. The lesson continued.

"People are going to watch the news tonight and say, 'Good for them.' But they're not going to get up and fetch the checkbook. If this thing had dragged on a while longer, it would have been us against the Park Service bureaucracy. We'd be martyrs. We could continue to beg for support. And we'd get it.

"Now, this fight is over unless we can find a spin that keeps contributors energized."

For a moment Pierce was troubled. Were they an organization bent on raising money or saving the environment? Why were they disappointed at an environmental victory? Who cares how it affects fundraising? *Wait a minute*, he thought. *This is Lester Crane, the ecological master. He knows what he's doing. I should trust him.* He quickly put his doubts back into an unused corner of his mind.

On the way back to the office, they stopped at a drug store so Crane could buy a bag of Green Savers for the volunteers who were answering the phones and licking envelopes back at PEW headquarters.

"Didn't you say a former intern runs this company?" Pierce asked, pointing at the bag.

"Yup. Dave Shenly worked for us a few years ago when we were fighting industrial pollution and food additives. When he graduated, he and a few of his friends started Enviro-Sweets, Inc. They marketed a few products, but Green Savers is the thing that really took off." He held up the bag. "See, the packaging is made of recycled materials and it's fully biodegradable. The candies don't have any unnatural additives or coloring."

Pierce was familiar with Green Savers. The breath mints were a sickly gray color, and they frequently stuck together. He learned the hard way not to keep them in his pocket unless they were first wrapped in plastic. But they tasted pretty good. They were a big hit on campus in Bloomington.

"I've always been proud of Dave," Crane added.

Pierce's former doubts were not only shoved to the back of his mind, they were also hidden under a layer of Green Savers. He knew his boss' guidance was partly responsible for the former intern's success. Pierce vowed to do equally well and, just maybe, earn Crane's praise.

"And that bear tape and the photos. That's the work of another former intern," Crane continued.

"I wondered how we got that footage."

"Bernie Wilson is still out in the park. He's my eyes and ears out there. Sometimes he's my hands too. He does a great job for us."

Back in the office, Pierce was determined to prove himself.

"Les, I know you want to put out another mailing. Let me take a crack at the first draft."

Crane smiled. "Sure. It should go to the people who already sent us money as well as our regular fundraising list."

"That's what I figured," said Pierce excitedly. He had learned the details of answering the phone and carrying stacks of paper from here to there. Big whoop. In fact he probably knew as much about the boring mechanics of PEW as Crane did. But this was his first chance to do something real. He wasn't going to college to learn how to stuff envelopes. He wanted to influence policy at the right hand of Lester Crane.

Now he had a chance.

Though he wanted to jump with joy at being given the job, he maintained outward calm, plopped down in front of a computer and began working the keyboard and mouse.

After 20 minutes, Crane called out from his office, "Read to me what you've got so far."

Pierce listened to the clicking and whirring of the inkjet printer. Then bolted to the doorway, clutching a piece of paper.

"I thought on the front we could have a graphic of a hand reaching down to help a struggling bear out of a hole or ditch or something," he began. "The banner would be something like, 'We're helping to save your bears.' Inside it could say 'Your bears are in danger in your park,' and underline the 'your's so they really stand out.

"The main text would be something like, 'The cherished grizzly bears in Yellowstone National Park are being viciously trapped and molested, all because one bear defended its territory against the onslaught of man. Recently, People for the Environmental Way won an important friend on Capitol Hill. But the fight is far from over. The American grizzly needs your helping hand now more than ever.' And here we could use one of Bernie Wilson's surveillance photos of a bear in a trap.

"Then we'd add something like, 'People for the Environmental Way is fighting tirelessly to protect the grizzlies' Yellowstone habitat. We want to do this not only for the safety of the bears but for the safety of the visitors. Your support will give us the tools to rebuild the grizzlies' home, to end the unfair treatment of the bears and to make sure they will be there for future generations to enjoy.' We could finish the brochure with the usual donation information."

Finished, Pierce watched Crane for a reaction.

After thinking for a few minutes Crane said, "I don't want to push the idea that people can go see the bears in the park for generations to come. After all, I want people out of the park." He thought a couple more minutes, then added, "It's a little rough, Randy, but we can work with it. Good job."

Once again, Pierce beamed.

**************

"Daddy, I'm hungry." Jason Hendricks peered over the top of his hand of cards to see if his father looked sympathetic.

Mike Hendricks didn't look up from his own cards. "No food in the tent. You don't want to attract bears do you?"

"You sound just like Mom."

The older Hendricks laughed and played a card. His wife didn't come on the family camping trip this year because she was afraid of the "wild" bear that was still running loose in the park. Every year the Billings, Montana, family drove down to spend a weekend at the Bridge Bay campground. It's not like the park was full of "tame" bears in previous years. He joked with her about being swayed by too much tabloid TV, but he didn't argue with her very vigorously. Since she was pregnant, she wouldn't have been able to do as much hiking and fishing anyway.

With the new baby on the way, Jason was going to have a big adjustment to make. For six years, he had been the singular object of his parents' attention. In a few months he was going to have to share. Mike thought it was important to spend one last long, active weekend with his only son before the new child arrived. They had been fishing on Yellowstone Lake all day, catching about a dozen fish, and carefully releasing each one to be caught another day.

"It's too close to bed time," Mike said as he looked at his watch. Just past 10:30 p.m. Well past Jason's normal bed time, but this was vacation. "In fact," he said, setting down his cards and reaching for his heavy metal flashlight, "Let's hit the bathroom one last time and call it a night. We want to get an early start on the geysers tomorrow."

"Can't we just finish this game?" Jason was clearly tired and ready for bed, but he was obligated to put up a small argument, for the sake of habit if nothing else.

"Not this time," Mike answered as he reached over to get their shoes. He looked back at his son, then froze.

Over his son's head, he saw the tent being pressed inward from the outside, as if someone were poking it with a baseball bat. Then he heard loud sniffing and smelled a strong animal scent.

"Jason, don't move!"

But it was too late. Jason had seen his dad's alarmed expression and glanced over his own shoulder to see the indentation pressing further inward. He spun around and began scooting backward toward his father.

Without warning another object joined the first, but this second one had a dark brown three-inch hook on the end that cut a fast slice through the nylon wall. The first protrusion slid into the new tent opening revealing a huge furry brown head with an enormous open mouth that quickly clamped down on Jason's leg and began dragging him out of the tent.

Just as quickly, Mike swung his flashlight, smacking the bear on the side of the nose. The grizzly pulled Jason completely out of the tent and Mike followed, resisting the temptation to grab his son, which would only result in a macabre tug-of-war in which the "rope" would be the loser.

Again, Mike connected the heavy flashlight against the bear's snout. This time the bear released its prey and lunged forward with a roar. Mike jumped backward just before the powerful jaws could catch him. Off balance from the sudden jump, he fell and felt the sting of numerous twigs and pine needles that carpeted the ground. Immediately he curled into a fetal position, covering the back of his neck with his hands and tried to play dead, a maneuver recommended by most pamphlets on bear encounters.

The bear wasn't buying it. Mike sensed the bear pounce and felt its enormous weight land on top of him, knocking all breath out of the man's body. Concentrating on keeping conscious, trying to breathe and holding himself into a balled position, Mike hardly felt his flesh tear as the bear knocked him around on the ground with big paws and sharp claws.

"Daddy!" screamed Jason, catching the attention of

Mike and the monster. The father watched as his son tried crawling away, dragging one bleeding leg behind him. With that the bear lost interest in Mike and turned back to his original prey.

Drawing any strength he could find, Mike rolled to his feet and jumped toward his son, getting there at the same time as the bear. With a yell summoned from deep within his DNA connection to the first primate who protected his young, the father smashed the flashlight against the hard skull of the angry grizzly. The loud crack sent vibrations up the man's arm and momentarily stopped the bear.

Unharmed but furious, the monster stood with a loud roar, revealing a muscular, nine-foot frame. The animal reared back then swung a massive paw at the older Hendricks.

Mike raised his arm to try and block the blow to the head. He heard the loud pop as his shoulder left its socket, but the arm was still attached and so was his head. Though his mind was foggy he could tell he was lying on the ground 10 feet away from the bear, still flailing his flashlight at whatever he might hit. He could also tell that his son's screams and the bear's roar had drawn a large crowd that was driving the bear back into the woods without its dinner.

*Thank God for a crowded campground*, he thought. The next few moments were difficult to grasp. He could still hear his son crying and calling out for him so he tried to stand but couldn't. Three men grabbed him and eased him into a seat at a nearby picnic table. The other sounds and voices were not as coherent. He looked at his motionless, numb arm and wondered when it would start to hurt. *If the arm never works again*, he thought, *at least it saved my head from being any more scrambled than it is now.*

Fighting unconsciousness, he watched one man apply a tourniquet to Jason's leg while another man backed up a van to the campsite. He looked around at his various saviors, and in the jumbled way a mind going into shock works, he could notice no details except the weapons each had brought to fight the bear. Firearms were forbidden for tourists, so the campers made due with whatever was at hand. One guy held a flashlight, much like his own. Two other people gripped smoldering sticks that were probably flaming when they brought them over. Another guy had a crowbar. And one guy clutched a weenie roaster.

*A weenie roaster?* he thought. *That thing couldn't puncture a half-frozen hot dog, but this guy brought it over to defend me and my boy.* He wanted to get up and thank the man. He wanted to thank all of them. But all he could manage was a strange mixture of relieved crying and laughter as they loaded him and Jason into the van for a trip to the hospital.

# FIVE

Lacy sprinted from her car into the park hospital and scanned the crowded room for body bags, victims or some other indication of the severity of the attack. Finding no clues she next searched for Steward. Because most of the crowd wore ranger uniforms, it took her a minute to spot him. He was in a corner talking to a couple of men who had the look of campers, dirty in the requisite places from sitting on the ground around a camp fire, hair untamed from a few days without a shower, and one of them was holding a weenie roaster.

*Must be witnesses*, she thought. She approached just as Steward was thanking them and sending them on their way.

"I got here as quickly as I could," she said as soon as the campers were gone.

"You doing naturalist talks?"

"Yeah. Over at the Madison campground. I was there to talk about geysers but the people wanted to talk about bears, ironically. It sounds like we could have done a bear talk at Bridge Bay and had a guest of honor show up."

Steward chuckled. Lacy studied his face, trying to read

the situation without asking. She looked around the small room at the other rangers huddled around maps, telephones and radios. Steward was watching the witnesses get in their cars in the parking lot and drive off.

"Did we lose anyone?" she finally asked.

He turned back to her. "Nope. The boy lost a lot of blood and the father was in bad shape. But the doctors got them stabilized enough to transport up Cody."

The park's hospital is a small building located near the Lake Hotel. Despite its unimpressive stature, the facility is equipped for procedures as sophisticated as open-heart surgery should the need arise. Usually, however, emergencies are sent to larger hospitals outside the park. The Hendrickses, who were camping only a couple miles away from the hospital, were patched up and on their way just two hours after the attack.

Lacy breathed a sigh of relief. "It was just the father and son right?"

"None of the nearby campers was hurt and the wife had stayed home in Billings. I already talked to her on the phone. She's a bit shaken up, but thankful that her husband and boy are going to pull through."

Lacy tried to hide her smirk. There was nothing funny about the bear attack, but she didn't overlook who had to call the nearest relative. It looked like Steward's reprieve from being the relative-caller was only temporary.

Under control again, she asked "Was it our bear?"

"Well, the bite wounds have been measured and some other data will be compared at the lab to find out for certain.

But my instinct is yes. The witnesses described a very big guy, which fits the Turbid Lake bear. He wasn't wearing a collar or tags, and our bear is unidentified. And then the way they described him." His voice trailed off as he turned back to look out the window, a troubled expression on his face.

"What do you mean?"

"I've got this suspicion that our bear is a little bit nuts."

"Uh huh," she replied. It was more polite than to say, *Yeah right. I think you are the one who's a little bit nuts.*

"Well, think about it," he said defensively. "Didn't the Turbid Lake attack seem unusually savage?"

"You're the bear expert," she said.

He glared at her and took a deep breath. She was obviously not on his good side. Right now she didn't care. If she hadn't volunteered to go with Steward to Turbid Lake she would be driving back to her cabin right now instead of hanging around a crowded medical room. Her own District Ranger wanted her to get out of this bear-chasing gig and back to her naturalist duties at Old Faithful.

But Chief Ranger Bobbie Marks was boss of her boss. And he said a job started should be a job finished. Because she and Steward didn't catch that bear yet she would be tied to Steward for a while.

When Steward continued, he was speaking formally and carefully.

"As you saw for yourself, the anger and contempt the bear showed for that trap he trashed was odd, to say the least. Most bears would either get trapped, or if they knew it was a trap, stay away. It's almost like this grizzly is angry and spiteful. Remember those trash cans I told you about?"

"Vaguely."

"I ran across five 'bear proof' trash cans that were torn up. I think our bear is responsible for it. They were smashed and torn far beyond what was necessary to get at something to eat. They reminded me a lot of that trap."

Lacy considered that for a moment. "So how do you make the connection to this bear tonight?"

"The campers who saved that guy and his son gave a pretty good description of the animal's size, which seemed close to how we had been picturing it. At least nine feet tall and heavy. Then they talked about how its fur was matted in several places and how awful it smelled. The light was pretty bad and the whole campground smelled like campfires, so it must have looked and smelled extreme for them to notice. It's not like grizzlies are especially clean or that they normally wear cologne, but the campers' description struck me as strange, even for a bear."

"To me it's unlikely that a normal bear would even get near that crowded campground," Lacy conceded.

"I hope we're not just lucky that he left a crowded campground without taking a couple of bodies with him."

Their conversation was interrupted by the park's public information officer, Sharon Reynolds. "Dusty, can I see the testimony from our witnesses?" She reached for the papers in Steward's hands. "I've got to work out some kind of statement to release to the media immediately." As she looked at the documents she added, "Nice job with the wife, by the way."

Steward shot a glance at Lacy, who grinned back at him.

The PIO returned the reports to Steward. "I'll bet Lester Crane is going to have a field day with this one," she said shaking her head as she walked away.

Steward winced. His reaction puzzled Lacy.

"Don't you like Lester Crane?" she asked.

He didn't answer. Instead, he walked out of the hospital and sat on a bench to watch the moon rise over Yellowstone Lake, leaving a shimmering pearly stripe from the mountains at the far side to the shore in front of him. She joined him and waited a few minutes, enjoying the view, before deciding to push the issue.

"I think Crane is truly dedicated to preserving this park and its wildlife," she started. "He's not afraid to stand up to the big businesses and corrupt politicians who would pave this place over and sell bear pelts to the highest bidder."

Steward smiled, not the reaction she expected, and stretched his strong arms to squeeze out the day's stress. As she thought about it, she probably should not have been pushing him. A bear mauling and his resumed duty of calling concerned family members was enough of a burden for one day. But still, she wasn't in a very good mood about being dragged back into bear duty. One trip was enough for her. If her unhappiness about being taken from her geysers to chase a bear caused her to pick at Steward, so be it. Besides, Lester Crane was a hero of environmentalists and naturalists everywhere. Who does this ranger think he is?

"Lester Crane is dangerous to this park and to every

issue he touches for a very basic reason," Steward began. "Everything he wants to do is based on the idea that people are evil."

"Aren't they? At the very least, they're stupid."

"Ignorant maybe. But not stupid, and definitely not evil."

"God, how can you say that?" She jumped to her feet. " I've picked up enough trash thrown on this beautiful ground. I've seen enough people harassing bison. I've found more than one elk that was killed by poachers. And I've seen plenty of the park's one-of-a-kind features vandalized for the sake of a souvenir. To me, that is evil."

He rose slowly and began walking to the shore. She followed reluctantly.

"Just because a few people don't understand what is here," he started. "Just because they don't understand their place on the planet, it doesn't mean they're evil. But the fact that we are in this park today, and will be in this park tomorrow and the day after that means that the majority of our so-called evil species had the sense to recognize how special this place is."

"I don't follow."

Steward continued. "Look. What is Yellowstone? It's a park, right? That means it's been set aside for the enjoyment of people. It says so on that big arch at the north entrance. The value of this place is its wonder and beauty. People come from all over the globe to look around and enjoy. If people were truly evil, there would be no park. There would be expensive homes built along the rim of the canyon. The animals would have long been killed and butchered. And there would be laundry facilities and health spas in the thermal features."

"Hah, caught you," she laughed. "In the early days of the park, there *were* laundry facilities and health spas in the thermal features. People *are* evil."

Steward grinned. "Back then there weren't any national parks. Nobody knew what to do with this place so a few people who didn't know better tried to do what people did everywhere else. They started businesses and tried to make a life for themselves. But in this place, the idea of a park was more valuable so those squatters were chased away. The aesthetic value of Mammoth Hot Springs is much higher than the possible monetary and therapeutic value of a bath house built on top of the Main Terrace."

They reached the edge of the lake. Voices and laughter revealed a party at the nearby, officially-sanctioned fire ring. *A group of employees must have gotten a permit to use the ring for the evening*, Lacy thought. Employees usually did a good job of cleaning up after themselves.

She shook her head. Seasonal park employees. Sometimes they were a real nuisance. Generally college-age, they behaved a lot like college students everywhere. Party a bit too hard. Drive a bit too fast. Risk a bit too much. Like Jenny Patrick camping by herself in a closed bear area. But their dedication to Yellowstone was admirable. If a comet were about to smash into the center of the park you could count on a gathering of employees trying to catch it rather than let it cause damage.

At the end of the summer they would go back to their

schools or new careers. Some would even volunteer with PEW. But all of them were irrevocably touched by the wonders of Yellowstone. They would spread the word of the park's glory.

And then there was Dusty Steward. *Where did he fit in all this*, she wondered. She had been warned about him, after all. Her friends said Dusty was a nice guy, but you don't want to get him started. He can ramble on like a misplaced professor. The other night over drinks he didn't seem so philosophical. Oh well, at least he's not shallow, even if he's wrong.

At the risk of setting him off again, she spoke.

"Don't you think Lester Crane and his group are working to preserve beautiful places like this?"

"The difference is that Crane is trying to preserve them by keeping people out. The early nature lovers made this a place for people to visit. Crane wants to lock the gates. But if people can't see the beautiful places, then those places are worthless. And people won't help protect things they can't experience. Once visitors can't enjoy the natural beauty, then there will be no reason to keep out the bath houses and laundries."

Lacy held up her hands to stop him. "Wait a minute. You don't think that if PEW gets a few bear areas closed that suddenly the park is going to be overrun with squatters."

"Crane isn't going to be happy just closing a few bear areas. We close them all the time. Jenny Patrick's campsite was closed. He wants more. He's in this game for power and he hates people. He isn't going to stop until the whole park is closed."

"Oh, even if he wanted to, he couldn't do that."

Now Steward faced her. "That's the other problem with people like Lester Crane. He doesn't really care if he wins. His whole mission is to collect more money for his cause. And I don't care how many bear areas we close, there will be run-ins between people and bears. Eventually one of those run-ins will be deadly for the bear or the people. Hell, look what's going on right now. Each time this kind of thing happens, he has an opportunity to whine to the media and solicit his contributors for more money. Eventually he might win. He likes bears better than people so he doesn't care if tourists get shut out. The question is how long can he keep the momentum going in his favor."

*I should let this drop, but I'm as bad as he is.* "Let's say, hypothetically, that Crane succeeds and closes the park to all but a few backpackers, bikers or some other limited number. Won't the park be better off because of the reduced traffic?"

Steward tossed a stick into the liquid moonbeam. "Let's say he only succeeds in eliminating overnight stays. Closing the campgrounds and hotels. I'm saying even that would be disastrous for the bears, the elk and everything else."

"Why?"

"The park is not a zoo. It's vast. Animals wandering around and minding their own business are not all visible from the road or trail. It takes time to see them. If Ed and Edna Smith from Athens, Georgia, know they probably will never see a bear in Yellowstone National Park, why would they come here?" Steward asked.

"To see the geysers," Lacy answered quickly.

"Maybe so. But even then, would they really care about the fate of the bears? How much outrage are they going to feel if poachers come in and start knocking off the bears? Ed and Edna have been told by Lester Crane and the government that they are too wicked to be able to look upon a grizzly, so why should anyone else have that opportunity? Are they going to write to their Congressman demanding protection for something they aren't allowed to see?"

"Even Ed and Edna don't want to see a species disappear," she countered.

"I'll bet every zoo within a day's drive of Athens has at least one grizzly bear. And the zoo will welcome the Smiths with open arms."

Lacy pondered that for a minute. "I hadn't really thought of it that way."

Steward continued. "As annoyed as you and I get with the tourists, as much trouble as they cause us, I'm glad to see each and every one of them. Granted, I wish more of them were a little more careful with the park and themselves. Believe me, I'm getting tired of talking to their next of kin. But as long as the people are interested in visiting this place, they will always help protect it."

She stewed over the idea, but the only conclusion she reached was that perhaps Steward was, indeed, nuts. He almost made a good case, but he's nuts. When this bear episode is over she will be happy to go back to her side of the park and talk about geysers. *Shame*, she thought. *He's kind of nice looking.*

Raucous laughter from the fire ring interrupted her thoughts.

**************

"Crane? Grossman," said the phone in the PEW chief's hand. "Don't you ever sleep in?"

Looking at his watch, Crane responded, "Hell, Phil, environmental warriors do more before 9:00 in the morning than most people do all day."

"Maybe I'll call the Pentagon next and see what they think about your take-off of the Army slogan."

"Ah, they're too worried about inventing the next bomb to kill us all. They don't have time to fret about me."

Crane looked at the stack of paper in front of him. He came in early because he had a lot of work to do. Handwritten thank-you notes to top contributors. New angles to develop for future fundraising. But there was always time to talk to a reporter.

"Anyway," he said, "I'm guessing that's not why you called."

"Nope. I've got something more interesting. I just got a short report over the wire. A bear attacked a little boy and his father in Yellowstone last night. Care to comment?"

"Of course. Give me some details first, please." Crane began digging through his "Yellowstone stack" for some relevant news clippings, recent position papers, anything. He was pretty good speaking off the cuff, but he preferred to have something in front of him to fall back on. As Grossman explained that details were sketchy because the Park Service was not scheduled to release an official statement until later in the day, Crane had time to re-read his relevant earlier news releases and fundraising propaganda.

"So no one is certain if it's the same bear that killed the Patrick girl, or if it's some other rogue," Grossman concluded. "And I don't know if they're going to resume trapping or what they're going to do. I'm sure the Park Service will tell us something later, but I'd like to get some comments from you to spice up this story before we send it out for the afternoon papers. I'm not sure their news conference will meet our deadline."

"You can always count on me for your deadlines, Phil." Crane paused, then continued. "It shouldn't matter whether or not it's the same bear that killed Ms. Patrick. The problem continues to be that the Park Service is cramming together people and bears. No American should be surprised at this outcome. As long as the park is overpopulated with people, we are going to see more and more injuries to people. And as long as the Park Service seeks revenge on the bears, we are going to see fewer and fewer grizzlies." Crane waited, listening to the clicking of Grossman's keyboard, then added, "How's that?"

"Just what I'm looking for. Thanks Les."

"No problem. And if the Park Service feeds its usual pile of garbage and you want a reaction, please call me again."

The two provided their polite talk-to-you-laters and hung up. Crane leaned back in his chair and smiled. This was getting good.

**************

Bill Penny decided to lock up his trash tonight. His restaurant in Cooke City, near the Northeast entrance to Yellowstone, had been a commercial success in recent years. The food was only average, the burgers-and-fries menu nothing spectacular, but Penny had one feature that drew a crowd.

Several years ago, he spilled a trash can out behind his restaurant and was too tired to pick it up. That night, he was awakened from his bedroom above the restaurant by a persistent noise. He looked out his window to see a black bear rooting through his mess. He opened his window to the cool night air and hollered at the animal. It grabbed a couple final morsels from his trash and scampered back into the woods.

He didn't think much of it at the time. If anything he felt bad for not cleaning up his spilled garbage. Without much concern, he fell back asleep. The next morning, when one of his breakfast patrons mentioned the bear, he was embarrassed. One of his neighbors must have heard him yelling at the bear and then told a tourist. When the next two customers came in and mentioned the bear, he laughed it off and admitted his mistake.

Then came the lunch crowd. Word about the bear must have spread through the tiny town as quickly as any juicy gossip. People who stopped for gas or a soda found out that a bear visited Bill Penny's restaurant the night before. The tourists were curious and wanted to hear about it themselves. His lunch business doubled that day, most people requesting a backyard view, and his story about the bear got better with every telling. By dinner, he could keep a table of tourists rapt with his tale about running downstairs in his pajamas to chase off a giant bear with a wooden spoon.

Not surprisingly, he spilled garbage that night too.

The following spring, "his" bear brought her two cubs with her to dine behind his restaurant. By the end of the season, he was able to move out of the upstairs of his restaurant into a nice home on the hill above town.

All three bears still came back to Penny's restaurant. Occasionally they fought, but that didn't exactly hurt business, so he never worried. The Park Service and Forest Service and others tried to get him to take better care of his trash since the first year. He complied enough to keep himself out of legal trouble, but skirted the law enough to keep the bears returning. His neighbors warned him that he was asking for trouble, but the profits had been too intoxicating, until the boy was hurt down at Bridge Bay Campground.

When Penny read about the supposedly wild bear that killed the politician's daughter, he began to wonder about his own furry visitors. But customers seemed even more eager to see a bear, so he didn't do anything. Then the boy got hurt in the big public campground, and he began to really worry. Last year, his lawyer warned him that if a customer went from diner to dinner, Bill could be held responsible.

*Perhaps*, he thought, *he should keep his garbage locked up inside his restaurant, at least until the bear scare passed.*

Bears are creatures of habit. Feeding grounds are

passed on through the generations like family jewels. Some well-worn trails to favorite spots are centuries old. Sure, they are always on the lookout for a new food supply, but for the most part, they will return to the same berry patches, the same trout streams, and the same garbage dumps year after year after year.

Their strange cycle of activity and hibernation requires them to eat a bounty of food during the months they are awake to prepare them for the long winter during which they will sleep. For females, the calorie consumption becomes even more important because they give birth and nurse while hibernating.

By now, the female who had been visiting Penny's restaurant -- at the back door not the front -- was a regular customer. Her first two offspring came back periodically as well, but she was more faithful to Penny's cooking. And now she was pregnant again and desperate for food. As she wandered up to the back door, she heard the usual squeals of delight from the people inside. Years ago it made her uncomfortable, but she was used to it now.

Tonight, for no reason she could understand, the cans of delicious table scraps were gone. So she sniffed around looking for something. Just a few grease spots from last night, but nothing else.

There had been other times when nothing was outside. But she was hungry, pregnant, and could smell a plentiful harvest behind the door and windows. Tonight, an empty plate wouldn't do. She raised up on her hind legs to pound and paw at the back door. It didn't budge so she scratched at it and the frame around it. Then she tried to dig under the door, but the stoop was made of concrete and she made no headway.

She could still smell the food. She was not ready to quit. Looking up, she saw people eating and staring at her. Never before had she tried to get through a window. She didn't like people and the sight of them kept her away. But she was hungry, and the window didn't look too difficult to dig through, maybe a little like the thin ice she saw on streams every spring.

She dropped to all fours to walk along the building, closer to the window. Then she raised up again and put her paws on the sill, which was now at the height of her chest. She had a good view of a lot of food, but she hesitated. Something was different. The people were making a different noise. High pitched, their mouths open. It didn't seem right.

Then she heard the door burst open. She looked over at the man. He was shouting and he smelled different. She had smelled his anxiety, his anger and his happiness. This was different. This was fear. Then she saw he was holding something that did not look like food. Everything was wrong. Take no chances. Go. She turned to drop to the ground and run.


Two booming shots echoed through Cooke City and the surrounding valley. A less resonating sound came from Penny's restaurant where several patrons were screaming or yelling. An even softer sound came from Bill Penny as he slumped against the scratched door frame, sobbing. No sound at all came from the lifeless bear.

# SIX

In media relations, a little continued effort can bring a huge return. Crane's relationship with AP's Grossman made the activist a known quotable source for the media. Most didn't call him themselves. Instead, they reported what the AP provided for them. But when Mr. Penny killed the bear behind his restaurant, that was the third news story to pop out of the nation's wonderland. News directors across the country decided their news teams should cover this story themselves. Lester Crane didn't have to go out and seek reporters. They came to him.

While Randy Pierce was on one line trying to secure plane tickets to anywhere near Yellowstone, Crane was on the other feeding the "line of the day" to newspapers, radio stations and TV reporters across the country.

"When the bears lose, we all lose. We lose a little bit of our heritage, and a little bit of our humanity. PEW has been trying to stop that loss for years, but the government continues to ignore us. Let's just pray that it's not too late," he told a reporter from Little Rock, Arkansas. Crane had been saying roughly the same thing to everyone who called, though he was getting even more polished as time went on.

As he answered a few more questions, he caught movement out of the corner of his eye. Pierce was waving with one hand and scribbling on some paper with the other, phone still crammed against his ear with his shoulder. The intern held up the sign reading "Billings and a rental car. Gardiner room."

Crane gave him the thumbs-up and continued his conversation with Arkansas.

**************

Early the next morning Crane, Pierce and two oversized carry-on bags were wheels up for Billings, Montana. Pierce watched the takeoff from the small oval window next to him. Most frequent fliers ignore, or at least try to, the fast acceleration, the quick hop-and-dip of becoming airborne and the sharp ascent of racing to cruising altitude. Pierce, however, was not a frequent flier and, while legally an adult, still viewed air travel with the excitement and awe of a child.

Though his family was well-off, Father Pierce preferred to drive on family vacations. Randy Pierce's complaints about the pollution of all the cars on the road led to more than one family argument, making the last family vacation the *last* family vacation. The current trip with Crane was the first time in ten years he had been on a big trip. It was his first business trip.

Once the plane climbed into the gray clouds and ended Pierce's view of the world around him, the intern turned to Crane who was scribbling away on a legal pad, recycled paper of course. Crane finished a thought, capped the pen and sat back, staring straight ahead.

"Good coverage last night," Pierce began.

Crane smiled. "That ought to bring in some money. I'll tell you Randy, this whole thing is playing out perfectly for us. People and bears have been clashing in that place forever. But this time it's actually looking like the Park Service won't be able to come up with another temporary fix. I gambled a few years back when I talked about closing down Yellowstone to save the grizzlies. It never played out right until now. We were the only ones who talked about it then, so now we're the experts on the issue."

"Is that why we have to be out there now?"

"Exactly. I want to be where the cameras are. All the networks will broadcast tonight's news from the park. The Today Show is spending the week out there. I'm not about to sit in Washington and let the Sierra Club or some other group weasel in on our air time."

Pierce had a troubled look and Crane noticed it. "All right Randy. What is it?"

The impatience in Crane's voice hurt Pierce. The man was teaching Randy a lot, but did he have to be so condescending about it? Pierce almost didn't respond for fear of sounding ignorant. Then he decided to say what was troubling him. If nothing else, he might continue to learn from the master environmental warrior.

"Tell me we have a higher purpose than just getting air time to raise money."

Crane rubbed his eyes for a moment, then looked at

his disciple. "Randy, we've got the highest purpose there is. We are the last defense against the long, perpetual, devastating attack on our planet. Look out the window. From this altitude you can almost make out the curvature of the earth. It's a big place and it's magnificent in its beauty. But when we pass a break in the clouds, look again. Below us, everywhere you look, you'll see highways, train tracks, houses, parking lots, farms, factories. When we get closer to cities you'll see smog. You'll see endless lines of cars and trucks. You'll see brown rivers that were once blue. As far as you can see, even from the highest height, you'll see the trail of man and the muddy footprints he has left behind."

Crane ordered a Coke from the flight attendant. Pierce asked for one too. Then Crane continued.

"Thanks to our environmental forefathers, some places have suffered only minor damage. Yellowstone is one of those areas. The roads cut through forests, ugly trash cans are placed next to the most scenic views, and hideous manmade structures draw travelers in their polluting vehicles to sleep and get enough rest to spend the next day tromping over worn trails. But by and large, it's a place where nature hasn't been defeated. Wild animals still roam. Fish can still live in the lakes and streams. We've even brought back the wolf, which had once been killed off."

By now, the other passengers had set aside their magazines and time-killers and were listening to Crane. Though he was only looking at Pierce, he was aware of his audience. He continued.

"The wild wolves are enjoying new life in the park, but the old, human wolves are continuing their endless vigil outside the gates. They wait, panting and slobbering for the park to show any sign of weakness. Then they lunge in, build a new hotel or road and keep a vicious grip on the throat of Mother Nature. Eventually, enough human wolves will break through the gate to kill her."

Pierce was amazed at the way Crane could work an audience. And the man wasn't done yet.

"My job and your job and the job of every other activist is to be alert for breaks in the fence. We must work fast to limit the number of human wolves that come in. Then we must try to beat back the ones that make it through. Our weapons for this defense are money and publicity. You can bet I will do everything in my power to get more money and more publicity if it means I can keep the predators of my species off Mother Nature's throat. There is no compromise. There is no accommodation. I'm fighting to total victory."

The crowd murmured. Crane still appeared oblivious to them, but Pierce knew better.

"And I'll tell you another thing." He quieted down. Enough for a dramatic effect but not enough so that his expanded audience couldn't hear him. "This issue with the bear is going to do more than patch the fence. This may be our chance to regain lost ground. I think we're close to chasing out *all* the human predators. You asked about our higher purpose. Well this is it. Chalk one up for Mother Nature."

With that, he sat back and folded his arms triumphantly. A middle-aged lady across the aisle applauded softly. A young man behind them joined in. Beaming, Randy clapped too.

The plane landed on time in Billings. The rental car was picked up with no hassle or undue delay. And Crane and Pierce were on their way to Yellowstone.

As the two drove west on I-90, the industrial landscape of Montana's largest city gave way to open country framed by buttes, stands of pine trees and distant mountains. The rough-looking Billings refineries were replaced by the even rougher-looking structures of Mother Nature.

Large, craggy rocks jutting through meadow and hill were unlike those Pierce had played on as a boy in the Midwest. These tough rocks did not have the same soft covering of ferns and grasses. The bare faces of boulders and cliffs, the heights to which they reached and the distance from which they could be seen, were all new to him.

Pierce was not prepared for what he was witnessing. His own bickering with his father had canceled a planned western vacation, so his only exposure to mountains came from the half-dozen times his family had driven through the Smokies on their way to Florida. He had grown up around the rolling hills of Southern Indiana, hills that, in the fall when the leaves turned colors, could rival an artist's pallet. Still, that colorful landscape was only hilly. This was mighty. He had seen the progressively rolling terrain of Kentucky and Tennessee. He had marveled at the height and beauty of the Great Smoky Mountains. But this, this was something grander than he had imagined. Sure, he had seen pictures of the Rockies, but no photograph, poster or movie could ever capture the feeling of being thrust into such enormous scenery.

The mountains towered above everything as their rocky peaks tore through the tree line. Only the bravest trees managed to hang on to an isolated spot here and there. But no tree had the strength or courage to survive on the upper slopes.

The gentle roll of the green mountains and hills he was accustomed to seemed meek compared to the violent angles of granite that left greenery behind, demanding to be seen and revered.

As they approached Livingston, where they would turn off the interstate and head south toward the park, the scenery became even more dramatic. The mountains pushed closer together, overlapping each other to present a wall of contrast and color. The big-sky Montana countryside formed a funnel, pouring rugged beauty into Yellowstone Park. Most of the early expeditions into the park followed pretty much the same route, through the funnel, that Pierce and Crane followed today.

Crane mumbled something. Pierce shook his head to clear it. He had nearly forgotten where he was and what he was doing, which was dangerous considering he was behind the wheel of their rented car.

"What?" inquired the intern.

"I said look at all that garbage."

Pierce turned his eyes from the towering peaks back to road level. He noted that Crane was staring at some billboards, a campground and a convenience mart that their car was just beginning to pass.

"Everywhere you look you see the muddy footprints of mankind," Crane said. "We'll just see what we can do about that."

What Pierce thought about saying, but did not was, *Quit seeking out everything negative. I'm having the closest thing to a religious experience that I've ever had and you interrupt it to point out a place where I would be happy to camp and grab a soda?* Rather than reveal to his boss that he might not agree with him, he kept quiet. After all, the environmental wizard was probably right. Perhaps the scenery was marred by the signs of civilization.

For certain, enough vehicles accompanied him on the road. Those big RVs sure chugged the gas. And they were hard to pass, he grumbled to himself as he glanced at his watch. Evidently, everybody was trying to get to rooms or campgrounds before dinner.

When they pulled into Gardiner, Montana, Pierce hunted down the hotel where he had made reservations. It had been tough finding a room anywhere near the park. All the rooms within Yellowstone's boundaries had been sold out six months ago. And the rush of reporters had gobbled up most of the remaining accommodations in the surrounding communities. Doggedly, Pierce had pursued rooms, finally finding a small, two-bed motel room just off the main drag in town. He referred several times to the directions he had scribbled while talking to the motel clerk over the phone.

Weary after the long drive the intern and his bags checked in.

Once in the room, Crane spread his stack of papers over one of the beds and began reorganizing them. He sent Pierce out to find a pizza or something to eat.

Pierce welcomed the opportunity to walk back out into the open air. A few families and couples were also strolling through the small town. Light was fading but he could still make out the peaks of mountains at the edge of town. He walked along the bridge crossing the Yellowstone River and continued in the direction of the park's gate. Gardiner ended near a building that sported a sign reading "K-Bar" and in smaller letters "Pizza."

"As good a place as any," Pierce said and stuck his head inside. The place was busy, and the smell of pizza was inviting, but before going in, he stood on the stoop for a few more minutes to watch darkness fall on the mountains.

Inside, he stood near one pool table and a bar. The table, and most of the bar, were in use. Toward the back of the room several dining tables were filled with people consuming various amounts of pizza and beer. He settled into one of two empty bar stools and grabbed a menu. His attention was divided between the menu and the end of the bar, where the pizzas were being prepared for the ovens. Finally, a waitress approached and took his order for a meatless pizza to go and a soft drink while he waited.

Sipping on his soda, he turned around to watch the pool game in front of him. A large, tough-looking man in his late twenties sank three striped balls in a row before missing. His partner was a muscular woman who looked like she wasn't going to need her partner's advice on how to shoot pool. The opposing team was made up of two scruffy guys about Pierce's age. The first challenger missed his shot. The muscular woman followed by nailing another stripe, but she didn't have a good shot left and missed. Too many solids on the table. The next young guy hit a couple before missing. Then the big guy finished off the stripes, pointed to one of the corner pockets with his cue, and put the eight ball into that pocket.

Pierce noticed a row of quarters lined up on the side of the pool table. He wasn't sure if it was a wager or what. But the winners didn't touch it. Instead, a Native American grabbed a quarter off the near end of the row, added three more quarters to it and put them in the slots on the side of the table to release all the sunken balls. He racked the balls for the woman who was preparing to send the cue ball into them.

With a loud crack, the cue ball scattered the other fifteen, dropping two solid balls into pockets. The game was on, and then it was over. She ran the table and smiled at her partner. He nodded to the Native American challenger and said, "We're done." The new player thanked him and waited for his challengers to insert the money and start the next game. The man and woman walked over to the bar and stood next to Pierce to order drinks.

"That was pretty impressive," said Pierce. He decided to see if these pool players were locals, and if so, he would try to get some inside information about Yellowstone's bears. Crane would be proud of him for uncovering anything useful.

"Thanks," the woman answered. She was sizing him up. But he knew she wasn't checking him out romantically, just seeing what he was made of. He figured he would pass the test. Long hair, goatee, sandals. The uniform of the environmentally aware. He must have looked harmless enough.

"I usually play until I run the table," she said. "It

always takes about five or six games, and then I stop."

"So you must be lucky enough to live around this beautiful area."

She smiled an acknowledgment. Her partner leaned over and extended a hand.

"Dusty Steward. This is my friend Eva Lacy."

Pierce accepted the man's hand. Though this guy looked extremely rugged, he had kind eyes and he didn't seem threatened that another guy was talking to his date. On the other hand, they may not be dating. They seemed friendly toward each other, but perhaps not more than that. Besides, Pierce's slight frame couldn't really be threatening to the hulk in front of him. The smaller man tried to give the hand a firm shake. "I'm Randy Pierce."

"What brings you here, Randy? Besides pizza," asked Lacy.

"I work for People for the Environmental Way. We're here investigating the treatment of Yellowstone Bears," he said proudly.

Steward choked on his beer. And Lacy laughed.

Pierce was puzzled. "What's wrong?"

Steward wiped beer off his shirt while Lacy explained. "Oh, Dusty and I have had a couple of conversations about your boss, Crane." She jerked a thumb toward Steward. "He's not a big fan. We're park rangers." She didn't offer more.

Pierce stared hard at Steward. Had he seen the ranger in The Scoop story on TV? If so, this ranger was much larger than he appeared on a 19-inch set. And suddenly more intimidating. Pierce's face flushed, embarrassed that he had started a conversation with the wrong guy. About then, Pierce's pizza arrived. He fumbled with his wallet to try and pay and exit quickly. Steward waved at the bartender. "Todd, put that pizza on top of the oven to keep it warm and refill this guy's drink. Randy, I think we need to exchange some information."

Lacy grabbed a table that was being vacated. The three sat down, Pierce's eyes nervously shifting between the two rangers.

"Relax, Randy," said Steward, placing his meaty hand on the young man's shoulder. "We help people who have been roughed up. We don't do much roughing up ourselves."

"He'll behave. I'm still mostly on your side," Lacy added.

"Uh, Mr. Crane will be expecting me back any minute."

Steward leaned forward in his seat, resting his big arms on the table. But the strong arms were not as intimidating to Pierce as the intense, deep eyes. "You're free to go, Randy, but let me ask you one question first. Why are you uneasy? PEW says it's interested in protecting the park. My employer, the National Park Service, is also interested in protecting the park. I can't imagine why our two groups are at odds. Don't we have the same goals? Shouldn't we be on the same team?"

Pierce breathed a short sigh of relief. "Oh thank God. You must agree with us then. You think the bears should be protected by keeping people out."

A sharp laugh escaped from Lacy. "I wouldn't go that

far. And you may have to sit here for a long time. He loves to talk about this."

Steward frowned at Lacy and turned back to Pierce.

Now Pierce was confused. The big guy was telling him that they should be on the same side, but also that he disagreed with Lester Crane. The woman was laughing it off, like she didn't agree with the big guy. And Pierce didn't know if either one was going to help him or punch him. And they were staring at him waiting for him to say something.

"Don't you think the bears must be protected?" he squeaked. It was the best he could do. A pretty safe line, wasn't it?

Steward continued his stare. "I know that every day Eva and I wander through the park physically working to protect it and to protect the people in it. And I know that every day your boss, Lester Crane, goes to an office in Washington and tries to raise money. Usually, we can protect bears from people and people from bears. But we can't protect the bears, or the people, from becoming PEW's next fundraising tool."

"Here we go," laughed Lacy as she leaned back in the chair.

Steward ignored her. "They haven't yet designed a fence, a radio collar or an ear tag that fits the political animal. Thankfully, those kinds of animals are usually content to eat each other. But sometimes they need to use something else as bait to lure another of their kind for the kill.

"The rangers can catch poachers. We can fine people for feeding bears. We can do lots of things to ease the relationship between people and bears. But we are powerless to protect bears from becoming bait in some political animal's trap."

"You're wrong." Pierce startled himself by responding. Perhaps this guy's lecture was reminding him of his dad, and Pierce's natural instinct to argue with Pop was overriding his natural instinct for survival.

Whatever the reason, he dove in. "We're above politics. Lester Crane cares about the environment. That's his priority. He may know how to play the political games, but only because he has to. If it wasn't for him, people would run over this park, chasing out bears, killing elk, mining for minerals. You should be grateful for Lester Crane. Without him there wouldn't be any park for you to work in."

Steward smiled at the upset student. That was the last response Pierce expected. He had been bracing for a broken jaw and his own ascension to the ranks of martyr.

"Randy, did you notice, outside the front door, the mountains?" Pierce nodded, so the ranger continued. "Did you notice the great big one with the pointed top?"

The intern's frightened, angry eyes softened as he thought about the breathtaking view that he had watched from the doorway. He hadn't wanted to come in until the sun set so he would not miss a second of the scene.

"You mean the one that turned more and more orange as the sun went down?" he spoke, more a whisper really.

"That's the one. It's called Electric Peak, one of the tallest mountains in the park, nearly 11,000 feet above sea level. It got its name during one of the early Yellowstone explorations. A scientist climbed the mountain to take readings and measurements. Then an electrical storm rolled in, forcing him to race back down to safety. As he approached, the others in his camp noticed that his hair was standing on end and none of them could touch him because the built-up static electricity shocked them."

Steward sipped his drink, staring steadily at Pierce. He continued.

"The mountain still attracts lightning. Two years ago, a couple of guys about your age ignored approaching storm clouds and climbed to the top. They reached the summit about the same time a strong thunderstorm did. They tried to retreat but weren't as lucky as the early explorer. One of the men was hit directly and killed instantly. His friend suffered serious burns but lived. I led the team that brought them back to ground level."

Pierce stared and said nothing. Lacy shifted uncomfortably in her seat. Steward went on.

"Should we have protected those young men from that mountain? Should we have protected the mountain from those young men? You may not think that's a tough answer. To Lester Crane and probably to you, it seems perfectly clear that we should keep people away."

Steward paused. When Pierce nodded, slightly, the ranger leaned forward and spoke very firmly but not in the least bit threatening.

"But consider this, are you satisfied only looking at Electric Peak from the front step of the K-Bar?"

Pierce thought about that for a minute. He had to admit that from the minute he saw that mountain he wondered what it looked like from other angles, how it felt to stand on top. He didn't answer. Was it really going to be taken away?

He glanced at Lacy and she was staring into her own lap. Her expression of contemplation must have been exactly the same as what was on his troubled face.

Steward continued. "You should get your pizza and get back to work. I'm sure you and Lester will be busy figuring ways to close our park. But I'll ask you again. Why are we not on the same team? What are you trying to achieve, really?"

Pierce left the two rangers at the table as he paid for his food and left the bar. The moon was bright enough that he could make out the silhouette of Electric Peak. Impressive. On his walk back, he began to question what he was doing. In rooting for keeping people away from Yellowstone, he had assumed he would be an exception, that *he* would still be allowed to wander through the park, even if all the stupid people were locked out. But the way Dusty Steward put the question to him, it occurred to him for the first time that perhaps he would not be allowed to see the park either. Where was that line going to be drawn? He looked over his shoulder at the jagged, elevated, skyline.

As Pierce put his key in the motel room door he heard voices. Two voices inside the room. Crane's voice he recognized instantly but the other was a mystery. Male. About his own age. Slowly, he opened the door.

Crane and the stranger looked up from a map they had spread across the desk. *Who is that guy and where did he come from?*

"Sorry that took so long. They were busy," Pierce offered.

"Randy, this is Bernie Wilson," said Crane. "He's one of our guys." Both smiled as Crane slapped him on the back. "He's my contact out here. This is the guy that calls and keeps us up to date on the Yellowstone action. Couldn't live without him."

"Smells good," Wilson nodded toward the pizza. "I'm ready for a short break."

As the three shoved gooey pizza in their mouths and drank soda from recyclable cans, Pierce evaluated the new arrival. Not more than five years older than himself. Hair hanging over his ears. Loose, comfortable clothes. *He looks like me with a little more seasoning.*

But something about the look in his eyes was kind of sneaky. Pierce wasn't yet sure if that was good or bad. A few frat boys with pilfered exam questions looked like that. Some of the true environmental guerrillas who visited PEW looked that way too.

As the dinner conversation progressed Pierce noticed the easy flow between Wilson and Crane. The elder man obviously viewed Wilson on nearly an equal level. For that alone Pierce regarded Wilson with some admiration and considerable envy.

*That's what I want to be*, thought Pierce.

"Did you find out anything interesting in town?" asked Crane.

The question startled Pierce out of his thoughts. "I talked to a couple of off-duty rangers."

Crane grinned. "I'm sure they were full of kind words."

"They weren't too bad. When I found out what they were I expected them to be more angry. They were more philosophical."

He took another bite and chewed slowly. Looking up, he saw Crane and Wilson staring at him, waiting.

"They did raise a good point," he ventured. "Why have we put them in such negative light? Shouldn't we be working with them?"

Wilson snickered, sending Pierce's feelings crashing into the ground.

Crane looked to the far wall and bit off more pizza. He seemed to be weighing the right statement, and the right attitude. Patient and nurturing won out.

"Randy, they're part of the establishment that's barreling down the wrong road. They're an extension of the Park Service. Deep down, the individual rangers care about nature and the environment, but ultimately, they're going to be loyal to their employer. They depend on millions of tourists coming to the park, much as this motel does. When it comes down to it, they'll sacrifice wildlife on behalf of people."

"Don't they do some good too? I mean, they catch poachers and try to keep people from damaging things."

"That's just a futile patch job on a sinking ship. Besides, we can't get enough public support by praising them. If we tell the public that the Park Service and its rangers have worked really hard to keep a bad system from being worse, then there's no crisis. People won't be motivated to support our agenda. It's much better, really, to go at them. Besides, they've got their own PR staff to save their image."

Crane and Wilson started a new conversation topic while Pierce felt out of his league.

*I'll do better next time.*

\*\*\*\*\*\*\*\*\*\*\*\*\*\*

"Seemed like a nice-enough kid," said Lacy after Pierce had left the K-Bar.

"His brain hasn't been completely washed yet," grumbled Steward. "But I don't give him much of a chance. He looked the part of a kook. Did you see him start to argue? He just started sputtering rhetoric, like I was his dad or something."

"At least he listened a little bit. Better than some of them do."

"Even you listened, again. I'll bet you're getting tired of my preaching."

She just shrugged.

"Well, thanks for letting me blab." He sat there, staring at his beer. "And thanks for coming along tonight."

She shrugged again. "Well, I didn't want you to have to face the pool tables alone."

"Man, I'm glad I didn't bet against you," Steward laughed. "I heard you were good, but that was some great pool."

She winked. "Accessible entertainment out here."

He was glad they had changed the subject.

He knew she was annoyed with his speech outside the hospital. He wanted to stay on good terms with her because they would still have to work together on this bear case. So he asked her to come to the K-Bar to unwind. *Now, the big question, is this a date?*

The conversation continued to loosen, from pool to volleyball to fishing. He was about to ask about the date status when the front door swung wide open, catching the attention of the two rangers. In tromped Sharon Reynolds, the park's PR chief. She headed straight for them.

"Please tell me this is a social call," said Steward.

Reynolds shook her head. "I know how you feel about this so I wanted to let you know before you heard about it from a tourist. We've decided to close the campgrounds at Bridge Bay, Fishing Bridge and Grant Village until we can be certain our visitors will be safe."

"Crap!"

"Dusty, it's important for the image of this park that no one else get mauled. We're getting beat up in the press. We lost face over trapping all those bears and we still didn't catch the right one. Plus, a little kid and his dad get attacked. We can't catch the bear and we can't keep people safe. And then that innocent bear got killed. We've got to do something to restore the public's confidence."

Steward was fuming. "So our plan is to cave in to that little weasel, Crane. Look, we'll catch that bear sooner or later and we can *never* guarantee that people will be safe. We're not rebuilding confidence or making friends by chasing people out."

"I understand your position. But the decision's been made. At least give me credit for finding you and letting you know."

Steward muttered a barely audible thanks.

"Sorry, Dusty. I'll see you guys later," Reynolds said as she left.

**************

"You're looking at Old Faithful in Yellowstone National Park," said the voice of Laurie Tomlison, female anchor of The Today Show. TV screens across the country displayed steam rising from the famous geyser cone. The producers hoped it would be erupting during this segment, but the geyser was too unreliable, at least by TV scheduled time. Within the next five minutes, give or take a few minutes, the geyser would surely perform.

Surrounding the natural fountain, at a safe distance, a crowd of people stood on the boardwalk that had been placed there years ago for their benefit. Even without checking on the next estimated eruption time, a visitor could get a pretty good idea when it was due by the size of the crowd hanging around on the boardwalk. At this moment it was pretty full. In the background the Old Faithful Inn, a magnificent log hotel, provided a pleasant visual distraction for those people who were not otherwise occupied by waving at the camera, an even more popular distraction today. The image was replaced by Tomlison's smiling face.

"The relationship between bears and people has always been controversial in Yellowstone. Our earlier segments this morning showed you how dangerous that relationship can be for people. But our next guest says it's the *bears* who are in danger. He says it's time for people to back down and stay out of this park." The picture changed to Crane, smiling and looking relaxed. "Lester Crane is the director of People for the Environmental Way. Welcome to The Today Show, Mr. Crane."

"Thanks, Laurie, and please call me Les."

Back to Tomlison. "Why is it that you think people should be kept out of Yellowstone?"

As Crane's face re-filled the screen, he took on a more serious look. "Well, Laurie, a growing number of people in this country believe in saving wildlife. Many of us think it's an embarrassment that hundreds if not thousands of species on this planet have died off as a result of mankind carelessly moving in and destroying them. Not always on purpose, but it happens nonetheless. Just because the grizzly bear is big and powerful does not mean it's not also fragile. We should do what we can to protect it."

"We're going to show part of a tape that you brought along," said Tomlison, looking at a monitor. Her face was replaced by the tape of the drugged bear being hauled from the trap. "This is the now-famous tape your organization secretly made of bears being trapped, drugged and tested."

"Yes. We've spent a lot of money trying to show people this tape, how the bears are treated in this park. This trapping spree followed the death of Senator Patrick's daughter. And you might remember that he used a photograph from this tape to ask the Park Service to quit abusing grizzlies."

"It must be nice to have such a strong ally."

"The senator is a brave man. We mourn his loss." The tape ended and the cameras switched back to Crane. "I might add that he was only partly successful. The rangers have scaled back their trapping, but it's still going on."

"Yet, your proposal to keep tourists out of Yellowstone is still controversial. Don't you think all these people who have come to see these geysers will be disappointed if they're locked out?"

"You would not believe the calls of support that PEW receives each day. The public is behind us. Yes, there may be some disappointment at not seeing Old Faithful, but that doesn't compare to the disappointment people will feel when the last grizzly bear in the lower 48 states dies and they know their own government caused it."

"The Park Service just announced this morning that it's closing three campgrounds and all back-country camping near the latest bear incident. Have they gone far enough, Les?"

The TV screens showed a color map of the park with red "Closed" signs over the affected camping areas. Crane's voice continued.

"Not at all. Bears are everywhere in this park. We can't worry only about the incidents that have happened in the past. We must try to prevent the ones that will happen tonight, next week or next month."

"How can people get in touch with PEW to offer support and find out more information."

Crane listed the toll-free number and web site address which were also printed at the bottom of the screen.

"Lester Crane, thank you very much. After our break," Tomlison paused while the screen changed to an image of a group of rangers standing at the side of the road looking at a gray, furry lump. "Last night a motorist hit and killed a gray wolf, one of just a few in the park. Our Nate Williams has the story. And then," the screen switched to a picture of a woman sauteing some vegetables over a Coleman stove. "Camp cooking with Chef Madeline. We'll be back."

"All clear!" shouted the crewman, alerting everyone that the cameras and microphones were off, allowing talking, nose-scratching, cursing and anything else not appropriate for a television celebrity or guest. Tomlison shook Crane's hand and thanked him for being on the show. He returned the thanks and walked over to the producer to make sure the man had his motel phone number in case they needed him to comment on anything else. As he left the set, Pierce caught up with him.

"Great job, Les."

"Thanks. How'd you do with CBS?"

"They weren't interested in a live shot, but I talked them into interviewing you for the evening news. I know that gives them editing power, but I think we brought along enough background footage to have some control over their story. The producer I talked to seems sympathetic to our cause."

"Where are they staying?"

"Down at Grant Village. They were grumbling that they couldn't get any closer to Old Faithful. Right now they're debating whether to try and broadcast from here or set up closer to their rooms with the lake in the background."

"I hope they stay where they are," Crane said as he narrowed his eyes.

"Why's that?"

"That Grant Village development is a perfect setting for us. That thing was built in a bear area. I'm sure it disrupted the feeding paths of many grizzlies. We can point that out. How about ABC?"

"They're worse off than we are," Pierce exclaimed. "They're staying all the way out at Cody. I found their producer scouting out a location around Old Faithful for their evening news. They're definitely interested in talking to you, but they're still working out their schedule. They've got two reporters here and they want to cover you, last night's wolf killing, the comeback from the 1988 fires and the huge crowds in the park." He laughed. "I think they got that idea when they couldn't get a room closer than Cody. Anyway, they haven't yet decided what will be covered when." He looked at his watch. "They need to decide soon or they're not going to have time to get it all. I gave them the cell phone number and beeper number."

"We're kind of stuck here for a while anyway," Crane said with disgust as he looked around at all the tourists.

"I hope they make up their mind pretty soon," said Pierce. "Man, I can't believe how big this park is. I would say we should go to Grant Village and check on CBS but that's an hour away."

"How's the web page coming?"

"I should be able to upload your hectic schedule as soon as I get it confirmed. You know, times, networks. Let the public know you're making good use of their donations." Pierce grinned.

Crane smiled back. "I'll take care of this next interview. You see what you can find out about FOX."

With that, Crane walked to the CNN camp, which was next to NBC. As big a park as it was, there was not much room for TV crews to get the perfect shot of Old Faithful without broadcasting each other.

*****************

Steward sat among the late-breakfast crowd at the Lake Lodge cafeteria, slowly scanning the *Billings Gazette*. Few daily newspapers were available in the park. The *Gazette* provided good-enough coverage of what was going on in the local world.

Normally he didn't have a great deal of time to read a paper, but Lacy hadn't shown up yet for their meeting, so he had the luxury. Meeting in the tourist cafeteria was a risk, because of all the possible interruptions. However, he didn't feel quite comfortable inviting her to his tiny apartment, which was hidden with other Park Service housing in a nearby wooded area. It would have been a cozy meeting, but perhaps a little too suggestive. He wasn't sure if it would have been more embarrassing to invite her or to hear her turn him down.

So he waited in a wide-open, public cafeteria. At least the view was much better here than from his apartment.

The clatter of a breakfast tray set noisily on his table startled him out of his reading. He looked up to see the tired expression of Eva Lacy staring back at him.

"Nice of you to wait," she said, gesturing toward his empty plate.

He set down his paper and grabbed his mug.

"I didn't finish my coffee yet," he answered hopefully.

She managed half a smile and dropped into the chair across from him. Between bites of scrambled eggs and bacon, she began to vent.

"I had to lead an 'Early Riser Geyser' tour at 6:30 this morning. That wouldn't have been so bad if I didn't have to rush all the way over here as soon as it was done." She set down her fork. "And then I was stuck behind a mansion-sized RV on Craig Pass."

"Uh, sorry," he said sheepishly. He really felt sorry for Lacy these days. She had ongoing duties at the Old Faithful geyser basin, but the Chief Ranger wanted her to stay involved with the hunt for the Patrick bear. That meant she had to meet Steward here this morning, so they could go back to the Bridge Bay campground for more tracking, to see if maybe the bear had come back.

"It's not your fault," she conceded.

They sat quietly for a moment. Steward stared out the

large window at Yellowstone Lake at the snow-capped mountains to the east. In the field between the lodge and the lake four bison were grazing. The usual perfect photo in this part of the park. Other people apparently agreed, as at least ten tourists were standing in the field, some too close to the bison, and taking photos. The bison seemed content to eat and the photographers did not seem determined to get any closer. Satisfied for now, Steward turned back to his partner. She had been watching the scene too.

"They're something, aren't they?" he pondered aloud.

"The bison or the tourists?"

He laughed. "Both, I suppose. But I was thinking about the tourists. At least they seem curious about this park."

"Almost too curious sometimes," she added.

He nodded vigorously. Vacationing in a land as large and legendary as Yellowstone requires lots of guidance. In addition to handling physical errors of judgment by visitors, rangers had to deal with a barrage of questions.

"What time does Old Faithful go off?" "Where can I see a bear?" "How come you let those buffalo wander around loose? Couldn't someone get hurt?" Rangers and service employees tried to do their best to patiently and politely educate visitors about this wondrous land. But Steward knew the desk clerks in the lodge kept a notebook of the stupidest questions they heard. Truly idiotic additions would be shared with the desk clerks at other locations. He had contributed a couple that he had been asked on the road.

"Curious as they may be, not one tourist has asked me about Lester Crane's news conference," he said.

"Dusty, how would they know about it?" she challenged.

"Good point," he said.

Few, if any, of those staying in the park would have seen Crane on the news. The mountains encircling the park made for poor television reception and there was no cable available. Only a few employees had satellite dishes. In fact, televisions were virtually nonexistent in Yellowstone, something that caught many visitors off guard. Perhaps one of the more magical aspects of the park was that people realized they could spend a couple of days away from TV and popular culture and still the sun rose in the morning. Visitors were amazed by the sights during the day and then warmed in the evening by watching the sunset while sitting in a rocking chair by a fire, reading or talking with a loved one.

"Of course, they might have read the paper." He patted the half-folded newspaper next to him.

"How'd we come out?" She pointed to the headline, *Momentum Building to Restrict Park Access*.

He shrugged. "Not surprisingly, the Billings people want the tourist dollars to continue to flow through their city. They're painting Crane as an extremist. But I don't know. The way they talk about the nationwide media attention, and there's some poll that they quote, it looks like the public is starting to be convinced it should lock itself out."

"Was anybody near a TV last night?" she asked.

"Joe Lowry was out at West," meaning the town of West Yellowstone, Montana, "and he said Crane was all over the news. From what Lowry said, other people near the TV were rooting him on."

They said nothing and resumed their watch out the window at the lake and mountains. The bison hadn't moved much but a different shift of tourists was taking pictures.

She bit into her toast and chewed slowly. Finally she said, "I don't know if you're starting to get to me or what. But I'm feeling uneasy about this whole thing. Do you think those people will actually be convinced to give up on coming to this park, so they can save it?" She pointed at the happy shutterbugs.

"Hard to say. Americans love to feel guilty. We're quick to accept the blame for everything, even if it's kind of stupid to blame an entire nation for one goofed-up bear. But they are our best defense." He nodded toward the tourist congregation in the meadow.

"Even the slow-moving RV I got stuck behind is important, assuming the pilot drives carefully," she said.

"And we have another important force on our side," he smiled. "As long as this park has its famous geysers, people will want to come. Crane may talk them into packing some guilt along with the rest of their bags, but they want to see Old Faithful and they'll make sure their politicians let them."

# SEVEN

About 15 miles northwest of Yellowstone, Tom Jackson cast a fly beneath the limb of a dead tree that stood about 10 feet out of the water. Earthquake Lake and the air above it were still. A few white puffs decorated the baby-blue afternoon sky. The lake remained calm as Jackson rowed his boat carefully, partly to avoid other dead trees that poked up from the water, and partly to keep from spooking the trout.

The bare trees he sat amongst had once been filled with green branches that shaded a popular camping area. In 1959 a violent earthquake dropped the side of a mountain into the Madison River, creating an instant dam, killing several campers, and forming the lake from which he was now trying to coax fish.

He was a little disturbed by the evidence that still remained of the old quake. He could see where the old road had broken and slid off the side of the hill, but he tried to ignore it. He could have fished around two dwellings that had been thrown from their foundations, their roofs still peeking from the water after all these years, but he didn't feel very comfortable with that. He had seen the quake's scars on the mountainside for several miles along the road leading to his present location, but he put those out of his mind.

*A few jitters are a small price to pay for good fishing,*
he told himself. It was a mantra often repeated on his fishing
trips here.

He refocused his attention on a #12 hook to which he
had tied a clump of feathers. The feathers were supposed to
look like a bug that might fall out of a tree. This creation sat
on top of the water. An invisible leader of about three feet
connected the imitation bug to a much thicker, yellow floating
line that led to an 8½-foot rod in Jackson's right hand. No fish
rose to take his feathers.

With a quick, graceful motion he lifted rod, floating
line, leader and fly off the water without disturbing the
surface. The line flew behind him like a slow-motion
bullwhip, then fluidly reversed course, shot out in front of
him, and set the fly on the other side of the tree, under a
different branch.

He watched the lure carefully, ready to set the hook as
soon as a fish could be convinced that the feathery concoction
might be tasty. No movement. At first.

Looking back at that moment, he wasn't able to
remember if he noticed the water move first or the tree. But
both moved and then he heard small rocks sliding down the
steep slope that was responsible for this lake. He was not in
the immediate path, but that was not especially comforting.
Where an earthquake had once shrugged off tons of earth into
the river, more rocks were sliding, and fast. He could no
longer ignore his uneasiness about Earthquake Lake.

In the bar that evening he re-enacted his experience for his friends. "I'm sitting in my damned rowboat thinking, 'O God, it's happening again.' So I grabbed my oars and started rowing like hell to get back to my car. I forgot all about my fly rod until the lure snagged a tree and started pulling line out.

"At first I think I got a trout on, and can you believe I actually forgot about what was going on. I grabbed my rod to set the hook." This drew hoots from his buddies who had also felt the tremor but weren't fishing at the time, though they were good fishermen and understood his predicament.

"The hook don't come out on the first two tugs and the rocks are still coming down the old landslide. So I'm thinking, 'Do I chuck my Orvis and save my butt or do I face Kingdom Come ready to fish.'" Now his friends were laughing so hard they were in tears.

Jackson took a long pull off his beer then continued. "I grabbed my knife, cut the line and started rowing again, but not 'till I kiss my Orvis first. So I'm rowing like crazy, adrenalin pumping, and I'm slamming into trees and anything else in the water. I don't know how I didn't break my boat in two. Finally I get back to the boat launch and I jump out, water up to my waist and then climb onto the shore. I'm tugging the bow up on the shore and that's when I finally stop and look around." He paused again to take another drink and build suspense.

"There ain't no more rocks falling. Nothing's moving anymore and the only sound out there is me panting and water dripping off me." His pals erupted again. By this time they all knew it had been a minor tremor. Other than some broken glass and plates, no damage in the area.

The conversation continued with lots of laughing and teasing.

A loud voice from the end of the bar cut through the chatter. "Shut up you guys! Look at the damned TV. Something's happened in the park."

\*\*\*\*\*\*\*\*\*\*\*\*\*\*

Perhaps that wild bear the rangers wanted would come out of the woods and eat his family. That's what Randall Beaman could hope for at least.

"Take me too," he muttered looking from the Old Faithful geyser cone to the tree line where, unfortunately, no bear was present.

"What honey?"

"Nothing," Beaman replied to his wife. Then turned to his kids, "Dammit Shelley, don't feed the ground hogs."

"They're marmots," she replied, in a snotty tone that she had gradually perfected during the long hours spent in the car this family vacation. She tossed one more Dorito off the boardwalk that snaked around Old Faithful and the rest of the thermal features in the Upper Geyser Basin. The waiting rodent happily grabbed the bounty and waddled under the boardwalk to devour its prize. Shelley and the other Beaman child laughed and glanced back at their parents to see if discipline would follow.

Day one, from Ohio across Indiana, Illinois and into Iowa, he had pleaded with his children to behave. His wife was not much help, because she was still mad that they hadn't gone to Myrtle Beach, a much shorter trip, she pointed out to him each night as they went to bed. During the rest of Iowa and most of South Dakota he changed tactics and used sterner warnings. Their whining skills became more finely honed, though, partly because of the previous day's practice and partly because his wife had joined in with the children. He even made the mistake of threatening to turn around and go home if they didn't behave. In unison, the other three yelled, "good," and laughed at him for the next 35 miles.

The Badlands and Mt. Rushmore were barely enjoyable because of the nagging. The third day, leaving South Dakota and traversing Wyoming was even worse. He screamed in the morning and, when that didn't work, started grudgingly accepting that this vacation had been planned by the Devil himself to torment Randall into insanity. Wyoming seemed to drag on endlessly. Beaman had time to reflect on the trip from Hell and realize that while some parents could track the successes and failures of their parenting skills over time, he could do so geographically. He couldn't wait to see what Idaho, Oregon and California would bring.

But first, Yellowstone. My God it had taken a long time to get here. Rand McNally should be sued. In his atlas, his home state of Ohio got two pages. Wyoming, which was more than twice the size, only got one. He hadn't fully understood how long it took to drive these western states. It was going to take him longer to get to the Pacific Ocean than he had planned. So now he was in a hurry.

And his anger was starting to spill over from his family to his surroundings. Why did the park have to be so big? Why are there so many RVs on the road? Why can they only drive about 30 mph on the winding roads with no passing lanes? And what is taking this stupid fountain so long?

He had always thought of Old Faithful erupting every hour, on the hour. That's why they called it Old Faithful. But when he and his "cheery" bunch got to the park, they found out that the world's most famous geyser was not so predictable. A friendly employee tried to explain to him that the interval was closer to 80 minutes and it was nowhere near reliable enough to set a watch by. Evidently, the park staff used some complicated formula based on the time and duration of the last eruption to predict the next one, give or take 10 minutes.

The employee was also very excited about an earth tremor that had just been felt in the area. *The Earth is quaking in Wyoming. I can't wait to see what California does to me*, Beaman thought.

On another day, on another trip, with a different family, he might have been interested in the details about geyser eruptions and he might have been thrilled to be in the park for an earth tremor. On this day, on this trip, with this family he merely sighed at the realization that the employee was telling him his long day of driving and waiting to get to this geyser would involve even more waiting to see water squirt out of it.

Again, he looked to the trees to see if his salvation might come bounding out to end it all. No luck. So he turned back to the mound of dry, gray earth and the distant pool from which steam rose.

His wife crabbed about the sun being too bright. His daughter complained that she was hungry. His son wanted to throw rocks into Old Faithful. His watch told him that the geyser was already five minutes past its margin of error.

"Come on already," he shouted to the geyser.

Around him others murmured agreement. He caught the eye of another man with an equally restless family. Though they didn't exactly smile at each other, their silent glance confirmed that neither was alone in his misery. Feeling just as bad, but no longer solitary, Randall Beaman sat back on the bench and waited for Old Faithful to erupt.

And he waited.

# *EIGHT*

"What do you mean it stopped?" Dusty Steward asked the voice on the phone.

Lacy was in the ranger station with him, helping to fill out a permit for some potential backpackers who planned to camp overnight in one of the areas not yet closed by the Park Service. Steward's tone caused her to pause and stare at him.

He met her eyes. "I see. Eva's here with me. She was just about to head back. We're finishing up a back-country pass, then we'll be on our way. Can we run with lights? OK." He hung up and rejoined Lacy.

After explaining to the hikers about the dangers of bears and of drinking the water without boiling it first, they ushered out the boot-clad visitors.

As soon as the door was shut, Lacy turned to him. "So?"

"Apparently, Old Faithful isn't."

"No!"

"They just called. It's an hour overdue. You're the best geologist and they need you."

Lacy sat--fell, actually--on a bench. "Whoa. Give me a minute. You can't tell me Old Faithful is out-of-order and expect me to march cheerily out the door."

Steward joined her on the bench and rested a hand on her shoulder, reassuringly.

"Feeling guilty?" he asked.

"What the hell is that supposed to mean?" she snapped.

*Steward, you doofus,* he scolded himself. *You like this girl. Watch what you say.* Out loud he added, "It's just that I know how you've always resented that geyser."

Her eyes were beginning to get wet in the corners. "I don't resent it." She paused for a moment and inhaled deeply. Then she pointed angrily in the general direction of Old Faithful.

"That geyser brings in thousands, no, millions of visitors who don't appreciate all Yellowstone has to offer. Sure, they think the other stuff is okay. The scenery. The animals. But they only look at the other features because they happen to be on the way to Old Faithful. I stand in front of groups of tourists trying to explain the intricacies of geysers and the only thing they're interested in is 'What time does Old Faithful go off?'"

She stood and paced angrily in front of Steward.

"The turn-off from the main road to Old Faithful looks like a regular interstate interchange," she continued. "The inn, the general store, the filling station, are all larger and more commercialized than the facilities in the rest of the park. Old Faithful is not just the symbol of the park, but the symbol of the worst pressures on the park."

"Yet, Yellowstone without its most famous geyser is unthinkable," Steward added carefully.

He watched her for a minute. He swore he could actually see it sinking in. A door was opening in her mind. New connections were being made. Her eyes widened and her mouth dropped.

"My God," she gasped. "What happens if they quit coming?"

*Ah-ha,* he thought.

She jumped up. "I've got to get over there." They headed for the car.

As they buckled in and sped away she turned to Steward. "I know I'm going to handle the geology end, talk to reporters. To see if this is permanent or not. But Old Faithful isn't in your district. Why do they need you?"

"Guess."

It took her a moment, then it hit her. "They need someone to console the tourists who are standing around demanding to see their geyser."

"Bingo. In fact, already some guy from Ohio was so distraught he tried to kill himself by jumping in."

*****************

"Every geyser eruption is a minor miracle," Lacy was telling the sea of reporters. "The plumbing of a geyser is complicated, remarkable and fragile. We should feel lucky that Old Faithful continued to erupt as long as it did." She was groggy from a long night of taking samples and looking at data.

"So it's your position that the earth tremor from yesterday caused Old Faithful to stop?" asked a reporter.

"There is a relationship between seismic activity and geyser activity, " she responded. "Many times the shaking ground preserves geysers or re-activates dormant ones. In the case of yesterday's tremor, we believe it terminated Old Faithful."

"Can you re-start it?" came a question from the back of the mob.

"It's not likely," she answered quickly, not wanting to dwell on that fact. Nor did she want to bring up the idea that the Park Service did not usually "repair" natural phenomena.

Another reporter spoke up. "Couldn't vandalism by tourists be partly responsible for the end of the eruptions?"

She didn't answer right away. She knew that ever since the geyser was discovered people had been inexplicably drawn to throw in objects. The truly persistent seemed to think the secrets of Old Faithful could be coaxed out by tossing in rocks, sticks, coins, chair legs or anything else at hand. Over the years many such sacrifices had been belched out during eruptions.

The addition of boardwalks, a fair distance from the geyser, helped ensure the safety of Old Faithful as well as its visitors. But the sneaky and tenacious managed to continue their unofficial experiments. A few of the college-age employees who lived and partied near the geyser all summer formed an elite group known as the "I Peed in Old Faithful Club," which revealed more about its members than about the geyser.

*But if Dusty knows what he's talking about, and I'm still not certain that he does, maybe I better not give any more ammunition to Crane.*

Finally, she answered. "No. It's true that vandals have done their worst to Old Faithful ever since it was discovered. But that remarkable geyser handled it all and continued to provide regular eruptions, delighting generations of visitors. However, the countless years of past service were never a guarantee of continued service."

Without emotion she continued to field remaining questions. Her answers were professional and smooth but her heart wasn't in it.

Enough vandalism could ruin a geyser. But that wasn't the problem here. Internal, intricate plumbing damaged by an earthquake was much more serious than hand-tossed debris. And it was not the kind of thing that could be repaired. It was, however, natural, and that was what Yellowstone was all about. She looked at the ground between her boots as if she could see the blockage holding back the flow of hot water. As eager as she had been to get away from bear chasing and back to her geysers, she didn't want it to be this way.

Slowly, she turned to watch a wisp of steam curl upward from Old Faithful. A small crowd sat quietly around the boardwalk like a vigil. The steam rose and dissipated. *Eventually,* she thought, *the crowd would too.*

**************

Was Lester Crane actually salivating? Randy Pierce wasn't sure. He did witness, however, that his boss, who should have been exhausted from his busy media schedule of the past few days, was given a shot of adrenalin by the news of Old Faithful's demise.

They had gotten back to Washington just two days before. Pierce was crawling but Crane was flying. He attacked the phone and the computer with renewed vigor, causing Pierce to admire him once again for his devotion.

Giddy and exuberant yet able to concentrate on minute details, Crane was rapidly talking about the opportunity that had been laid in his lap.

Simply put, Lester Crane smelled blood.

"Millions of visitors trample on the fragile ground around the geyser," he was telling a reporter on the phone. "They throw things in it. It's only a wonder that Old Faithful lasted as long as she did. I predict other geysers and park wonders will also be extinct before our children have a chance to see them," he said.

That call finished, he took a swig of bottled water while dialing another number.

Pierce gave a questioning look.

"Bernie Wilson," he responded to the intern's expression.

When the call was answered he ordered, "Bernie. People are going to act up around the geysers, more than ever. Get photos."

He hung up the phone, and said, "Randy, you know what to do."

Pierce jumped to his computer. The position paper Crane had just been working on would soon appear on the PEW web page. Pierce would work up some appropriate, gloomy graphics. Perhaps an out-of-order sign over the geyser. If he could tie in the destructive influence of man, perfect.

*It's really hopping now*, smiled Pierce, finally feeling that rush of energy that must be driving Crane.

\*\*\*\*\*\*\*\*\*\*\*\*\*\*

How could Old Faithful be done? Even though she understood all the science and geology better than anyone, Lacy still couldn't believe it.

She looked at the stack of phone messages on her desk. Reporters, those could wait. Friends, they could probably wait too. Strangers, most likely just to ask if it was true, those could definitely wait.

She got up and walked to the window. Not as many people wandering around as usual. How could Old Faithful be done?

It was not the biggest geyser in the park. It wasn't the most spectacular or even the most regular. Because of the crowd that had converged on it each hour, it wasn't even the most enjoyable to watch. But it was OLD FAITHFUL. The one and only. How could it be done?

Through the window she saw the strong, purposeful

stride of Dusty Steward. *Everything is falling apart around him and he still looks like he's got the whole park under his control.*

"Can Lester Crane really shut down this park?" she blurted as soon as he walked in the door. "Do you think anybody is taking him seriously?"

"Nice to see you too, Eva," he replied with a smile.

"Sorry." She turned away. "I'm just having a tough time accepting all this."

"It's hard to believe people would support shutting us down," he answered. "On the other hand, I just got word from the reservation office, 10 percent of the winter reservations have canceled already and 5 percent of next summer's reservations have canceled too. That's only two days into this thing. They expect the cancellations to continue through the next week, with few people calling to take their place. If it weren't for all the reporters coming in it would be much worse."

"Why are people staying away? What's wrong with them?"

"People equate this park with that geyser and with wildlife. If the geyser's not working and the wildlife is trying to kill them, why should they come?"

"But there's so much more here," Lacy protested.

"Granted. You and I know that because we live here, but most people don't."

"This place isn't a secret," she insisted. "Millions of people visit Yellowstone every year. Even if they only think of bears and Old Faithful when they come in, it can't take them long to realize what else we have to offer."

"Yeah, and they've already seen it, so what do they care if the doors are locked behind them?" he snorted.

"But what about you and me and all the other 'lifers' who come back year after year? Can't we spread the word?"

"I wouldn't count on it," he said quietly.

Lacy frowned. The "lifers," the people who worked year-round or came back each summer season tended to claim ownership of the park. Because of their vast experiences in the Yellowstone area they would be well-equipped to sing the praises of all the hidden features that the general public may not know about. However, they also tended to dislike all the tourists -- plodding along in slow-moving RVs, stopping to take pictures of every bison within a mile of the road. Tourists get in the way. A seasoned hiker in a hurry to get to the next adventure had little patience for a family stopping in the middle of the road to take a picture. Many lifers would probably be happy if hotels shut down and people quit coming.

Steward rapped his knuckles on her desk. "If only we had gotten that bear quickly. At least that part of the controversy would be over."

"Anything new with that?"

He shook his head.

*Screw the bear.* She looked back out the window. What in the world was happening to Yellowstone? What was going to happen next?

How could Old Faithful be done?

**************

Senator Phil Patrick watched the traffic from his office window as he listened to the pair of colleagues behind him.

"Phil, you understand we're not talking about going out on a limb here. We're not going to pursue this if the President isn't behind us," said Senator Harris, the older of the two senators, a long-time lawmaker with a reputation for budget-cutting and deal-making.

"And it's not like we're asking you to take an active role here," added Senator Freemont, the other visitor, an up-and-coming influence peddler in the Senate.

The first man jumped back in. "Right. *If* we get the President on board, and *if* the public looks supportive and *if* it looks like your support will give us the votes we need, then we'd like to be able to tell people that you're with us."

Finally, Patrick turned around to face the two senators, friends really. In a legislative body of 100 people, with a little over half from his own political party, Patrick got a chance to know who his colleagues were and how they worked. He liked the two men before him now. Still, he was uncomfortable.

"You know," Patrick said, "I've been to Yellowstone. There's a lot more there than Old Faithful and bears."

"I know, I know," said Harris. "I took my family out there after the fires. Big place. Beautiful. But it's expensive and we have to get a grip on this country's budget."

"Pfffft," snorted Patrick. "How much money are you going to save by closing Yellowstone's gates and turning it into a wildlife refuge? The Park Service budget is not going to amount to anything in cutting the deficit. When are we going to start looking seriously at entitlements. That's where we've got to start cutting. It wasn't that long ago we were talking about surpluses. Now we're still dancing around the real issues and talking about cuts to the Park Service. Meaningless."

"Not exactly," Harris replied. "You're right that Yellowstone has nothing to do with our spending problems. But we've got to convince this country that we've trimmed back absolutely every piece of fat before we start snipping Social Security checks."

Patrick said nothing.

Harris continued, "The fact that we are still in Washington when we should be home with our own families on our own vacations is another reason this issue can fly now. It's hard for the membership to get worked up in defense of a vacation spot when we can't take our own vacation until this budget is straightened out."

"And Phil," chimed in Freemont. "Out latest polling suggests that people are beginning to see Yellowstone as fat, as one of those things that can be cut." He began to pull some papers out of his briefcase.

Patrick got angry. "Put that damned thing away. I don't want to look at the poll of the week. When are we going to stop following those things around here? We pay a bunch of reject political science majors ridiculous sums of money to ask people questions that they haven't really thought about. Everybody is able to come up with an opinion if you ask them. They don't care much but they answer anyway, without carefully considering the issue. Then we let those results control our every move. Nuts."

Nobody spoke as Patrick walked around his own office, like a futile, desperate lap around a prison cell.

"If I agree to join you on this issue, it will have nothing to do with that damned poll," he said.

"I hope that if you join us, that it's because it's the right thing to do," said Harris. "People in this Senate trust you, especially on the Yellowstone issue. If you agree to close it, they know it's not because of a poll," he paused to glance at Freemont. "That's why we want you on board. Hell, Phil, I want you to join us so I can convince myself I'm doing the right thing."

Patrick sat down in his chair and sighed. This issue wasn't going to go away was it? What would Jenny have wanted? She usually believed what Lester Crane preached, but would she support actually closing Yellowstone? If ever the park were to be closed, the federal budget and the current problems out there provided the opportunity. He glanced at the family photo on his desk. In the photo Jenny stood next to him, smiling her beautiful smile. *Stand next to me now*, he thought. *Tell me what to do.* The photo remained silent.

Finally he stood and looked at Harris and Freemont. "I'm not ready to commit yet. But I think you may be on to something. It may be time to lock it up."

# NINE

Since his retirement Charles Corbin had become an artistic fly fisherman. The graceful arm-rod-line movements masterfully presented carefully tied lures to waiting fish. Fly selection, fish finding, choice of casting technique were all skills crafted over time.

Today, standing thigh-deep in the crystal-clear Yellowstone River, somewhere in the calm stretch between LeHardy's Rapids and the thunderous falls, Charles reflected on his clumsy beginnings in this craft. In his late fifties he had stumbled upon a copy of Norman Maclean's *A River Runs Through it*. He was not far into the story before he could never look at bait fishing the same way again.

His wife was pleased when he sold all his poles and tackle at a garage sale. She was less thrilled when he quickly replaced it all with new, more expensive and time-consuming fly fishing equipment. But she grew pleased again when she discovered that his new hobby would bring them to the beautiful mountains every summer.

The first time he ventured into the water was comical. Though he didn't fall, he came close more than once. His action with the fly rod was no better. He was rapidly whipping his arm back and forth, slapping the water with his line and, he was sure, scaring every trout within a mile of him. He lost three flies, one in a tree on the shore and the others flew off the end of his line because he hadn't tied them on right.

While most people would have been discouraged, Charles was not. After a half hour, he waded out of the river, the Yellowstone, and sat on the shore, exhausted and laughing. It had been fun! He sought lessons from an employee at the Bridge Bay Marina and honed his craft with each succeeding vacation.

The typical fly fisherman wears oversized rubber pants, a big hat and a many-pocketed vest while standing in cold water waving a long stick back and forth. Forget the skill needed to catch a fish, a fly fisherman needs a great deal of skill to keep from being mistaken for a clown.

Over time, Charles achieved that level of talent and more.

He loved his hobby. And he loved practicing it in this part of the Yellowstone River best. Between rapids and falls the river was wide, shallow and smooth. The current was evident, but there was no rippling action. Rather, the river moved as a single piece. It was strange to step into. One would expect it to act more like an airport moving sidewalk than a body of water. But the foot broke the surface, same as with any river anywhere in the world, and the fisherman could walk out to just the right spot.

Another reason he enjoyed this section of the Yellowstone was that the park's road followed it. He was pushing 70 years and did not have it in him to hike to a back-country fishing spot, though he had been told of several that rewarded younger fishermen. Here, he could park near a picnic table, walk 50 yards and step among the cutthroat trout.

The clear water, too, seemed designed for the fisherman. Not only could he see the fish, but also their food. Periodically, Charles would stop casting and survey the different kinds of insects that were floating by. He carried with him a good selection of dry flies to mimic the ones that were on the surface and wet flies to mimic the nymphs that were under water. Without bending too far, he could identify the nymphs bouncing off rocks on the riverbed.

Such a nymph had been used to catch three fish already, which had been immediately set free in accordance with the "catch-and-release" regulation for this part of the river. He hadn't moved a fish in the last several casts, even though he saw his targets ahead of him. Patiently, he stopped casting and watched for a few minutes.

Whereas when he started fishing this morning the fish were not rising to the surface, now they were. He took quick inventory of the bugs floating by and tried to determine which were being eaten.

After selecting a matching lure and attaching it to his leader he paused to study the fish again. All morning he had worked his way from his car toward the middle of the river. He decided to go toward the other shore where few other fishermen ventured. No others were around currently, but he knew the river was popular, at least this side of it was.

About 20 yards from the far shore, he spotted a fat cutthroat upstream from him. He watched and waited. The fish floated in place, despite the current. Without any sudden movements, it rose to the surface then quickly popped a meal off the top of the water. Charles found his prey.

He cast way off target a couple of times to get his line out without spooking the fish. Then, during his back cast, he aimed for the forward throw and followed through, dropping the fly five feet in front of the fish's nose. The fish saw it and rose to let the current bring it in. Then the water surface broke and Charles felt the familiar tug of a fish on line.

He also heard an unfamiliar "woof" from the nearest shore.

Trying to keep his concentration on bringing in the fighting fish, he glanced to see what had caused the noise. A big, brown, furry face stared at him from out of the shadows of the trees. Instantly the fish was forgotten.

Charles slowly and carefully backed away from the bear. As it stepped out of the trees into the sunlight, he recognized it as a grizzly. He had run across them before while fishing. He knew the best thing to do was remain calm as he tried to get away.

"That's okay buddy. I'm getting out of your way." No sudden movements. No running. Backing up slowly.

His arm jerked once more and he quickly grabbed his fly rod with both hands, suddenly remembering the fish on the end of his line. He let out some additional slack and the fish shook loose. Thank God he had been using barbless hooks for catch-and-release.

He hadn't acted too suddenly had he? He refocused his attention on the shore just in time to see the bear lunging off the bank.

**************

Even with his car lights flashing, Steward had trouble getting through the people and the line of cars crowding the road along the Yellowstone River. He had left Lacy's office about 20 minutes before he got the call.

Traffic jams were common in the park. Some of the more popular wildlife don't shy away from the roads, or at least open areas visible from the roads. When a big animal wanders into view, brake lights flash, doors fly open and camera-clutching tourists rush toward the thing.

Park veterans can figure out what kind of animal has emerged based on the size of the traffic tie-up. Bison are plentiful enough near the roads that they only draw a moderate crowd. More cars will stop for a close-up of an elk, especially if it's a bull elk with antlers. Moose can draw an even bigger crowd. But bears are the true celebrities of the Yellowstone animal kingdom. Once the rangers began to effectively enforce the "Do not feed the bears" rule, bear sightings from the road became uncommon, almost rare. But occasionally, one would stroll out into a meadow, and the vacation paparazzi would appear instantly, cars clogging the narrow road.

Bear backups were big. On his way to the scene, Steward wondered just how large a bear-mauling backup would be. It was huge.

When the car could drive no farther he put the vehicle in park, lights still flashing, grabbed his shotgun and ran to where the crowd was gathered. He was the first ranger on the scene, having taken the distress call himself, but he expected other rangers, including Lacy, to be here any minute.

He yelled "Where?" at the front of the crowd and followed the response point to a spot on the other shore. He could see a hat lying on the bank. Nothing else.

With a loud splash he ran into the river. Through a strong current of bone-aching cold water, over slippery rocks and with a shotgun held overhead, one can only move so quickly. Steward did his best and reached the opposite shore, amongst the cheers of those on the other side.

More slowly and deliberately he approached the trees. He could easily follow the trail of disturbed grass that led to a trail of disturbed pine needles and undergrowth. Something, someone actually, had been dragged along. But he knew better than to run, shotgun or not, he didn't want to be the subject of an even longer trail.

Once his eyes adjusted to the tree-filtered light, his vision was good. The lodgepole pines formed a thick-enough canopy that bushes and undergrowth were minimal. The only obstructions to his sight were the straight trunks that didn't send out many branches below about eight feet.

Neither did the trees do much to obstruct his sense of smell. The fresh scent of pine was quickly covered by the heavy musk of bear and another, more pungent, odor. *Not that smell again.* About 30 yards into the trees, at the end of the trail, lay the lifeless body of Charles Corbin. After only a glance Steward knew he needn't bother checking for vital signs. So he carefully pressed on, gun ready.

*The damned bear should be here,* he thought. *They don't abandon their kill like this. So where is he?*

The bear must have heard the commotion of Steward splashing across the river. Was it possible it also saw the gun and knew what it was? Steward wondered. In any case, the bear had stopped dragging the body which enabled it to move faster and made it harder to track, not that bears are especially careful where they walk.

Steward slowed. If the bear was running, he would not be able to catch it anyway. Bears are too fast. If the bear was not running, then it might have something else in mind. Confronting the bear would be one thing. Confronting it on its terms would be another.

The odor was around, but he couldn't tell if the animal was near or far. Which way was the wind blowing? A golfer might bend to pluck some grass and watch in which direction it would blow. Too cumbersome for a deadly hunt. Steward merely concentrated on his own arm hairs. He could feel that they were blowing from his back toward the trail. The bear was downwind of him and would know he was coming.

Time to be even more careful, if that was possible. It was getting to be late evening. The sun was out, and was still coming through the trees, but its position in the sky was causing many odd-looking shadows here in the woods. Is that a bear? How about that? He couldn't really tell.

The light breeze rustled branches and plants. Yet he could pick out the occasional crunch that sounded like a heavy animal moving. And he still had a trail to follow. He took more careful steps in the direction where the bear should be.

By now, the automatic response to duty had subsided and the realization of where he was and what he was doing began to sink in. A human carcass lay about 100 feet behind him. A vicious bear was somewhere in front of him. And he was alone, though armed with a powerful shotgun. It wasn't really fear that gripped him now, but a sense that he needed to be extra efficient at his job. No mistakes allowed.

He continued along the fresh, winding trail, thinking and evaluating his next move. What would a bear do? Normally, a grizzly would have stayed to defend its dinner. But what would *this* bear do. By now Steward was convinced it was the same bear that killed Jenny Patrick and mauled the campers. He couldn't tell from the tracks or anything physical. But he sensed it. Proof or not, it was the same bear. Was it trying to lead him away from the shore, where more humans were within helping distance? Would it try to circle around? He stopped cold.

Was it his imagination or was the bear scent a little stronger than it had been? Slowly he turned. He heard the rustling, then saw the large shadow moving about 30 yards from him. It *had* circled!

"You're done now," he yelled.

The bear stopped, stared, then charged while Steward brought his gun into firing position.

"Dusty!" called Lacy. From her voice he could tell she was on the other side of the bear, not 60 yards away. He could not fire and risk hitting her.

Her shout startled the bear who instantly changed course and headed into the trees and out of view. Steward wanted to take a quick shot at him, but he didn't know if other rangers might be out there too. The bear was gone. Damn.

He kicked a clump of pine needles and stomped over to Lacy. "Eva, why didn't you shoot him?"

"The same reason you didn't. I might have missed him and got you."

*Not likely*, he thought. Her marksman skills were legendary among the rangers. Even though she didn't carry a firearm in her duties as a naturalist, she spent time on the shooting range to keep her law enforcement commission. Maintaining those skills enabled her to be drafted into this mission. *Just what she wanted. But I'm glad she's here. She is a good shot.*

"But you don't miss," he said.

She ignored the compliment. "A better question is what the hell were you doing wandering around by yourself?"

He didn't have a good answer. Instead he looked away and swore under his breath.

She answered for him. "You were so wrapped up in getting this bear that you ignored your own sense and your training."

He wasn't happy about being reprimanded by this ranger. For one thing, she was of lower rank. Secondly, he was beginning to consider her as more than a friend. But he deserved this particular berating, so he let her continue.

"You could have waited by the body. If the bear had decided to protect its kill then you would have had a shot at it. If it didn't come back, then you could have waited for your backup, me included, and we could have gone back in an organized fashion. But you had to go charging in there so that when we arrived we couldn't take a shot without risking the lives of each other." Then she softened. "Dusty, don't let this stupid bear take away your common sense. Don't lose your instincts."

"Yeah," was his only response. They walked back along the trail in silence. Back at the body two other rangers were finishing their collection of evidence. The body was covered by a sheet. Steward and Lacy paused to look at the lifeless shape.

"His wife is on the other side," said one of the other rangers. "We haven't told her anything official but there were enough witnesses that she probably has some idea by now."

Dusty knew it would be his job to break the news.

"What do we know?" he asked quietly.

The ranger stood up and walked with Steward and Lacy back toward the river. On the other side they could see a large crowd. Steward could make out two rangers working to keep the crowd back and another one corralling a smaller group, probably witnesses and Mrs. Victim.

"The guy's name was Charles Corbin from DesMoines. He was fishing out here, closer to this shore than the other. A couple of tourists were driving by, and saw a big bear bound out of the woods, knock him down and drag him up here. Several other motorists pulled up in time to see that last part. Three different guys tried to run across the river and help him but they couldn't make it very far."

Steward nodded. Though it was August, the water was much too cold for unprotected legs. He glanced at his own wet legs and was not looking forward to wading back. The other rangers, at least, had the sense to put on insulated waders.

The ranger continued, "They could just stand back there and watch. Fortunately, the bear took him out of site before it killed him. The wife is an avid photographer. She was taking pictures of fish jumping up at LeHardy's Rapids. She came back here when she heard the sirens. Figured it was a fishing accident."

"Thanks," said Steward, first to the ranger for the information and again to Lacy for the scolding. He would not make the same mistake next time.

After the run across the river, the discovery of another body, the hunt through the woods and the meeting with the bear, he felt as if he had put in more than a full day's work. But half way back across the river he picked out the waiting Mrs. Corbin. Even from this distance he could see the small glimmer of hope in her eyes. Hope he knew he would have to crush. His job had just begun.

**************

"What's the Park Service doing about all the vandalism?" was the question that accompanied the microphone thrust into Steward's face. It was only two days since the death of Charles Corbin and Steward was not in the mood to be chatty with the press corps.

Rangers all over the park were being stopped by the seemingly endless supply of reporters. Steward felt he was handling more than his fair share because other rangers were used to referring people to him for questions about bear attacks or serious accidents. His colleagues had no incentive to start answering questions themselves so, if they could get away with it, they would send the microphones, cameras and notebooks in his direction. He tried to send reporters to the park's press office until he discovered they were also sending reporters to him. Only Lacy was handling comparable press duties because of her expertise on geysers.

Truthfully, he could have pleaded with his boss that he needed to return to his own district, away from Old Faithful. He suspected the West District Ranger had requested Steward stick around the geyser as retaliation for pulling Lacy away so often. Regardless of the real reason, Chief Ranger Marks ordered Steward to assist the Old Faithful crew, in addition to keeping things running in his own district near Yellowstone Lake. So the constant press briefings continued.

"We have added guards to the Old Faithful geyser basin." He gestured to the noticeably beefed-up security at the basin. "But it's a big place with a lot of visitors. We can only do so much," Steward replied calmly, without emotion. By now, this answer was rote recitation.

He had to admit to himself that the extra security hadn't done much good. The angry tourists from the first day Old Faithful quit were followed by other angry tourists each successive day. Apparently, many people stuck with their vacation plans, even knowing that they would be disappointed by the geyser's tranquility. During the long trip to the park, he figured, some of the tourists brooded and planned ways to take revenge.

"Old Faithful itself now has a full-time sentry to stop people from filling it with debris," he told the latest group of reporters gathered around him. "Several other rangers patrol the boardwalk that winds among the other thermal features in the basin." *Yet, some folks manage to leave their mark,* he thought.

"Could you please explain how people have been able to write messages in the streams around the basin?" asked another reporter.

Steward let out a sigh. No escape from these guys yet.

"The run-off from geysers and springs gradually cools as it makes its way toward the Firehole River. At different temperatures, different colors of bacteria grow. A few degrees difference is lethal to one color and paradise for another. The result is usually a mossy rainbow running from thermal feature to river." How many times had he recited this?

"But this bacteria is as delicate as it is lovely," Steward continued. "Some tourists also think it's perfect for writing in. The color can be scraped away with a stick, or finger. Unfortunately it takes a long time for the bacteria to grow back in."

While the reporter scribbled his quote, Steward looked around the basin. Within a week of the non-eruption "Old Faithful sucks!" was a prominent message along the boardwalk. "Who forgot to flush?" was another message. Some of the language was more colorful than the bacteria it destroyed. All of it was vandalism, and it covered every section of the thermal growth within reach of the boardwalk.

It made for great TV.

"Have there been any arrests?" asked the reporter.

"Since we increased security patrols we've apprehended several culprits. A few people had to turn themselves in when they discovered the hard way how hot this water can be. They were treated and ticketed." Steward replied.

He knew the news that night, and probably for the next week, would show the Old Faithful geyser cone littered with soda cans, chip bags, film boxes and other trash in addition to the more-natural rocks and sticks thrown from the boardwalk. Some objects made it into the cone, but the geyser accepted it and lay still.

"With all this vandalism and the most recent fatal bear attack, is the Park Service considering closing Yellowstone? Have you lost control of the park?" the reporter continued.

Steward knew his own philosophy was getting lost. The vandalism on top of the other problems would make it difficult to convince the public of how crucial it was to keep the park as accessible as possible. "Yellowstone is still a magnificent place. There is still so much to offer. And people belong here because–" Steward never finished.

Out of nowhere, a slim young man in properly rumpled environmental fashion appeared next to Steward and began ranting, "Of course they won't close the park. They're after every tourist dollar they can grab today while Yellowstone crumbles into nothing but a heap of garbage for the future."

In response to the startled looks of the press corps and Steward, he revealed, "I'm Bernie Wilson, on behalf of Lester Crane and the People for the Environmental Way. I am the eyes and ears of Yellowstone Park."

Wilson now had the full attention of the reporters, the cameras and anyone else within 50 feet. He held up a bright orange ID card with his photo on it.

"Bears are being tortured, people are being killed and our rare and beautiful thermal features are being destroyed, all because the Park Service is too greedy to do what's best for the people of this country who own Yellowstone. People for the Environmental Way are not afraid to stand up to the big money and the big dollar because we know the real people out there want Yellowstone saved." And on he went.

Steward had completely lost the spin. The story now belonged to PEW.

*Maybe I should just kick his butt,* Steward thought. His radio interrupted thoughts of how *that* would play on the evening news. He wandered away from the reporters to take the call.

"Dusty," said a familiar voice on the radio. "It's Eva." Did his heart just jump?

"Hey," he said. "Some PEW goon is over here playing the media like a fiddle. Do you think I should wrap some bacon around his neck and tie him to a tree where bears hang out?"

"Uh, let's talk about that later. We're needed at Heart Lake."

He knew what that meant. Around Heart Lake were back-country campsites and bears. So far this summer that was not a good combination. He went to his car as quickly as he could without drawing the attention of the reporters.

# TEN

Unlike the campground at Bridge Bay, or even the campsite at Turbid Lake, Heart Lake was *really* in the back country. Granted, there was a small ranger outpost nearby and a fire watch cabin at the top of neighboring Mount Sheridan, but the campsites were about 10 miles from the road.

Both Steward and Lacy were physically fit enough to knock off 10 miles without wearing down too much. But who wants to walk that far to work? They took horses.

On the long drive to the Heart Lake trail head and the seemingly longer trail ride into the camp, Steward and Lacy talked about the details they had so far. According to the two-way radio reports -- radio traffic was purposely sketchy and guarded lately because of the media's intense curiosity -- there had been bear trouble but no fatalities. If they had injuries or bodies to deal with, they would have taken ATVs or something even faster to get back to the camp.

Another subject they discussed, to Steward's consternation, was the fact that this would probably be the last outing Lacy would spend with him.

"Dusty, I have got to stay around the geysers. Even

Marks agrees, whether the bear case is solved or not. He's a stickler for finishing a job once started, but he knows I'm needed at the geyser basin," she told him.

"I understand. I'm surprised he wanted you to come with me today." He hesitated. "But we can still get together some time when this is all over, maybe."

He risked a look at her. She did not say a word. And she kept her eyes on the trail.

The trip seemed longer than it was.


"You ready?" asked Ranger Norm Miller, who was stationed at the Heart Lake ranger cabin.

"What've we got?" Steward dismounted his horse and shook Miller's hand. Lacy followed him.

Miller led Steward and Lacy from the cabin, around the lakeshore, to the campsite where three young men and a young lady sat on a log, dirty and tired-looking.

"You said on the radio that a bear stormed into the camp last night and dug up some food near the fire ring," Steward said to Miller.

"By their description, a grizzly," he replied. "No one hurt, thank God."

"Must not have been our elusive friend or else they wouldn't be sitting here," Steward said to Lacy quietly as they reached the unhappy campers. Toward them, and in a louder voice, he said, "I'm Ranger Dusty Steward. I know you've been through your story already, but I'd like to hear it again if I can."

One of the guys, still excited from the night's events, began, "We were in our tents settling down for the night."

Steward glanced over at two small dome tents, still standing. The camper continued.

"About 12:30 we hear this snorting and growling. We've all heard the news reports so we think 'bear' right away. I grab Alex here," he pointed to the girl, "and we headed up that tree over there." He gestured to a pine tree nearest one of the tents.

"These two," he pointed toward the other guys "were already up that tree." He nodded toward the tree closest to the other tent. The other guys grinned sheepishly. It was early afternoon already so Steward figured they were recovered from the night's scare.

Steward continued, "Did you see the bear very closely? Did he charge you?"

"We weren't exactly quiet or fast climbing the trees. The bear looked at us but he didn't come our way. Only stopped what he was doing long enough to 'woof' at us. But we could see him pretty well. Full moon last night."

"What did he look like?"

"He was a grizzly. A big brown one. I know the difference between black bears and grizzlies. This one had the big head and the hump on his back. I think he had a radio collar on too."

Steward glanced toward Lacy. *Not the killer*, his eyes said. His initial impression that this was not their target bear was correct.

The camper continued describing his evening. "He

kept sniffing and digging around the campfire."

Steward interrupted. "He must have smelled your food. Did you cook there?"

"Hey, we cleaned our camp when we were done," said the camper, a little annoyed. "We know what we're doing. All our plates, utensils and even the shirts we wore when we were cooking are hung up in the bear bag. You can check it if you want. It's still there."

The ranger noted where the man was pointing. About 100 yards from the tents a rope stretched between two trees. From that, about 12 feet off the ground, hung a plastic trash bag.

The camper continued, "After a minute, he dug up some fish. I couldn't tell how many from where we were, but they looked fresh. I mean, not more than a day old."

"If you couldn't see how many fish there were, how could you tell how fresh they were?"

"They were more than just bones. Plus, if they were fairly fresh and buried a little ways, that would explain why we didn't smell them ourselves."

Steward pondered that a minute. Why would someone carry their fishing equipment 10 miles to this lake only to bury what they caught?

This time the girl spoke up. "Is there any way you can find out who camped here last night? They must have buried the fish."

Miller spoke up. "I already checked. This site's been vacant for the last couple nights."

"And I guess it will have to be vacant for a few more,"

said Steward. The policy was to close back-country campsites where bears were active. "Thanks for your help, but I hope you weren't planning to stay another night."

The campers laughed at that one. "I've donated enough blood to the Yellowstone mosquitoes for one summer," said their leader.

Steward and Lacy thanked the campers for their cooperation and made preparations to close the area. As the campers were breaking camp, Lacy split off and walked down to the beach. Steward realized he was staring at her. She was standing beside the shimmering Heart Lake. To one side of her Mount Sheridan, still snow-capped even in the middle of summer, caught the angle of the afternoon sun to show off its rugged texture. *She really looks good here,* he thought.

*Dusty, get your mind back.*

He rubbed his eyes and took a quick survey of all the scenery around him. On this clear day, the blue sky and the blue water weren't exactly the same shade, but their colors would have made a great outfit. The green of the grass and the trees were backed by the always-impressive Mount Sheridan. Had they been standing on top, they would have had a spectacular view of the pointed Teton Range to the south. Rising to impressive heights from relatively flat surroundings, the sharp, rugged, mountains looked like their namesake breasts only to the French fur trappers who named them, apparently after spending a bit too much time alone in the wilderness. But at the level of the heart-shaped lake, Sheridan blocked their view, though its own presentation was pleasant enough.

His mind went back to breasts. He glanced again at

Lacy. *Cut it out!* he scolded himself.

Then Steward's radio called.

"Dusty, we've had a mauling up by Electric Peak," said the ranger messenger.

The hair on the back of his neck stood. "Special assignment?" he asked, his code for whether he was being asked to console grieving survivors about the death of a friend or loved one.

"Close, but not this time," the ranger on the other end answered. "Five campers, only one injured."

Steward looked to Lacy, who had come back when she heard the radio. He spoke into it. "Did they say the bear came into their camp and dug up food?"

"Affirmative. And they swore they hadn't left it there."

The rangers signed off and Steward walked over to the hole where the fish-eating bear had found his reward. He stared into it for a moment. Electric Peak was too far to realistically be the bear he was hunting. For that matter, Heart Lake was pretty far from the original trouble area. But now other bears were being more aggressive than usual.

"What do you think, Dusty?"

"I think if we dug a little deeper, we'd uncover a big orange PEW sticker."


**************


Crane hung up the phone and smiled, leaning back in

his chair, staring at the ceiling.

Pierce watched him for a moment. He knew his boss had been talking to Bernie Wilson, probably getting another Yellowstone update. Crane's habit of building suspense by not saying anything was beginning to grate.

Finally Pierce blurted out, "What's up?"

"Well, it looks like our work is half done. Most of the back-country campsites are now closed. It appears bears bothered campers in them, and in a couple of the large campgrounds too."

"Why did the bears act so suddenly?" asked Pierce.

"Dirty campsites I guess. The bears found food. That should keep them coming back for a while, which means the campers will have to stay out."

Pierce was shocked. "Anybody hurt?"

"No bears, if that's what you mean. A few people got bitten and knocked around. No fatalities."

Pierce was trying to read Crane's face. The look was … well … creepy.

**************

Lacy and Steward answered their summons to headquarters. Mort Lightfeather, the superintendent of the park, greeted them. He was a tall, solidly built Native American who was well-liked by the Park Service employees. The two rangers had each met him a few times over the years and were infected by his warm smile. Today he was grim-faced. Steward felt his own heart picking up speed and he could tell by Lacy's fidgeting that she was anxious too.

Lightfeather began, "Steward, Lacy. We need help and everyone I've talked to said you're the people to handle it." He paused, apparently searching for the right words, then spurt out, "We're closing for the winter. No winter lodging at Old Faithful or Mammoth. No snowmobile trips. We're closing."

"That's stupid. That won't solve the bear problem. The bears are sleeping during the winter. What're they thinking," Steward blurted out, momentarily forgetting that he was talking to his boss.

"Steward, there's more to this issue than the bears and even Old Faithful. Our Congress is still trying to control national spending," the superintendent said.

"Yeah, but how much money are we going to save by closing the gates for one winter."

Lightfeather's look answered him.

Steward was stunned. "You think they're going to close every winter? Still, that can't even amount to much savings."

The superintendent's dark eyes narrowed as he stared at him more intently. He said nothing.

Suddenly Lacy sat up straight and gripped the arms of her chair. "They're going to close us next summer, or at least they're going to try to," she choked.

Lightfeather leaned back in his chair to open a desk drawer and pull out two plane tickets.

"And so the game moves to Washington, D.C.," he said.

# ELEVEN

"I'm sorry, Mr. Steward," said the desk clerk at the Washington hotel. "But we only have one room reserved for the two of you." The young woman was trying to be polite but was obviously weary. Judging from the long line he and Lacy had waited in, and the one behind them, Steward could understand the weariness, but not the lack of a second room.

"Yes, but that was a mistake by someone. Can't you just add a second room to our reservation now and let us work out the paperwork later?" Steward asked, as patiently as possible. He glanced at Lacy. She was staring straight at the desk clerk. Her eyes revealed nothing but he could tell she was clenching her jaw.

"Again, I'm sorry," said the clerk. "We're booked solid and we don't anticipate any cancellations."

Lacy finally spoke up, still not looking at Steward, "What about other hotels in town?"

"I'd be happy to call around for you, but as you can see, Washington is very busy today. I don't think we'd have much luck finding very good rooms nearby," the clerk said. Then she added, "This room does have two queen-sized beds."

Steward was beginning to feel the mass of the line behind him. He could sense the growing impatience. *One of us has to bring this up first*, he thought. "Well, Eva. Our big meeting is in less than two hours and I don't feel like riding all over town in taxis. As far as I know I don't snore."

Lacy looked at him quickly, then back to the desk clerk. "Fine," she said curtly. Steward thought he detected a faint blush in her cheeks.

"Why are all the people here this weekend? What's the big convention?" Steward asked the clerk.

"Everybody seemed to pick this week I guess. The teachers' union, a cosmetics convention.... . Oh. And People for the Environmental Way is having a big rally on the mall for the next few days. They can really pack 'em in."

"As if I didn't have enough reasons to hate Lester Crane," Steward mumbled to himself.

They took care of the final paperwork and made arrangements for their baggage. Then they marched, together but keeping a safe distance between them, toward a phone.

"Um, I guess I'll call," Steward volunteered.

Lacy just nodded and turned to walk around the lobby. Steward definitely detected deepening crimson in her cheeks. He wasn't sure how much was embarrassment and how much was anger. It was bad enough that neither ranger understood exactly why they were chosen to be here instead of Marks or Lightfeather. And now this. He chose to focus on the phone as he punched in the numbers.

After speaking with Lightfeather for five minutes, Steward hung up the phone and scanned the lobby. He caught

Lacy's attention and motioned her over.

"Well, he apologized and said he would try to fix things. But it looks like nothing can be done for tonight at least."

"How did they screw this up?" she asked.

"Um ... apparently ... he was under the impression ... I guess someone told him ..."

Lacy looked him right in the eye.

He finally blurted it out. "Somebody told him we were a couple."

"Who?" she demanded.

"He didn't really say. He said it was kind of common knowledge around the office. I guess we *have* been spending a lot of time together."

"What!? That was work!"

"Don't look at me, Eva. I can't believe it either. If we're dating, I wasn't told about it." He looked back at the phone. "Man, I always miss the juicy rumors."

Lacy laughed for the first time since their arrival.

"I bet he just made the whole thing up," Steward continued. "Tight wad was just trying to save money by making us double up."

She laughed again, pulled her key card out of her pocket and started walking toward the elevators. "Might as well make the best of it."

He followed her. "Like I said, I don't think I snore. How about you?"

She punched his arm.

**************

The room worked out fine so far for the rangers. If they took turns changing clothes in the bathroom, they could get ready for their duties and still maintain some privacy. Steward had made a mental note of how far apart the beds were. Then he realized he didn't know how apart he wanted them to be so he tried to push it out of his mind.

"Secretary Hershauer will see you now," said the receptionist, freeing Steward from the burden of having to think about it any more. He stood up, looked around the reception area of the Department of the Interior. His thoughts had taken him away from his surroundings. *Quit thinking about her*, he scolded himself. He and Lacy were going to meet with the Secretary of the Interior, an honest-to-goodness cabinet-level official, to talk about keeping the park open. Steward glanced at the national park posters on the walls and at Lacy standing next to him. She seemed to be impatient.

The two followed the receptionist into an office tastefully decorated with historic paintings and polished wood furniture. Steward supposed it would be considered large, but given that his own office was an entire national park, no room ever looked too impressive. Behind a finely finished desk stood a gray-haired man with confident eyes and a practiced smile. *Looks taller on TV*, thought Steward.

"Rangers Steward and Lacy. I'm pleased to meet you. I hear you are the two who can turn this mess around," said Hershauer, shaking the appropriate hands and smiling the appropriate smile.

"We'll do what we can," said Lacy, a quiver in her voice. Neither ranger was used to dealing with the polished world of Washington and it was especially evident in Lacy.

Hershauer directed them to a group of three seats away from his desk. They sat in the remarkably comfortable chairs as Hershauer directed the small talk for several minutes. He praised the rangers for their service. He learned that the flight was fine. He confirmed that the weather in the park would be getting cold before too long. He said he would try to fix the room problem at the hotel. Eventually, he got around to his plans.

"Eva, you're the most articulate expert we have on geysers. Until I read that brief you wrote for Mort Lightfeather I didn't completely understand why we couldn't just turn Old Faithful back on. I would like you to accompany me to Capitol Hill on Monday. There is a Senate committee meeting and they want to know more about what has happened to Old Faithful. They're not the most technical bunch and not really the brightest bunch either. But still, they are our Senate and they deserve a good explanation, one better than I can give them by myself."

She smiled and nodded at him. He turned his attention to the other ranger.

"Dusty, you have a gift for helping people deal with unpleasant situations. Also you're well-versed about our grizzly bears. I want you on the Sunday morning news programs."

Steward's mouth fell open. "Sir, I'm a ranger. I'm proud of that but it doesn't mean I can take on the Washington press corps."

Hershauer raised his hand to silence the protest. "Look. We've decided we need a real front-line ranger to fight our battle. The American people have seen enough polished spokespeople debating this issue. They're tired of seeing me. They want to see what a working man thinks. You're the guy. Just be yourself. Besides, my staff will brief you on the kinds of questions to expect and the kinds of traps your opposition will try to set."

Steward perked up. "My opposition? Who is my opposition?"

"Lester Crane from the People for the Environmental Way."

The ranger leaned back in his chair, a dark look in his eyes and a tight smile across his lips. "I'll be happy to do it."

With that, Hershauer shook the rangers' hands, thanked them again for their service, and showed them out a door where his staff spent the next two hours briefing them on their next duties.

**************

While he was on hold, Lester Crane jotted notes on a pad of recycled paper on his desk. He glanced up at his intern who was on his own phone, but listening to the same line. Crane observed that his protege was sorting through his own pile of work. The older man smiled as he realized Pierce had picked up his habit of keeping work handy during phone calls in case they were stuck on hold. *Got another one trained.*

Finally, the call went through and both men shifted

their full attention to their respective phones. Pierce covered his mouthpiece because he was allowed to listen but was instructed not to talk.

"So that ranger is going to be the guy," Crane said after listening for several minutes. "He's the guy who doesn't want any restrictions on people going in? And you told him to be himself?" He chuckled. "I'm going to cream him."

Crane grinned at Pierce. The intern pumped his fist in victory.

"Thanks for the update, Jerry. Tell the President that we are continually pleased with his commitment to the environment. And take as much credit for it as you'd like."

After he hung up the phone, he turned to Pierce. "That Hershauer. Not too bad for an Interior Secretary."

**************

Across the room, Lacy was pulling out various accessories, getting ready for bed. The rangers were tired and edgy after the exhaustive briefings. And they were beginning to feel the pressure as the importance of what they were asked to do was sinking in.

On top of that Steward discovered a new problem. He stared at his open suitcase. *I don't wear pajamas. I don't own pajamas. I sure as hell didn't* pack *pajamas.*

Under the current rooming arrangement, he couldn't sleep in the outfit God gave him. It would be almost as embarrassing to wear the outfit Fruit of the Loom gave him. His fitness came from hiking and an active job so he didn't work out. No sweats or workout clothes. If he just wore his jeans to bed he would look like a clod and it would be obvious what the problem was.

"Eva, I'm going to run downstairs and get a book or paper or something to help me clear my mind. Need anything?"

"Whiskey?" she replied through toothpaste foam.

He nodded and headed out the door. In the lobby he checked his options. Not many retail shops would be open at this hour, so he went into the gift shop. No pajamas but he found an acceptable pair of Redskins boxer shorts. After checking with the clerk to determine that the $45 price was not a misprint, he handed over the money, grumbled and walked into the lounge to get a couple of stiff drinks to go.

While waiting for the drinks he checked out the TV in the corner of the bar. The local news could barely capture his attention. The anchors smiled their way into a commercial. And then the TV screen won Steward's full attention.

"Could you turn that up please?" he asked the bartender anxiously.

The familiar scene of Old Faithful was smoldering in the background of the commercial. For years people only recognized the famous geyser by its eruptions. Photos and drawings of Old Faithful with water shooting from it were used in park logos and on the covers of virtually every book about the park. But due to all the recent television coverage of the geyser's demise, the small wisp of steam escaping the once-virulent geyser cone had become nearly as common a symbol of the park.

Just in case a few people didn't know the geyser in its new, quiet form, the commercial producers included the label "Old Faithful" in big letters across the top of the screen. In the foreground a man paced impatiently on the boardwalk in front of the geyser. He was made to look like the stereotypical tourist, complete with a camera and camcorder hanging from his neck. He stopped, looked at his watch and then tapped it as if to make sure it was still working.

Suddenly the scene changed to reveal the stunning beauty of the Grand Canyon. Not the canyon in Yellowstone, but the massive, spectacular, world-famous Grand Canyon in Arizona. A montage of hikers, rafters and sightseers entertained and beckoned viewers.

The picture cut back to the tourist standing in front of Old Faithful, at twilight, still waiting for an eruption.

Then the scene returned to the Grand Canyon at sunset, with a young couple hugging in front of the breathtaking colors and shadows that paint the canyon as the sun goes down.

Finally, a voice brought the first words to the commercial. "Need a vacation? Come to Arizona's Grand Canyon, where the scenery is always working."

At the bottom of the screen read, "Brought to you by the Flagstaff Chamber of Commerce and the Arizona Department of Tourism." A large toll-free number and web site address completed the scene.

"Damn," was all Steward could say.

He quickly paid for his drinks and carried them back to the room. When he walked in Lacy was sitting on the end of one of the beds, staring at the room TV. Her expression was one of shock.

"You must have seen it," he said.

"How could they do that, Dusty?" she asked. "You don't see the Wyoming Chamber of Commerce buying ads every time one of the tourist helicopters crashes in that damned canyon."

"I guess they couldn't resist twisting the knife."

"What are we going to do about it?" She was kneading the bedspread in frustration.

"You could start with this." He handed her a glass of whiskey.

"Can you take that out of the bar?"

"I'm not really sure. I didn't ask." He raised his glass to his lips. "Better hide the evidence."

She got up and set her glass on the counter. "I'm not in the mood now. I'm so angry about that commercial." She walked back to her bed and plopped down. "I'm just trying to figure out how I'm going to smile and be pleasant Monday when I have to testify to all those politicians."

She sat still for a moment, then smiled. "I'm trying to figure out how you are going to be pleasant debating Lester Crane tomorrow morning." She laughed.

Steward laughed back. "Who says I have to be pleasant to Lester Crane? If I screw up on TV they'll either fire me or punish me by making me keep my job in Yellowstone. I hear all the top ranger jobs are going to be at the Grand Canyon next summer."

Lacy threw a pillow at him. "I'm going to sleep. You should do the same thing." Then she nodded at the package he had carried in the room with him. "I thought you were a Broncos fan."

He tossed the pillow back at her. "I like Washington so much that I decided to start rooting for the Redskins."

**************

Across the room Steward listened to the steady rhythm of Lacy's breathing. He was trying to lie still in his own bed so he would not wake her, but he was restless. He had been glancing at the clock enough that he could make a pretty accurate guess she had been asleep for an hour. He hoped the next hour might bring him some sleep too. Or maybe the hour after. Any sleep this night would be welcome.

His thoughts switched between two distinct images, like his mind was powered by a TV remote control in the hands of an impatient sports fan trying to watch two games at the same time. One vision was the rise and fall of the shapely chest only six feet away. The other, more troubling, picture was the gaunt, arrogant face of Lester Crane.

*Please, God. Torture me with one image or the other, but end this game. My brain is going to split.*

He tried to imagine what he would say to the pasty faces in the hot TV studio and to the millions of Americans who were either interested in Yellowstone or killing time before Sunday dinner. Hershauer's staff had tried to make him relax and not worry about the impact of his actions.

At first, they didn't believe him when he told them he had never seen the show on which he was going to appear.

"Look, I'm usually busy working at that time of day," he explained. "And even if I was inside doing nothing, TV reception is terrible."

As preparation for his appearance they asked him the questions that would likely be asked the next day so he could practice his answers. Then they suggested ways he could make his answers better, more in-line with the administration's spin.

At one point he asked, "So the President and Hershauer agree that for the park to be saved we have to keep people visiting."

"Well, you could say it's important to consider that, but remember that the administration is committed to protecting wildlife too," corrected an especially skinny member of the staff. James, his name may have been.

"Listen. You can't save the wildlife by chasing out the people," barked Steward. "That's what I'm trying to tell you. How can I say the tourists are the key to saving the wildlife and then weasel around that we might have to keep them out to save the wildlife. Am I supposed to contradict myself?"

Skinny James looked as exasperated as Steward felt, but the ranger suspected it was for a different reason. "Look, Dusty. I know you're supposed to be yourself. At the same time you're representing the United States Department of the Interior. I'm just trying to help you keep from painting us into a corner. This is politics. The scene will change each week. We need to leave some wiggle room."

"Then what the hell am I doing here?" Steward replied. After looking around at the concerned looks of the staff, he added, "I bet that's what you've been asking yourselves for the last hour."

They chuckled, but seemed to fight the urge to nod. "You'll do fine," said Skinny James.

*Yeah, right,* thought Steward.

With the image of that troubling meeting replacing the others in his mind, he drifted … no … tumbled into sleep.

# TWELVE

Showtime.

Steward sat stiffly in the padded plastic chair behind a woodgrain table. A few feet to his right, in striking distance if it came to that, was Lester Crane. Steward wore a freshly cleaned and pressed ranger uniform. Crane had on his own uniform, of sorts. Open collar. Comfortable. The environmentalist looked a little better groomed than in most pictures Steward had seen, but he still looked as if he was either on the way to, or just back from, some sort of commune with nature. It occurred to Steward that his own uniform would make him look like a member of the police state while Crane appeared to be an honest friend of the Earth.

*I always thought dressing for this type of situation meant dressing up*, the ranger thought.

Across the table sat four media pundits who handled the questions and commentary for the show. *Pundits*, thought Steward. *That means they have some expertise. But just because they are experts at politics, does that mean they know anything about Yellowstone? I know a lot about Yellowstone but I don't understand anything about politics.*

Steward tried to remember the briefing with Hershauer's staff. They showed him a few video clips of the program and told him a little bit about each of the panelists. The older guy on the end was Thomas Haines, a well-respected journalist of many years. He had been one of the pioneers of TV news, known for his coverage of government and elections. Now he was the moderator of this program and imposed a calming influence when things got heated. Steward was told to throw a panicked glance at Haines if he needed to be saved from the discussion. The old man always saved his guests.

The next guy in the row was a current member of the White House press corps. Peter Wilson. A very loud reporter whose opinions usually marched a couple steps ahead of his knowledge.

Next to Wilson was Mabel Torrence, the only woman on the panel. She hosted a public opinion and news program for National Public Radio. She believed she had a good read of public opinion but couldn't comprehend that the opinions of her NPR audience did not necessarily match those of the rest of the nation. It didn't matter too much, though, because she seemed to take the most pride in always disagreeing with Wilson, regardless of what the man said.

Finally came Phil Grossman, from Associated Press, the only print journalist on the panel. He was fair but tended to follow the PEW line. Looking at him in person, Steward thought he looked familiar. He wondered if he may have talked to the man during the Yellowstone press crunch a couple weeks ago.

Around him, people scurried. Two guys connected and

disconnected wires. A young lady clipped tiny microphones to the lapels of panelists and guests, except for Crane whose mike was clipped to a wad of cloth just below his collar. A flow of different people carried stacks of papers in and out, placing them in front of the panelists and removing them again. Two other workers positioned and repositioned a Teleprompter in Haines' line of sight. Two young ladies brought coffee in and out, glasses of water too. Steward got one of each. The crowd and commotion were nothing like Steward envisioned and nothing like the segments of programs he had watched.

Then there was the noise. Steward assumed a broadcast set would be somewhat like a library, everyone being as quiet as practical until the director finally announced, "Quiet on the set," at which point even the slightest noises would cease. But the ebb and flow of personnel did not creep on tiptoes. Nor did they whisper. They conversed as if in any office. Steward was instructed to talk in a regular voice for his mike check, but he didn't have anybody to talk to. Then Wilson asked him about a good place for steak near the park. He told the reporter about a great place near West Yellowstone. Wilson told him about a good one in Washington, then he resumed his conversation with the other panelists.

For their part, the panelists were very verbose. Wilson and Torrence shared jokes. Haines and Grossman exchanged gossip. Then the partners switched and the banter continued. Sometimes they pulled Steward or Crane into the conversation. Occasionally one of the panelists would ask Haines a question about the show they were about to do, which would momentarily focus the discussion. Then back to normal.

As air time approached, a man with headphones and a clipboard shouted out the time remaining. No one seemed to hear him except Steward. He thought when the man said "Two minutes" that everyone would quiet down. But nothing changed. At one point Steward wondered if he should interrupt the journalists and make sure they were aware that the program was about to start.

He glanced at Crane. The PEW chief was smiling and relaxed. *Of course*, thought Steward, *he's done this about a hundred times before.* So Steward sat back and sipped his coffee, certain he was the only nervous person in the entire building.

At the one-minute mark, the staff began to vanish and so did the noise. A suprising number of people settled into position, as if they were staying. The camera may only point to six people, but twice that number were apparently going to be just out of view. *Okay, now the stomach is churning.*

At twenty-seconds-to-go the remaining background talking ceased. However, Haines and Torrence were having a pretty good conversation. Wilson and Grossman were discussing the finer points of NFL officiating. *I have to pee, but I'll ignore it.*

Ten seconds. The staff was quiet. The panelists were still mumbling. Steward looked at Crane, who was staring straight at him with a sneaky grin. *What the hell am I doing here?*

Five, four, three. The last two seconds were counted

off silently by the clipboard man's fingers. And the panelists were still conversing. A red light on one of the cameras came on. Haines, who had just finished talking to Torrence, started talking to America.

"Good morning." Haines voice was calm and steady. "The vacation season is coming to a close. Some of you may have spent your vacation at Yellowstone National Park. But will that park be open for vacation next year? Should it open for tourists ever again? A summer of tragedy and destruction may have changed the world's oldest park forever. Mike Scallatti has the story."

Everyone at the table watched the report on the monitor. Scallatti was apparently a reporter for the network. Steward realized that the TVs were showing this report and not the room in which he and the journalists were seated. In fact, it occurred to him that he had not been on camera yet. The story was a re-hash of the Yellowstone issue, complete with video of his colleagues dragging a limp bear out of trap. *I wish that was never taped,* he thought.

The report ended and Steward saw Haines on the monitor. It startled him when he saw the monitor face talking and realized the guy sitting nearby was saying the same thing. Then he looked up, saw the camera light on, and tried to act cool. He thought it best not to look at Crane.

"… has been a hot topic on Capitol Hill," Haines was saying. "In a moment we'll be back with our panel and guests Lester Crane from People for the Environmental Way who says the park should be closed for its own good."

Steward knew what was coming, he sat up straight and looked at the camera in front of him, hoping that was the one he was supposed to stare at. It must have been, because one of the clipboard people was looking at him and pointing at that camera. The red light turned on. Steward gave his best effort at smiling.

"And park ranger Dusty Steward, who has been closely involved in all aspects of the Yellowstone turmoil. Please stay with us."

Someone yelled "clear" and the crew got back to work adjusting things. Haines spoke to all of the panelists and guests this time. "Les, you will make a brief statement. Dusty, you get a brief rebuttal. I get the first question. Then each of the others will get a turn. We'll let the conversation direct the rest of the schedule."

"On in five," yelled the clipboard man. Followed, in five seconds, by a signal to Haines.

"Welcome back," Haines said to the camera. "As you saw in our earlier tape, Yellowstone National Park has been the scene of much tragedy and controversy this summer. Lester Crane is the director of People for the Environmental Way. Mr. Crane, your group has been gathering support to close the park to the public. Why?"

Crane smiled. "Tom, Yellowstone is a treasure. Not just to our country but to the world. Unfortunately, the treasure has been tarnished. The bears and scenery that symbolize that wonderful park are becoming damaged beyond repair. Our nation had the foresight to create the world's first national park when we made Yellowstone. Now we need to demonstrate the foresight to save that park by limiting access to it. As the crowds continue to swarm into the park, the park continues to deteriorate."

Back to Haines. "Ranger Dusty Steward works very closely with the bears in Yellowstone. In fact, Ranger Steward is the man who found the body of Jennifer Patrick early this summer. You personally have witnessed the rise and fall of bears in Yellowstone, Ranger Steward. Yet your National Park Service is fighting to keep the gates open."

*Relax. Forget that millions of people are watching you. Concentrate on what you are supposed to say. Remember what you worked on with Hershauer's staff.*

"Well, Mr. Haines and other panel members. It's very important that we –"

"Not everybody in the Park Service wants to keep abusing the park," Crane interrupted. "My group hears from countless park employees and even from many tourists who know it's best for Yellowstone to protect it from too many visitors."

*I should have expected him to cut in.* "It's kind of pointless to have a park if you don't let people in it," Steward stammered.

"But it's definitely pointless to have a park with nothing left in it," Crane fired back.

Haines reasserted himself. "Just a minute. Now, Ranger Steward, you believe the public is not having an adverse impact on Yellowstone."

"Of course people are leaving their mark, intentional and otherwise. But people are going to have an impact on that land one way or another. We are best off using it as a park that everyone can enjoy. Take that option away and it will be used for something else, like mining or ranching."

Mabel Torrence spoke up in her broadcast voice that was both lyrical and pointed. "Are you saying the Park Service won't continue to protect and preserve Yellowstone if you can't run it as a park?"

*Boy I'm way off script now. And that briefing yesterday didn't help much.* "No. But it's a big park. If the public isn't there and if they don't feel ownership of it, I don't see how we can protect it," tried Steward.

"Other nature preserves are doing just fine. People respect them for what they are," said Crane.

Wilson boomed in, "I'm with the ranger on this one. If we can't use it for fishing, turn it over to the lumber companies. At least we'd get something useful out of it."

"I wasn't really saying we should–" Steward's voice squeaked.

"Oh, come on, Peter," laughed Torrence. "You don't believe there is any value to protecting nature?"

"We should definitely protect nature," said Wilson. "But do we have to protect all of it? Yellowstone is big and it's expensive to maintain … kind of like public radio." He and Torrence laughed.

"Okay, folks," said Haines. "Let's get back on track. Phil?"

Grossman leaned forward. "Ranger Steward, are you saying the Park Service won't be able to protect the park without a large public presence?"

"As I said, it's a big park," Steward replied. "Look how much trouble we've had locating one bad bear. It would be difficult to–"

Crane again. "And in the process of searching for that one bear, you've harmed a dozen innocent ones. In the meantime, tourists who are upset about the end of Old Faithful have been vandalizing Yellowstone beyond repair."

Grossman followed up. "But shouldn't the Park Service be concentrating on protecting people, even more than the thermal features?"

"Times have changed," said Crane. "People are in danger only because there are too many of them in the park and they have pushed into areas they were never meant to go. We are long past protecting people from the park. It's time to protect the park from people."

"What about the logging and mining companies that are ready to exploit Yellowstone?" asked Torrence.

Crane adopted a very calm, caring manner, as if he was reassuring a child that there was no monster under the bed. "That's just not going to happen. The President has made it very clear that he is dedicated to protecting the environment. I believe he is sincere." Then his voice changed, becoming more severe. "That's why I'm surprised the old Yellowstone policies have not been updated. It's time to save the park."

*I don't really understand politics,* thought Steward, *but I think that was a significant statement.*

Haines spoke up. "I'm afraid that's all the time we have. Again, our guests were Lester Crane from People for the Environmental Way and Ranger Dusty Steward from the National Park Service. Thank you, gentlemen."

Steward realized his face was probably in the nation's

living rooms again. He also realized his current, bewildered expression wasn't helping his cause.

Haines continued. "Up next, the chopping block is getting heavy use on Capitol Hill. It's time for budget talks. When we come back."

The floor manager gave the "all clear" signal. Steward stood to shake Crane's hand. The environmentalist smirked and shrugged his shoulders as if to say, "You didn't stand a chance."

Steward gripped his hand a little too tightly. The smirk left Crane's face as Steward stared into the man's eyes. The ranger squeezed even harder until Crane's expression contained fear, and doubt. Then he leaned forward so that Crane alone would hear him.

"Next time we meet on my turf."

With that, he released Crane's hand and followed his escort out of the studio.

# THIRTEEN

"Nice job, Ranger Steward." "Way to go." "All right." "There he is."

As Steward was being ushered into a conference room outside Hershauer's office, all the staff were shaking his hand or patting him on the back. Next on the schedule was a debriefing on the TV show that took place less than an hour before.

Lacy watched him come in. She heard the praises of the staffers but she could read on Steward's face that he didn't believe they believed it. Honestly, she wasn't sure if they were sincere or not. She had watched the program with the staff in this very office. Some of them appeared distressed. Others seemed pleased. For her part, Lacy felt like Steward had been cast in the wrong role.

*He can't make his case in the short time they gave him,* she thought. *Not with all that chatter and competition. Shoot. He's been working on me for two months and I'm still not fully convinced.*

Steward sat in the chair next to her.

"Well, Dusty. You sure showed them. The TV

audience is ready to burn their PEW cards and go kill a bear." Lacy whispered through a smirk.

"You're next," he whispered back.

"… and I think we may be able to straighten out the rooming situation," said Skinny James, breaking into the duel. "We found another room on the floor just below where you are staying now. Again, I apologize for the mix up. But we've got it fixed. If you two want to flip a coin or something, you can decide which one gets to move."

"I prefer things the way they are right now," Lacy blurted out, too quickly for comfort.

Immediately her face reddened. She stared directly at Skinny James, not daring to look at anyone else in the room. But judging from the sudden silence, and by the look on James' face, she knew, absolutely knew, everyone was staring at her. Their expressions would range from the snickering grins of adolescents who just heard a dirty joke to the judgmental glare of prudes who just encountered a slut.

"Um. That works for me too," added Steward, breaking the tension. "She doesn't snore very loudly."

A few people laughed. Skinny James mumbled something about taking care of it. And the meeting continued.

When the burn of embarrassment receded from her cheeks and finally faded from the back of her neck, she glanced at Steward. Hopefully, her eyes said, "Thank you."

\*\*\*\*\*\*\*\*\*\*\*\*\*\*

Ranger Joe Lowry was already at the Turbid Lake campsite. His partner, Bill Kruse, was back at the truck piddling with something.

"Man, it takes him a long time to get his equipment together," Lowry said to the bear trap.

While Steward and Lacy got to jet-set around Washington, he and Kruse were stuck checking the few remaining bear traps. After Senator Patrick's speech back … seemed like a century ago … the rangers cut way back on the trapping. But they quietly maintained a few traps in the spots most likely to attract THE bear.

"This was almost glamourous before the trouble started," he said. Lowry used to love to check the traps. With a masters degree in biology, he was usually called to run tests on the captured bears. That's the kind of thing he had gone to school to be able to do.

Now, however, he was seen as a circus trainer. A torture chamber overseer.

"We're still finding important information about bears. We are helping them," he pleaded with the trap, which he had determined was empty as soon as he reached the campsite. The trap didn't answer, not that he expected it to. The recent stress of the job had led him to talk to traps, trees, rocks and anything else nearby, but he figured he was fine, as long as he didn't believe they were talking back to him.

"Let's see. The bait is still in place, though the flies are adding some maggots to the mix." He started speaking with an infomercial tone of voice. "A tasty, high protein treat for any bear."

He laughed. "There's a commercial I'd love to see."

Regaining seriousness, he walked around the trap in widening circles. "No tracks from wary bears who didn't have the guts to go in. In all, I'd say this was a wasted trip."

Then he looked up. Down the trail, standing on its back legs, towered an enormous creature. Nine feet tall. Silver-tipped brown fur. The pan-like face with a brown snout, pointed at him and sniffing. On top of the head two wads of jaw muscle the size of sofa pillows hinted how powerful a bite from the animal could be. It was all grizzly bear.

It roared. The volume startled Lowry, who began to slowly back away from the animal. He knew the drill. If you run from a bear it might chase you because of instinct. If you can get up a tree, it's not a bad idea to do so. Lowry knew no low-enough branches were near.

If the bear charges you, drop to the ground in a fetal position and cover your neck with your hands. It may bat you around but it might lose interest and move on before it kills you.

*But not this bear,* thought Lowry. *This is the one.*

When in danger the mind can work with incredible speed. Lowry noticed the lack of a collar or tags. More importantly, he noticed the approaching bear looked ... well, different. It was larger than most Yellowstone bears and it looked considerably meaner. Lowry had seen his share of grizzlies up close. Looking at the current beast, he finally understood what Steward meant by saying the bear they wanted was unusually brutal.

Lowry continued backing up as the bear dropped to

the ground and started loping toward him. He glanced around, looking for a low tree limb anywhere within range. Just as he thought. Nothing.

*The trap!*

It was still 30 yards behind him. But the bear was only about 20 yards in front of him. If the bear started running, he was done for.

The bear roared again. Lowry jumped and started moving faster, still facing the animal.

Then the creature leaped forward. Instantly Lowry turned and sprinted for the trap. He dived into the tube just as the bear reached him and slapped at his feet. The force of the blow knocked his boot off and he could only hope his foot was not still inside.

Lowry's momentum carried him most of the way into the trap but the sideways blow from the bear smashed his legs against the outer edge of the tube. He had felt the metal cut his flesh but he was more afraid of feeling the bear's teeth.

Quickly, he grabbed the hook the slimy, bloody bait was hanging from and used it to pull himself deep inside. The bear sniffed at him and began to lunge into the trap.

Lowry jerked the meat hook one more time, sending the heavy, powerful grate at the end of the trap crashing onto the bear's head. The bear went down and lay still.

"Got you! I killed you, you bastard," he hollered.

He tried to catch his breath and check his wounds. He was relieved to see that he was missing a boot but still had both feet. Further up, his leg was bleeding, but apparently not broken.

"Hah!" he shouted triumphantly at the dead bear. The smile left his face. No carcass lay at the end of the trap anymore. In fact, he saw no bear at all. Slowly, he turned to look out the other end of the trap. It was still welded shut.

He sat quietly, listening for any sound of the bear. Then he remembered Kruse.

"Oh man. He doesn't know what he's walking into." He grabbed his radio.

"Bill. It's Lowry. There is danger here!"

The radio did not answer.

Carefully, Lowry lay on his stomach and inched his way toward the end of the tube closest to the trail Kruse would be taking in. He didn't see anything.

He tried yelling out the end of the trap. "Bill. The bear is around somewhere. Be careful."

No response.

Lowry scooted forward even farther to get a better look. From the side of the opening he saw a flash of brown and felt the power of a massive bear claw against the grate, bending it inward and hitting him in the face.

Slightly dazed he pushed himself backwards and waited. The brown face appeared and roared at him again. Then it vanished.

Lowry looked around the corrugated metal tube. He knew the beast was out there somewhere. He tried to call Kruse on the radio again. No luck.

Then it came. The loud slam against the top of the cage bent the roof inward, pushing the meat hook down, pinning his leg against the floor of the trap. It was an instant motion but to Lowry it played out as a slow-motion film that he was unable to stop. Only the immediate pain told him it was real.

He yelled at the agonizing wound. The sound at the end of the trap quieted him.

He turned his head to see the belly of the bear outside the tube. The claws from two massive paws were being worked into the edges of the grate. Then he saw the body convulse as it put its enormous strength into pulling at Lowry's only protection. He felt the entire trap move and saw the grate bend some more.

*Two more pulls, I'll bet*, he thought.

The next pull yanked the trap even farther and nearly removed the cover.

A loud pop, interrupted the bear. Lowry could see the animal jump back. It was looking toward the trail.

Then another loud pop sounded. The bear roared toward the trail and then bolted away.

For a moment all was quiet.

"Joe!" came a voice at the end of the trap. Then appeared a face to match.

"Bill. Did you get him?"

Kruse faced the direction the bear had run. "I might have hit him, but he definitely is not down. I don't know how far he went." Then he looked back inside the trap. "You okay?"

Lowry took a moment to survey the damage. It was hard to tell which blood came from him and which came from the rotting meat resting on his legs. Infection was practically guaranteed.

"I don't think anything is broken, but I'm pinned in here."

Fortunately, Kruse had packed enough tools to dismantle the hook assembly. Otherwise he would have had to hike back out for the equipment, leaving Lowry alone, and exposed.

"And to think I was griping about how long it took you to get your gear packed," said Lowry.

After Kruse freed him, Lowry gladly took the rifle the ranger had brought along. And prepared to limp back to the truck. Together the men crept out of the back country, holding guns ready and startling at every noise in the trees.

**************

"I'm not sure which was worse, my performance on TV or the debriefing," said Steward into a cold can of cheap beer. The rest of the six-pack was crammed in the flimsy plastic hotel ice bucket. He sat propped against the headboard of his bed, legs stretched out near the end.

"You're not making me any more relaxed." Lacy sat cross-legged on her own bed, surrounded by notes and a couple of thick reference books.

"Don't sweat it, Eva. You should thank me for lowering the bar. Regardless of what you do, you'll still look good by comparison."

She kept her eyes on her work. "Would you please

shut up. If I knew you were going to be so damned noisy I would have taken that other room."

*Oh yeah, that other room.* Steward didn't really need to be reminded. She actually had said, at great embarrassment to herself, that she wanted to continue sharing a room with him. Despite all the other thoughts and pressures working on his mind, her little admission stayed with him all day.

He quietly sipped his beer and watched her work. It is not supposed to be fascinating to watch someone sort paper and jot notes on a legal pad. But something about the intelligent look in her eyes and the graceful movement of her arms as she assembled her notes was compelling. *Good grief. She's just sorting paper and writing on a yellow tablet. Get a grip.*

Shaking his head, he stood and walked over to the plastic bucket on the dresser. Drain one beer. Open the next.

"Got an extra?"

She was looking at him. Nice eyes. Inviting?

"You sure you can take the break?"

She leaned back, knocking a small stack of papers off the bed. "I've gotta quit. My brain is turning to mush."

"I don't know if this stuff will help." He held up his beer. "It's been responsible for turning my brain to mush on more than one occasion. In fact, I think there's a Surgeon General's warning on here somewhere."

She laughed. "Cheapskate. You just don't want to share."

He grabbed a cold one and carried the dripping can over to her.

*This is it. I'm going to sit next to her. We'll sip. We'll laugh. And then we'll see what happens.*

The phone rang.

*But first we'll answer the phone.*

"Probably our Yellowstone friends calling to congratulate me on that great TV show," he said.

Lacy grabbed it first. Her expression changed from fun to concern.

"Is he all right?" she asked.

# FOURTEEN

Capitol Hill. Center of world power. Lots of people. Lots of people in suits. Congressmen sitting, standing, talking, listening. Wealthy lobbyists sitting, standing, talking, listening. Reporters writing, talking, listening, recording. Staffers talking, listening, writing, scurrying.

Eva Lacy sitting, trembling.

"Just relax, Eva. You are going to do fine," said Jerome Hershauer.

"Thanks," she squeaked. She looked around at the crowd. She and Hershauer were sitting at a table facing a Senate committee. Behind her sat a murmuring crowd of lobbyists, reporters and any other person who could fit in the room.

"Why is the crowd so big? Isn't there anything else going on in Washington today?"

"Sure," said Hershauer. "But this is the most interesting thing right now. You've got to understand, though. You might be nervous about making a mistake, but don't fret. Something more interesting will eventually happen in this town and you will be forgotten. So just relax." He smiled and he looked genuine.

She relaxed a little, then peeked over her shoulder to where she knew Steward was sitting, two rows back. She caught his eye and gave a look that said, "Can you believe this?"

He mouthed back, "Remember what I told you."

She caught herself before she laughed and then scratched her nose with an extended middle finger. He smiled at her.

Lacy turned to face forward, slightly shaking her head. Last night, after the call about Joe Lowry's bear attack, she had been a wreck. The pressure of today's hearing, and Steward's tough day on TV, then finding out that her friend had nearly been killed by that bear, it was too much.

Steward had stomped around the room for 20 minutes, complaining about how he should have been there, in the park, not wasting his time in Washington. Finally he vented enough that he noticed she was distraught. She needed his help and he responded. He held her hand, in a friendly manner, not romantic. And he listened to her cry. When she had pulled it together he talked to her, though his conversation didn't seem especially effective at the time.

To help her relax Steward had offered less-than-helpful advice. "Eva they're not going to be listening to what you're saying," he told her. "They're going to be staring at your chest."

Last night she threw a shoe at him. Today the subtle finger gesture would have to suffice.

*At least he is aware of my chest,* she thought. *I still*

*don't know how I feel about sharing a room. Why did I have to bring up keeping the situation the way it was? That was almost a blatant invitation to my bed, but I didn't want it that way. He understood. How did he understand? On the other hand, maybe I want to invite him. Either way, he didn't end up there.*

"Eva." Hershauer was talking to her.

She jumped. *What have I been thinking. This is not the time. Damn that Dusty.* She regained her composure.

"They're about to start. I'll speak very briefly then introduce you."

"I'm as ready as I'll ever be."

She glanced one last time at Steward. He smiled and adjusted in his seat and made an obvious effort to stare at her chest.

Quickly, she turned back around and noticed that at least one senator was staring at her chest too. *Damn that Dusty.*

After the droning opening comments of the committee chairman it was Hershauer's turn.

"Thank you, Mr. Chairman and members of the committee. I know America has been concerned that Old Faithful is not cooperating with us these days. Your offices have been swamped with letters demanding the geyser be fixed. Believe me, my office has gotten its share of mail too."

The Interior Secretary was really pretty good, noted Lacy. He was very smooth and his tone and demeanor projected outstanding charisma. Hershauer continued.

"Old Faithful has served us so well for so long that it's

hard to believe it could quit. But it did. I would just ask you and the American people to remember that we never turned it on in the first place and we did not turn it off. Unfortunately, that means we don't have the kind of power over nature to start it again. We have claimed Old Faithful as America's treasure but now we need to think of it as a gift from God. One that perhaps he took back."

Hershauer paused for a moment, then continued. "With a lead-in like that you may think I'm about to introduce a minister." A chuckle rippled through the room. "Instead, I'd like to introduce Ranger Eva Lacy. She is a geyser expert in Yellowstone and she will be able to explain the situation to you better than I can."

Lacy could feel all the attention in the room turning toward her. Deep breath.

"Thank you, Secretary Hershauer and members of the committee." Her voice cracked. "Secretary Hershauer suggested I explain how geysers work and let you take it from there. I suppose I have done this a million times for groups of tourists." She stopped and looked around. "You don't look much like a group of tourists."

Another chuckle drifted through the room. She relaxed.

"The idea of boiling water bubbling up through the ground is unbelievable. In Yellowstone, it comes up in the form of hot springs and mud pots. Sometimes the heat comes out through drier openings called steam vents and fumaroles. Walking through the park and seeing mud volcanoes, sulphur caldrons and all the evidence of the tremendous heat of the earth's core is exciting and terrifying at the same time."

The room was quiet and she had the attention of the committee.

"As remarkable and unbelievable as those other thermal features may be, a geyser is truly incredible. The complexity of plumbing and conditions required for a geyser to exist is baffling. Yet Yellowstone has been blessed with two-thirds of all the world's geysers.

"For now let's just accept the fact that extremely hot water is coming out of the ground. If you want an explanation on how that happens, I'll be happy to give it to you. But for the sake of time I'll concentrate on what has to happen to make a geyser.

"Picture a large pipe filled with water. Under the pipe is a flame. As the water at the bottom is heated it rises. As it cools at the top it sinks. Hot water goes up. Cooler water goes down. This little current continues and everything is fine."

She looked at the faces of the senators. One of them looked lost but the rest were grasping what she was saying. She continued, using her hands to help illustrate her talk.

"Now picture that somewhere along that pipe, someone has squeezed the pipe nearly closed. At that point the current of hot and cool water stops. The hot water below the narrow part can't escape and the pressure builds. The lower water gets hotter and hotter, well beyond the boiling point. But see, because the lower water is under pressure it doesn't yet boil. It's waiting for something."

She paused a moment. When she gave talks to tourists she tried to build the suspense at this point in her presentation. It seemed to be working here too.

"Finally some of this heat below the squeezed part breaks free. When the pressure is released, the water underneath turns to steam in an instant. It expands with amazing force and pushes its way up. All this water that has expanded and all the water above the constriction is pushed out in a violent and marvelous eruption until the pressure and heat can calm back down."

A couple of the committee members applauded the imaginary eruption. Lacy smiled.

"For this little eruption to take place everything's got to be just right. You've got to have the right kind of plumbing and the right amount of water and heat. The kind of geyser I explained to you is very simplified. Most of the geysers in Yellowstone are far more complicated. Their plumbing is intertwined in ways we don't understand. If one geyser has a long, powerful eruption, then a nearby geyser may have a small one on its next turn. The Yellowstone geyser basins are like giant, fragile ant farms filled with boiling water that squirts out of some of the holes if the ants happened to dig them just right.

"It's as delicate as it is magnificent. So you can understand that if the crust of the earth shifts, like it does during an earthquake, some geysers are going to break. I'm sorry that Old Faithful is the one that suffered."

Lacy sat back and let out a breath. Surveying the eyes of the Congressmen, she felt she had reached most of them. They seemed to understand the situation.

But not ones to stay silent for long, the committee members started to ask questions. Hershauer played traffic cop, handling all the policy-related queries himself and only deferring to Lacy on technical questions about the geysers specifically.

An hour later it was all over. Hershauer rose so Lacy did the same as a small crowd of staffers from both the committee and Office of the Interior gathered around. Just behind them lurked a few reporters who had follow-up questions. Lacy saw Steward on the fringes beyond them.

Hershauer grabbed her hand with a firm handshake. "Well done, Eva. You are truly a credit to this country's rangers."

She thanked him and worked her way, with pride, through the crowd. After clarifying a technical point with one of the reporters, she found Steward and joined him.

"Why do you get to be the hero and I have to be the goat?" he asked her.

She placed a hand on his shoulder. "Because that's the way nature decided it should be."

"Yeah, thanks," he said. "Listen, Skinny James said we're done here. We fly out this evening."

"Thank God."

\*\*\*\*\*\*\*\*\*\*\*\*\*\*

"Our government policies are designed to pave the way for overcrowding in our beautiful parks. In fact, they are designed to pave the whole damned park," Crane roared into the microphone.

The crowd on the mall roared back with laughter and cheers. Pierce was on the stage about five feet from his boss.

He was trying to estimate the enormous crowd. Ten thousand? Twenty thousand? He really couldn't tell, but he knew he was looking at a big crowd.

Years ago the agency responsible for counting the crowds for events on the mall stopped counting. The problem was that protest groups accused the agency of undercounting their crowd. Surely, they claimed, their important group drew a larger following than the so-called official count. The government was obviously trying to cover up the true might of the marching organization. Since protest groups like to protest, they were eager to start new protests directed at the agency. Interestingly enough, the agency that used to count crowds was the National Park Service.

Even though they were not counting anyone today, they were still the target of the protest on the mall.

Crane continued his sermon. "The Park Service is juggling the life of our bears and other animals. They are juggling treasured natural features that are as fragile as they are beautiful. They are juggling all our most prized natural resources." He paused for effect.

"But those clowns aren't any good at juggling and they have dropped the balls."

More laughter and applause broke out in the audience. A few spontaneous chants picked up here and there. Pierce couldn't quite make out what the various chants were. He looked at some of the signs and banners that the environmental masses had brought along. "Save our parks" was kind of to-the-point, but not too original. "Quit drugging our bears," "Mankind isn't so kind," and "PEW not NPS" were a little more clever. But Pierce's personal favorite was

"Bears shit in the woods, but men do much worse."

He continued to scan the crowd for interesting signs and activity while Crane talked on. Then he caught a relatively odd commotion at the edge. *That can't be.* Many of the protesters were wearing various shades of olive or green. But those colors and outfits were a little more earthy than the well-pressed shade of green he glimpsed. The rumpled drab green shapes were beginning to surround the two formal-looking greens. The chanting near the two shapes began to catch on and spread through the throng like a sound wave. *What are they doing here?*

Even from a hundred yards out, Pierce recognized the tall, powerful shape of Ranger Steward and the shorter, yet equally powerful, shape of Ranger Lacy. They walked with confident steps that showed they were in control of the space around them. It was odd, he thought, because they really were not in control of their current surroundings. Scores of people were hurling taunts, though none had yet hurled anything physical.

Still it was an interesting contrast. The PEW legions walked, talked and gestured as if they were in touch with the earth. But it was in a kind of loopy, flowing way. The two rangers also carried themselves as if they were in touch with the earth. But they seemed as if they were in control of it. Two purposeful strides cutting through a hundred grooving waves.

Perhaps that was why the taunts were directed at Steward and Lacy. Other rangers and security officers were near the mall. The PEW crowd largely ignored them. But the two Yellowstone rangers ... They could not be easily ignored by the activists. Pierce understood the feeling, though he couldn't exactly explain it. He had felt their presence ever since he met them in that bar by the park.

Steward and Lacy were so like the protesters at the same time they were so completely different. Steward's ilk would march into the wilderness as an equal. The PEW group would whine their way in as if they were going to confession. The ripple of PEW must have been a reaction to that incompatibility of attitude. Pierce was certain of it because he could sense that irritation from here. It must have been overwhelming in close proximity to the rangers. He marveled at the flow. It reminded him of the mountain streams he saw in Yellowstone, the frothy whitewater bubbling over hefty boulders.

Then something bounced off Steward's head. It was probably just a wadded up poster but Pierce was taking no chances. He jumped off the stage and began tearing through the crowd. By the time he reached the rangers, more objects were flying. Posters, cups, lunch bags, Green Savers. Through the crowd he saw security officers converging on the scene.

"Stop!" he yelled as he wedged his way between the rangers and the crowd. This required him to circle the rangers, with his back to them. He was attempting to face down the protesters while waving his own PEW identification tag that hung from his neck. It was, of course, bright orange like the fabled PEW stickers.

"This will only hurt our cause," he pleaded. "We can't look aggressive. Come on. We've come so far. Stop. Halt." And on he went until the rain of objects subsided.

"Sorry," he said over his shoulder as he led the rangers

farther out of the crowd. The rangers had been on the fringe of the mass to begin with, so they only had to make it through the people who had converged when the fun started, most of whom were already going back to hear the speakers. Pierce waved at the other security guards to show he had things under control and they went back to their posts.

"Thanks, Randy," Lacy said when they were in the clear.

"This is the second day in a row I've had crap thrown at me. At least yesterday it was only verbal," said Steward. "Is Washington always like this?"

"Some people enjoy it this way," replied Pierce. *I thought I did*, he added for his own benefit. "What are you doing here?"

"We were walking back to our hotel so we can pack and get the hell out of here," said Lacy.

"Besides," added Steward, "You saw where we work. We thought it was polite to see where you work."

Pierce looked around at the pile of junk that had accumulated where the rangers had been standing. Fortunately, a few of the protesters were picking up some of the trash, but he was sure a lot would remain. Crumpled at his feet was one of the posters he thought was so amusing. *Bears shit in the woods, but mankind does much worse. And here's the proof*, he thought.

"Thanks again, Randy," Lacy said. "We're going back to our office in the mountains. We like it better there."

*I don't blame you.*

*************

"What the hell was that all about?" Crane was glaring at Pierce back in the PEW offices.

It had been a long, quiet walk back. Pierce was waiting for the explosion and now he was getting it.

"We've got the mall full of people. The momentum is with us. We're feeling our power. Then a couple rangers wander in, two of the same rangers that have been causing all the trouble. They start to feel our power and here comes our very own intern to save them." Crane continued. "Whose side are you on?"

Pierce looked at the floor. "I just thought it would look bad if things got out of hand and somebody got hurt."

"Grow up, Randy. Tonight we're going to get a slight mention on the news if we're lucky. If things had played out the way they were headed, we would have been the top story."

"But how does it help us if we injure a couple unarmed rangers?"

Crane just shook his head. "Do you really think we would have hurt those guys?"

"Somebody sure seemed to be trying," Pierce said sheepishly. He got the feeling, again, that he had missed something.

Crane sighed and plopped down in his chair. "Randy, let's think about this a minute." His tone was that of a remedial teacher. "The security guys were moving in. Now, who do you think they were moving in to protect?"

"The rangers," Pierce said quietly.

"That's right. They were preparing to protect your ranger *friends*," Crane said with a slight sneer. "Now, if the protesters, who took time out of their schedules to come to Washington and make a stand for the things we believe in, hadn't let up right away who would have been arrested and possibly roughed up?"

"I suppose the protesters."

"And what image would have appeared on CNN and the networks?"

Pierce looked at the floor again. He understood, exactly, what his boss was saying. He accepted his licks and answered. "The TV would have shown a bunch of men in uniforms arresting PEW protesters."

"Exactly. The Americans trying to defend our environment being hauled away by the police state that is destroying the environment. It would have made for great TV. Probably would have brought in more donations than our bear video."

Pierce sat quietly for a moment. "Sorry," he said at last.

Crane let up. "Don't worry about it too much. It was an otherwise-successful rally. And the PR is still going in our favor."

Pierce went back to his own desk. Strangely, he didn't feel the way he usually did after these discussions. Instead of feeling like he had learned another lesson from the master that would motivate him and help him hone his own skills, he felt that he had learned a lesson that was much more troubling.

More than once since he had taken up the PEW cause he had started to wonder if he was doing the right thing. Each time, with Lester Crane's help, he had ended up renewing his commitment to the supremacy of nature. Man and wildlife were to be kept apart for the sake of wildlife.

Sitting back at his own desk, he started sorting through incoming donations.

*Thanks for the money,* he said to the checks in front of him. *If we get our way, you will never get to see the places you are protecting. This sucks.*

Ever since he met those two rangers in Gardiner, their words had stuck with him like a pebble in a hiking boot. By shaking his foot around he could keep hiking but the stone was always there. *If I help close the park to people, will I ever get to go back?* Sooner or later he would have to stop, remove his boot, and take care of the pebble once and for all.

"Randy." Crane's voice startled him.

He looked up from his thoughts and saw the environmental warrior standing next to him. But Crane looked different somehow. The lines, receding hair and thin frame had once looked like seasoning earned through dedication and time spent in the trenches. Now it looked kind of old, even impotent. The voice from this creature spoke again.

"Since we are riding a great wave of momentum, I think it is time for another fundraising mailing. And Randy, I think you are ready to handle this one yourself, start to finish." He reached out and squeezed Pierce's shoulder and handed him a piece of paper he had filled with notes. "And take a look at this. I just got off the phone with Jerry Hershauer."

Pierce could read enough of the notes to make out what was happening. He beamed. *This is perfect.*

***************

Nearby in the Hart office building Senator Patrick was having his ear bent.

"You have done so much for the environment already," said Kenneth Spilman to the senator. Spilman was a successful attorney and lobbyist who claimed a home in Jackson Hole, Wyoming, about 10 years ago. Because of his skills of persuasion and his familiarity with the legislative process, he was chosen by other wealthy Jackson Hole landowners to lobby Capitol Hill.

He continued, "But the greater Yellowstone area really needs your support."

Patrick leaned back in his chair and contemplated the man in front of him. He had worked with Spilman in the past. And he had been a senator long enough to know what lobbyists did and why. He really didn't need another beggar in his office, claiming a vote would provide some great deed. The true desire was usually somewhere else. The man's own pocketbook, most likely. Patrick knew the power of lobbyist money but he was not afraid to make a lobbyist squirm.

"Mr. Spilman, you aren't here on behalf of any ecosystem. You are here to protect the value of your home and the view out your window. What do you care about protecting bears and other wildlife?"

Spilman was unfazed. *Why should he be worried?*, thought Patrick. *Crane probably showed him the same thing he showed me. Polls say my constituents favor closing the gates.*

A faint smile crossed Spilman's lips. "The view out my window is the Yellowstone ecosystem. Even if I was being purely selfish about this, which I am not admitting, the fact is that your constituents and I share the desire to protect the same real estate. We are on the same team. We share the same interest."

Patrick leaned forward quickly. "Don't think that for a minute. *My* constituents are interested in saving wildlife, scenic beauty and the working geysers in Yellowstone. Your interests are much more narrow. The first time a bear takes a dump in your swimming pool, you are going to be back in this office asking permission for a hunting license."

Spilman said nothing. Patrick knew he was waiting for the "but." He gave in.

"But it looks like we are riding the same bus to different stops," said Patrick. "I'm not thrilled about this legislation. People should not be kept out of that park."

"They cause a lot of damage," helped Spilman. "They do threaten the animals and the thermal features."

"Yeah, but they also protect them because they are proud of them and they want their kids to see them. Take away that pride in the park and you also take away the protection. No one is going to be proud of a park they can't see."

"Well, the tide seems to be moving in a different direction," noted Spilman. "I hope you can help us on this. I've taken enough of your time, but thank you." The lobbyist rose to shake hands and leave.

After Spilman was gone Patrick sat quietly. *Of course, I'm riding that tide. I'm supporting them and helping close the park. He knows it and is probably reporting back to his neighbors and Crane right now, with glee.*

*What is going on with this issue?,* lamented Patrick as he stared at a photograph of his daughter. Typically, liberals line up on the side of the Crane bandwagon and conservatives line up on the side of the businesses and developers who make money from the continued use of the Greater Yellowstone Area. The two camps choose up sides and start swinging, much to the delight of the fundraising machines of various special interest groups who stood to make money off the controversy.

But something changed this time. The rich who had admired the beauty of Yellowstone during vacations began buying property to build second homes. Or, thanks to computers and modems, they built their primary homes and ran their businesses just as if they were back in their home states.

As this new breed of wealthy outsider began to bulldoze hillsides, Patrick heard the complaints of long-time residents of the Rocky Mountains, those who had worked with their hands to brave fierce winters and keep cattle healthy.

"Senator," they had grumbled. "These people have no respect for the scenery or nature. They have no respect for us.

Our favorite taverns and restaurants are replaced with trendy, pricey restaurants and cappuccino bars. In our schools our kids are made to feel like garbage because we can't afford the designer clothes that they can buy for their kids."

"I'm sorry," he had told them. "This is a local issue. I can't do much about it." But their complaints were ignored at home too. The economic vitality of the new residents proved too tempting to city planners, and the development continued.

However, a few years before Old Faithful quit spouting, the newcomers were no longer so new. The developments they had created, ones that overlooked beautiful scenery, now overlooked other developments. They resented the growth they had started, without, of course, taking the blame for its initiation. When they turned to the city planners to keep growth in check, the planners called them selfish and let the sprawling continue. Patrick knew it was only a matter of time before the issue reached beyond local politics.

He wasn't surprised that Lester Crane was the first to bring it to Congress. PEW fought the early developments every step of the way but Crane was quick to offer the hand of friendship once the great geyser opened the door of opportunity.

Patrick realized what was going on. PEW had fought development before and lost. By holding hands with the homeowners, the PEW tactics could now be successful. Besides, the new partners had money.

The budget. The environmentalists. The selfish homeowners. And then his own daughter. *I can't stop this momentum*, Patrick thought.

Then the bell sounded, informing senators that it was time to vote back at the Capitol.

**************

"I still can't figure out what that was all about," shouted Steward. He wasn't yelling because he was angry but because the plane from Denver to West Yellowstone was very small and very loud.

"Gosh, Dusty. Do you think fretting about it while flying over three-fourths of the country will solve things?" Lacy replied with immense sarcasm.

He frowned at her. "I'm just afraid that they are back there right now planning to shut the gates to the public. And I don't think our presence helped one bit."

"Speak for yourself," she laughed. "I think I did a fine job."

"That's not what I meant." He grabbed her hand. What a natural thing to do. Why didn't he do this long ago? He stammered just a second, then continued. "I think you did a fine job too. But the performance didn't matter. We were just there to play a role while the decisions were being made by somebody else." He didn't let go of her hand.

"Who?" She gave his hand a squeeze.

"I don't know exactly. Maybe some of the senators in the committee. Maybe Lester Crane has more power in Washington than we know. Maybe the President. And to tell you the truth, I don't really trust Hershauer. He seemed like a decent guy but I don't understand the world he lives in out there." He thought for a moment, then added. "And I don't know if he understands the world we live in either." He squeezed her hand back.

They sat quietly, or as quietly as one can sit in propeller-driven aircraft.

Finally, she turned to him. "Dusty, the other thing I don't understand is why we had a room to ourselves for two nights and you didn't try to hold my hand until now."

He visibly flushed and stared at the ceiling. But he didn't let go. "Well, I thought about it until the phone rang last night." Then he faced her. "Eva, I have been so far out of my element lately. Washington is not my kind of place. God knows I wasn't at home on that TV show. And you ... Well, I would be perfectly comfortable pulling you to safety off a mountain cliff, but it's awkward for me to pull you into my arms."

"And I probably didn't make it any easier on you," she said.

"Believe it or not, I had never thought about us very seriously." He was feeling the tingle of nausea and excitement that creeps from the stomach to the limbs and up the back of the neck. He had been attracted to many women before. That was no big deal. A very physical kind of thing. It usually passed within a few days. But he had known and liked Eva for a short time that seemed much longer, but not nearly as long as he wanted. Perhaps he was merely unaccustomed to feeling this level of physical attraction and profound respect for the same person. Confronting an emotion like this could overwhelm a guy.

"But now I do." He would have scooted closer to her. But it was kind of irrelevant. He was a big man on a small plane. He had been sitting as close to her as possible ever since they boarded.

"And we're almost home," she said.

He bent his head down and kissed her. Planes bounce with turbulence. Engines roar with the duty of keeping heavy metal thousands of feet off the ground. Passengers shout to each other in attempted conversation. Smells of disinfectant compete with smells of traveling bodies and airplane food.

Yet somehow, the kiss was romantic. At least to Dusty Steward and Eva Lacy.

As they approached the airport and the kiss was over for the moment, Steward shook his head. "And we had that room to ourselves."

She laughed.

"Not taking advantage of that will go down in time as one of my biggest regrets," he said. "It will rank right up there with not smacking that first protester who hit me with a poster."

She laughed again. "I think that's what they wanted."

"He came to the right place," he said. "I don't know what held me back. And what about that guy who was screaming in your face. I was expecting you to give him a serious headache."

"Yeah, that PEW kid showed up at the right time. What's up with him anyway?"

Steward thought about that a moment. "Maybe he has some common sense. He won't last long with PEW."

They continued to laugh about their adventure with the protesters, her appearance in the committee and his on TV. And they continued to hold hands. Even when they got off the plane and met Joe Lowry, who was going to drive them back to the park.

"Driver, you have a stretch limo I presume," Steward asked Lowry. Lowry still sported a few bandages and a limp from his bout with the bear. Steward tried not to stare.

"Yeah, right." He didn't seem too amused. He looked at Steward and Lacy's clasped hands. "I thought you said you guys weren't dating. You called the office from Washington and gave us all hell about that room thing."

"Long story," said Steward, somewhat embarrassed.

"Anyway, I'm taking you straight to Lightfeather. Take a look at this." He handed Steward and Lacy each a sheet of paper.

Steward saw it was a news story downloaded from an online Washington newspaper.

# News You Can Use

## Here's what's breaking NOW:

### Yellowstone Gates Likely to Close
by Phil Grossman (AP)

The gates at Yellowstone National Park may close for good in an effort to "preserve and protect its treasures for the future," said Secretary of the Interior James Hershauer.

The announcement comes at the end of a tumultuous summer season that was marred by the demise of the Old Faithful geyser, fatal bear attacks and vandalism. Hershauer revealed that his latest budget proposal reflects reduced fiscal requirements of a closed park. But he added that fiscal considerations during the current budget squabble in Congress were only a minor aspect of the plan.

"Yes this is drastic but it is also necessary. Our priority must be to maintain the park's wonders and protect its full-time residents, the animals that live there."

He acknowledged that his department had conducted public opinion polls indicating growing support for a closed park. He credited People for the Environmental Way for helping people understand the need to lock the gates.

"This is not just a victory for People for the Environmental Way. It's a victory for all people,"

# News You Can Use

## Here's what's breaking NOW:

said PEW founder Lester Crane. "Once people understood the negative consequences of Yellowstone's 3 million annual visitors they were ready to do whatever it took to protect their nation's park."

The National Park Service had already made the decision to close facilities to winter visitors. If the budget is accepted in its current form, the gates will not re-open in the spring.

Under the new proposal only park rangers would be permitted inside the park boundaries. Researchers and selected naturalists could apply for special permits to enter the park to check on the wildlife and thermal features. Hershauer estimated that the park would remain closed to tourists for at least the next five years.

"Our hope is that if the park recovers in the next several years we will be able to let a few guided tours back onto the premises. Until then Americans will still be able to visit our other national parks and wildlife areas that have not been closed," Hershauer said.

"We are not just doing this because of the tight budget," he reiterated. "Sure budget considerations made us evaluate our spending priorities for the future, but it is the current condition of the park that makes us act to close

# News You Can Use

## Here's what's breaking NOW:

the park now."

Budget talks will continue on Capitol Hill, but insiders predict the Park Service's Yellowstone plans will not change. The only opposition to the plan comes from businesses near the Yellowstone area who thrive on tourist dollars. However, they seem unlikely to overcome the strength of Hershauer's endorsement and the lobbying weight of other property owners near the park that want to see the gates closed.

-end-

**Get the New news**

New York

Chicago

D.C.

L.A.

U.S.

World

World's Best Auction

**<<Prev.**    **^Home^**    **Other News>>**

# FIFTEEN

"We're closing," Steward asked/answered. It was a question in that he wanted to be sure he read correctly, a statement in that he knew he had.

Lightfeather looked grim. "We lost the damned thing early. PEW jumped on the bear attacks and our procedures. Then when That Geyser stopped ..." His voice trailed off. Many park employees were so frustrated with Old Faithful that they stopped calling it by name.

"We didn't have much of a chance," he continued. "PEW has been waiting for years to do this. We might have been able to weather just the bears or just the geysers, but we couldn't handle both of them."

Lacy spoke up. "Why did Hershauer seem so happy? When we were out there he seemed to be on our side but in the media he seems to be on Lester Crane's side."

Lightfeather smiled. "It's politics Eva."

"So whose side is he on?" asked Steward.

The park superintendent's smile faded. "I don't really know. But I've been concerned lately that Lester Crane is reacting to things that I haven't even heard about yet."

He paused a moment, considering if he should go on.

"Now, don't go spreading this around, but I think Hershauer calls Crane more often than he calls me."

Steward looked around the quiet room. Lacy was staring at her boots. Lowry was tapping a pen on a notebook while glaring out the window. Lightfeather was drumming his fingers on his desk while staring at a light fixture.

"What's next?" he finally asked.

Lightfeather shifted in his seat. "Well, we begin letting people out of the park as the lodges close and we stop letting them in. Effective immediately."

Steward thought that over a minute. "So they've actually done it. They've removed the entire reason for the park's existence. Welcome to Yellowstone National Big Plot of Land That You Pay For But Can't Visit."

"Maybe they have a point. Visitors have done some damage over the years," Lightfeather sighed.

Steward jumped up from his chair and leaned forward, placing his big hands on Lightfeather's desk. "The only point they have is on the tops of their heads. If it weren't for visitors, there would be no park. We would have homes, farms, mines and God knows what else spread around here. This place wasn't set aside for the benefit and enjoyment of the bears, elk, moose or any other furry creature. It was created for the enjoyment of the people. Even if every footprint on the Yellowstone trail wears away part of the park, every person taking every step gives this park a purpose. Their visit, their hike, make Yellowstone valuable.

"Take away the person's ability to come here to camp, hike and sightsee and you take away the person's desire to keep development out. The bears are not going to write to their Congressmen. The wolves can't keep out hunters and trappers. Only people can do that. The value of every set of eyes that comes here far outweighs any perceived damage caused by feet, cars and tents."

He stopped and looked around the room. Three sets of eyes were wide open and staring at him and three mouths hung open. Slowly he stepped away from the desk and sat back in his chair.

"I suppose I should have said all that when I was on TV. Sorry to take it out on all of you," he said quietly.

"But Mort," he added, looking squarely at Lightfeather. "This park will disintegrate."

**************

At PEW headquarters a cork flew from a champagne bottle and landed noisily in a box of empty aluminum cans. Other noises included the usual cheering and loud conversation that follow a victory.

"Randy," bellowed Crane's voice, cutting through the din. "We're going back to Yellowstone to hold a big news conference."

"That's great, Les. I'll set it up. And here," he handed Crane several sheets of paper. "That's the next fundraising mailing, ready to go to the printer."

Crane studied the brochure and letter Pierce had designed. "Outstanding, Randy. This is really going to help our cause. Great job." He went to his desk, pulled out a purchase authorization form and signed it.

They tapped their plastic champagne cups together. Then Pierce walked to his desk and slipped the signed form and the mailer proofs into his briefcase. After downing his drink he set out on foot to the print shop a couple blocks away.

At the shop he gave the printer the purchase form then pulled out a folder. He opened it to confirm the brochure and letter were different from the ones he had shown Crane and then gave it all to the printer.

To save money, PEW usually relied on a team of volunteers to stuff envelopes and lick stamps. That gave the volunteers who were too old, young or disabled for marches or clandestine sabotage to still feel like they were PEW warriors. But if Crane wanted a mailing to go from computer to mailbox in a hurry, like he did with this fundraising plea, he hired mailing companies that had the ability to label the envelopes, sort the mailing list by carrier route and apply postage. These companies could move mail very quickly.

*How efficient,* thought Pierce.

# SIXTEEN

"Well that sure didn't take long," said Steward as he and Lacy examined the dead elk. It had been shot, even though it was well inside park boundaries where hunting was illegal. The antlers had been sawed off.

He looked around at the evening sky. Insects hummed around and a few birds sang to each other, preparing for the night. "They only started closing the park two days ago. How did the poachers move in so quickly?" asked Steward. "I mean, I knew it would happen. I just thought it would be later."

"We've had poachers ever since hunting here was outlawed, Dusty. Maybe we would have found this poor elk anyway."

"Maybe, but it certainly didn't help his chances by notifying all the poachers that 3 million potential witnesses were not going to be here anymore."

"I wish we could catch them," Lacy said bitterly. "But that's just not realistic. The few dozen of us remaining rangers can't patrol this huge place."

"I hear Lester Crane and his goons will come

swooping in to the park tomorrow. Maybe they are coming to help out," Steward said with an angry and sarcastic look.

"The sad thing is that this poor guy just plays into his hands," said Lacy, kneeling close to the elk.

"Exactly. This is just further evidence that people should be kept out, or so he would say."

"Well, this is a more convincing argument than the ones he used to close us. I mean, look at this poor thing." Lacy touched the animal's face.

Steward squatted next to her and grabbed the elk's head, twisting it to reveal the bloody stubs where the antlers had been. "Now think a minute, who had a use for these antlers? Where was the value?"

"I expect the elk had a use for them," Lacy answered with a smirk.

He had already decided she told jokes at inappropriate moments as a way to relieve stress. He snorted at her, then continued. "Now that he isn't using them I guarantee they are on their way to someone's mantle or being ground up for an oriental aphrodisiac."

"If you wanna get horny ..."

"Eva, for Pete's sake I'm trying to make a point here."

"Sorry, Dusty. For some reason it's hard to be too serious when you're starting a philosophical discussion with a dead elk head in your hands."

He put the head back down and stood, wiping his hands on his pants. "That, and the fact that you've heard me say these things about a thousand times," he said with a smile. "But the point is, until the park was closed the elk's antlers were important to the tourists, as long as they were on the elk's head. Now trophy hunters and sex chasers get top billing."

The two stood silently for a moment contemplating the morning's carnage, neither smiling anymore.

"The real tragedy here is that these animals would have shed their antlers in a few weeks," said Lacy.

"Enough of this crap, Eva." Steward took off his pack, plopped it on the ground and started rummaging. "We've gotta get this park back."

"Any ideas?"

"I don't have the whole plan worked out but I know where to start," he said as he checked his shotgun and ammunition.

"Where?"

"That one bear started this mess. I'll start there. I'm going bear hunting."

*****************

"You do the hunting, Dusty. I'll take care of the cleaning." Lacy said to herself as she stood near the Old Faithful geyser cone with a flashlight and a bottle of dish soap.

She checked her surroundings carefully. Even though the geyser was no longer erupting, even though the tourists were gone, even though there were few rangers spread throughout a large park, there was something about the Old

Faithful area that caused people to congregate. It was the biggest draw when the park was open. All signs pointed there. People were just plain drawn to the icon and Lacy would not have been surprised to see several other rangers, or even strangers, nearby, even on this moonless night.

But no one was around. Taking a deep breath, she stepped off the boardwalk and advanced carefully toward the geyser, her flashlight guiding the way. Walking around geyser basins was treacherous even in the daylight. The crust of ground could break underfoot and you would find yourself standing in seriously hot water, your boots being the only thing keeping your flesh on your feet. *This is worth the risk,* she thought.

For some reason, soap affects geysers. Some park storytellers say this was first discovered by Chinese laundry operators who tried to set up shop on geysers in the early days of the park. Things didn't work out so well for these entrepreneurs who mistakenly caused scalding eruptions at inconvenient times. Once the park features were protected, first by the army and then by the rangers, one of the biggest challenges was keeping impatient tourists from "soaping" geysers to get them to gush.

Lacy assumed people had tried to soap Old Faithful ever since it stopped, but she had not heard any details. And if she had caught someone doing it, she would have been obligated to aid in their arrest.

"I guess I'm under arrest then," she said to no one. She took the cap off the bottle and emptied the contents into the gurgling geyser. Quickly she stepped back and waited.

Soap bubbles and nothing else.

"Damn. I hope Dusty is having better luck than me."

She was answered by the sound of distant gurgling hot springs, hissing steam vents and the snort of a feeding bison.

*****************

*This is too damned easy,* thought Al Rennison. ("Rhymes with venison," he told his hunting buddies.) He was a big man but he managed to get comfortable in the cab of his Dodge pickup. A pillow was propped between the driver's door and seat. One foot stretched across the bench. The other hung to the floor of the passenger side. A heavy sleeping bag was opened like a blanket to cover him. He supposed he would toss and turn a little during the night but right now, on his back, he felt all right. Through the sunroof he could make out the uncountable stars of the clear Yellowstone sky.

All day he had driven the empty park roads looking for elk. The stupid things hung out near the road, almost like they missed tourists. He must have seen 50 but he only had time to shoot 10.

By the time he got to his 10th trophy the process was smooth. See a group of elk. Stop the truck while grabbing the shotgun from rack. Get out and walk to can't-miss range. Shoot the biggest bull. Cut the antlers off the dead elk. Throw the antlers in the back of the truck. Drive to the next victim.

For the first catch, he needlessly approached the bull cautiously. He forgot that many of the animals would be used to harmless humans and would not automatically bolt. He couldn't get too close of course but his big gun and good aim assured that he didn't have to. A couple of times he got spooked when the rest of the herd did little more than flinch at the sound of gunfire. They hadn't a clue what the noise was and didn't understand it meant danger. He got two trophies out of one herd before the rest of them figured out that they should run.

With a truck full of valuable antlers he pulled into the closed Fishing Bridge campground to rest before leaving the park. It was a perfect spot. No other campers nosed around because the park was closed. And he was far enough off the road so a passing ranger wouldn't see him. If he could hold tight until 2:00 a.m. he'd be sure that none of the skeleton ranger crew would be on duty. He could drive right out to the East gate, use a barricade key he had pilfered, and head home.

On the way in he'd done something similar. Came in late at night. Slept until morning. Went out to find elk.

Contentedly reviewing his day, Rennison began to drift off to sleep.

WHAM!

A hard jolt against the driver-side window knocked Rennison awake. He lurched into a sitting position, instinctively reaching for the shotgun in its rack on the rear window. Looking in every direction as alertness replaced weariness in his eyes, he saw nothing but the stars in the sky.

WHACK!

Another blow against his window. This time the force caused a thick web of cracks to obstruct his view. But through the windshield he could make out a large shape moving slowly.

Bear? He jerked around with his gun, accidentally hitting the barrel against the windshield and knocking the weapon to the floor.

CRASH!

A large brown paw smashed through the window. Just as Rennison reached his gun two claws dug into the back of his neck and tore their way toward the top of his head.

Nothing vital was cut but the pain was immense. Rennison screamed and tried to both look up and bring his shotgun into position.

The paw slid off Rennison's head and grabbed the window frame. A second paw joined it and tore the door from the truck as if it were a child's plastic model.

The bear leaped forward. One paw pushed Rennison's gun back to the floor. The other paw smashed his face back into the seat. And a steely set of jaws clamped down on the back of his neck.

Al Rennison's poaching trip was officially over.

# SEVENTEEN

"Outside the Rennison family, not many tears are going to be shed over this one," Steward said to a wallet he had found in a bloody scrap of pants lying near a battered pickup truck filled with antlers. The carcass of the wallet's former owner lay in a heap between two pines. A dusting of pine needles and dirt covered the body, minus several pounds of flesh that were currently being digested elsewhere.

After calling in the situation to headquarters and a friendly heads-up call to Lacy, he tossed the wallet back into the truck and continued his conversation, this time with an antler he pulled from the back.

"Okay, so maybe this guy had it coming. But our grizzly wasn't passing moral judgment. He doesn't know the difference between a poacher and a boy scout. Hell, *I* have taken naps in my car when I've been out too late. Doesn't mean I should get eaten."

He replaced the antler and grasped his rifle. "So, my dear bear, one act of justice does not make you a saint. Parole denied."

He shined his flashlight around the vacant

campground. The trail was not difficult to find. Bears don't feel the need to walk carefully as they go.

"I'll bet I could find you," he said in the direction of the trail. Then he started walking in that direction. Abruptly he stopped. For one thing it was not very smart to chase a grizzly bear in the dark. And if he did find it, then what. He remembered what had happened in Hayden Valley when the bear got between him and other rangers. Nobody had dared to take a shot and the bear got away. It would be even worse if they were all stalking around at night. He was determined not to let the bear escape again because he was too impatient to wait for his backup.

Before leaving he unzipped his pants and urinated near the trail. "Yeah bear, I'm here. I'm leaving *my* scent because this is *my* park and I'm coming back."

He shined his flashlight around in all directions before trotting back to his truck. Looking around one more time he slid behind the wheel and started the engine. He thought better of it, turned it back off and grabbed the radio to hail Lacy. She answered quickly.

"Eva, I'm staying here tonight. I want to be around in case something happens and I want to get an early start in the morning."

"Understood, Dusty. I am on my way from That Geyser. Lowry is coming down from Mammoth. See you in a couple hours."

Steward dug a camera out of his bag and flashed some photos of the Rennison display. He didn't need to draw a chalk line around the victim but he wanted to preserve as much of the scene as possible for future study. Then he placed the body in a body bag that he had begun to carry as standard equipment in his vehicle.

"Lucky me," he said.

He stuffed the corpse into the back of Rennison's truck, among the antlers.

"That bear isn't going to like me taking his late-night snack," said Steward as he glanced around at the darkness.

After thoroughly rinsing off, he settled into the seat of his own truck to get a quick nap and soon discovered just how many sounds a national park can make. Wind rustles through pine trees. The nearby Yellowstone River makes an occasional gurgle. Bugs bump into car windows. Wind changes course and speed to rustle trees, bushes and grasses in sporadic directions.

And every single noise sounds like a stalking grizzly bear.

***************

Pierce tossed fitfully in his hotel bed. Once again he was in Gardiner, Montana, the night before a news event he had helped stage. Tomorrow, he would stand next to Lester Crane, who was now sleeping peacefully across the room.

He glanced over and checked to see that his boss was really sleeping. Crane was.

*If you only knew,* he thought.

The cameras would be there. The tape recorders. The

reporters' notebooks. Crane would make an opening statement full of clever sound bites. He would give the media an opportunity to ask questions.

*Then all hell will break loose.*

Pierce knew he would not be back in this room tomorrow night. In fact he had no idea where he would spend the next night or even the afternoon. *Maybe I should sneak out now.*

*Too late for that. I have to face this sooner or later.* He rolled over and vainly tried to rest.

**************

Tap. Tap. Tap.

Steward bolted upright at the sound on his driver-side window. His head whirled around to see a flashlight shining in. He opened the door to hear Lacy laughing at him.

"Remind me not to put you on watch next time we go camping," she jabbed. "That bear could have led a parade of elephants right around your car and you would have slept through it."

Steward checked his watch. "I haven't been out long. I think I was so wound up from thinking every fart of nature was a rampaging bear that I finally shut down."

"Well, rest or not, I'll get us alert in the morning." She held up her camp stove and coffee pot.

"You're wonderful," he said. "Where's Lowry? Maybe he brought eggs and sausage."

"He's staying at Mammoth. Crane is having a big news conference at the arch tomorrow. Probably to gloat. Lowry said he wanted to stick around there."

"He scared?" asked Steward.

Lacy thought for a moment. "Would you blame him?"

Steward looked around at the dark wilderness and thought about Lowry's ordeal with the bear. Steward shook his head.

"Of course I don't blame him," he said. "The manly side of me wants to say we don't need him. But we probably do."

Lacy shrugged. "There just aren't enough of us around here now. Besides, Lowry will contact us as soon as the news conference is over. It's the fastest way for us to find out what Crane does."

"Crane does what he always does. He'll whine. He'll fuss. He'll hate people. Crane will be trying to protect the park by holding a news conference while we are trying to protect the park by hunting down a killer bear."

"You know, Dusty. Even if we get rid of the bear we won't save the park."

He was quiet for a moment, then nodded. "That Geyser."

"I tried to soap it," she said.

Steward was shocked. "I can't believe you." Then, more quietly, "Did it work?"

"It bubbled."

"If I knew you were going to do the laundry I would

have had you take some of my T-shirts."

She lightly punched his arm. "Or those Redskins boxers."

"Hey, speaking of that. I can't offer you a fancy D.C. hotel room, but I have a pretty luxurious ranger truck."

They climbed in and she was immediately in his arms. After a long, long kiss he looked at her and stroked her cheek.

"Eva, I am willing to overlook the fact that we are in a cramped car seat, like a high school prom date. And I am willing to overlook the fact that sex can attract bears. But then I think about the fact that we are parked next to a dead guy's trashed truck and that his body is in the back. That's more effective than a cold shower."

She laughed. "I'm not even willing to overlook that part about the sex attracting bears. If that bear drags our naked bodies out of this truck, can you imagine Crane's next TV commercial? That video would be even better than the trapping one."

He chuckled at the image and then pulled her closer. Feeling the safety and comfort of a shared embrace, he dozed off much easier than he had before.

*****************

A watch timer awoke them just before the sun peeked over the mountains. Between flashlights and approaching sunlight, Lacy could see well enough to make a pot of strong coffee. Steward dug around his pack to find a couple apples and a bag of GORP. He never went anywhere without this legendary trail mixture. Technically, GORP was supposed to stand for granola, oatmeal, raisins and peanuts. Steward's preferred blend was peanuts, raisins and M&Ms. Whatever the mix, it would provide the energy the rangers would need for the coming challenge. They quickly gobbled up what they could, eagerly downed the hot coffee and then checked their equipment for the hunt.

Even in the middle of summer, mornings in Yellowstone are cold. This time of early fall, frost was common and snow was not unheard of. Steward and Lacy moved quickly to get the blood moving and to try to stay warm, each breath a visible puff. They said little as they concentrated on the task ahead.

In what seemed to take forever but was actually less than an hour, the sun had risen enough that flashlights were not needed. Steward squinted into the morning sunlight and began to follow the trail that was less than 12 hours old. Lacy walked a couple yards behind him, both rangers alert and conscious of everything around them.

Normally, Steward would have been trying his damndest to make noise so he didn't surprise any bears. For *this* bear, however, he was more concerned about the bear surprising him. Steward had removed the bear's kill. He didn't need to make extra noise. It knew they were here. They chose their steps carefully.

That the bear was around he was sure. From the fatality at the truck Steward followed a trail of crumpled plants. Obviously something big had come tromping along. It didn't take a cunning Indian scout to see the trail. After a time the trail became less obvious but Steward felt that he was going in the right direction. He found a dead log that had been thoroughly scavenged for bugs and grubs.

"Nice to see he's not living exclusively off people," he said, carefully checking his surroundings.

"Shall we claim he's reformed and call off the whole thing?" Lacy's voice quivered with nerves.

Steward stopped and looked at her. "You sure you're up to this?"

"Let's just get it done," she replied quietly.

They didn't say much else for the next mile or so. Between the intense concentration on sticking with the fading trail and trying to avoid a grizzly ambush, there was not a lot of interest in talking.

"Crap," said Steward as he stopped. "He's gotten on a game trail and I can't tell for certain which way he went."

Animals tend to follow the same paths from prairie to water hole. Over time they wear trails that are easy to walk along. The Yellowstone wilderness is crisscrossed with countless paths left by animals. They are a great discovery for hikers who are bushwhacking off the trails marked by the Park Service. As long as the game trail is going the same direction the hiker wants to go, the trip will be a bit easier than trudging through thick weeds and deadfall. It's an easier trail for a bear to use as well.

To Lacy and Steward, it looked like the bear came to a game trail, padded around and then chose one direction. Or the other. They couldn't tell which one.

"I don't think I want to split up," said the cracked voice of Lacy.

Steward didn't say anything. He stooped over and

walked around the intersection of the bear trail and the game trail, examining every stalk of grass. Finally he stood up and looked at her.

"Okay. Let's go toward Storm Point. At least the scenery is better there."

She smiled back at him, weakly.

\*\*\*\*\*\*\*\*\*\*\*\*\*\*

The sun was not quite over the mountains, but already Pierce and Crane were hard at work preparing for their morning news conference. Pierce was double-checking the press packets that would be handed out and Crane was talking on the phone, probably with Bernie Wilson.

He hung up the phone and danced around the room. "Whoowee. Another one down."

Pierce looked up expectantly.

"Some hunter was killed last night," said Crane. "He was out poaching elk and sawing off their antlers. When he stopped to sleep for the night in his truck a grizzly smashed the truck and killed him." He let out another whoop.

"Serves him right, I guess," said Pierce.

"Bernie gets great stuff listening to the ranger frequency. And the timing is perfect. We are going to be celebrating the closing of Yellowstone and we get one more example, on deadline, of why it has to be done."

"Do you want me to change anything with these?" Pierce gestured toward the press kits.

"No, they'll be fine, but I'm going to stop by the ranger station where Bernie is hanging out and see how much more information I can get. Just finish up here and then check the setup for the news conference."

Then Crane was out the door.

Pierce gathered the press kits and stuffed them in a box to be carried to the news conference site under the historic arch at the north gate of the park. Before hoisting the box, he sat down and took a deep breath. *It's not that the box is so heavy*, he thought, *but I've got to be prepared to carry my spirit.*

He reached into a pocket of his rumpled, olive-colored coat and withdrew a copy of the fundraising brochure he had designed for PEW. Crane, he knew, had not yet seen the finished product. Nor would the environmental boss expect it to be a topic of the pending news conference. But the reporters had seen it by now. And Pierce was sure they would bring it up.

# EIGHTEEN

"Hey, Travis. You hear about Al Rennison?" hollered Pete Crummel, a hunting guide based in Cody.

From his rickety chair at a small Formica breakfast table, Travis Raines yelled back across the busy diner. "'Bout the bear? Me an' Tommy was just talking about it."

Tommy the restaurant manager added "Heard it was that same bear that caused all that trouble."

As vast as the West is and as few people live there, the grapevine is surprisingly quick. Legends of strength and endurance in the back country are shared as soon as the first person who hears or lives the tale can make it to the closest bar. Tales of death move even faster.

Crummel joined his friends at the table. "I just *knew* he was poaching. He didn't have it in him to get a good buck the right way. And he couldn't of got that truck without going over his limit and selling the extras."

"Got his didn't he?" said Raines.

The men thought quietly for a few minutes. Then Tommy added, "Damned shame, though."

"If anybody deserved it, it was Rennison. But does

anybody deserve that?" said Crummel. "I heard the bear ate half of him."

He and Raines squirmed in their seats while Tommy wiped off the table next to them.

"I don't even know how guilty he was," said Raines. "In a way, since they closed the park, it ain't really a park anymore. Rennison wasn't really poaching."

Crummel looked at him carefully. "You've been thinking about going in there yourself haven't you." He saw Raines and Tommy glance at each other quickly and then look down.

"Man, I don't believe it."

"Hell, Pete," said Raines defensively. "They're overpopulated with elk and deer. The things are just going to starve. I've been saying that for years. I've never poached in there before. I hate poachers as much as anybody. But if it ain't a park anymore–"

"But it *is* a park," interrupted Crummel. "What's the damned sign say outside the entrance? 'Yellowstone National Park.'"

"And if I drove out there tonight and took down that sign, I ain't gonna do it, Pete, but if I did, who would put it back up? They only got a few rangers working. Nobody drives up there anymore. The only thing that makes it a park is that we're not supposed to hunt there."

Nobody said anything. Raines continued, "You've seen my shop, Pete. I sell T-shirts and other tourist junk. No tourists going to Yellowstone. Nobody to buy my stuff. You and Tommy ain't gonna buy enough T-shirts to keep my family fed. If I can't live off the land one way I'll have to live off it another."

Crummel thought about that. His own business would probably increase because hunting expeditions would be one of the few remaining ways to enjoy the Yellowstone area. Some people would be determined to enjoy Yellowstone and would come out to the area to do *something*. He would guide them through the mountains even though he wouldn't lead them into the park itself.

People in the West all lived off the land, he knew. Some, like himself, lived off it directly by hunting for food. Helping other people hunt for sport also provided him with a living. Others lived off the land by mining and selling the natural resources. And many more survived because of the rare and rich beauty. People who lived in far less-beautiful parts of the country come out just to look at the land. While visiting they eat in restaurants. They buy souvenirs in shop's like Raines'. They sleep in hotel rooms. They provide a living for a lot of other people.

*That's right,* thought Crummel, *Raines and Tommy have been living off the land as much as I have.*

"Travis, wait here a minute," he said and went out into the cool air toward his truck. After digging around in the trash on his floorboards, he fished out a slip of paper and brought it back in the bar. He handed the crumpled paper to Raines.

"On the way over here I got a call on the cell phone. I took down the name and number thinking he was going to be a client. After a couple minutes I thought he sounded a little bit shady. He was hinting that he might want to do some hunting in the park. I told him I couldn't help him."

He patted his friend on the back. "You do what you have to, Travis. I don't really like it but I understand. In case you can't read my writing, the name is Matt Wise and he's staying at the Hilltop."

*****************

"Look at this." Steward was pointing toward an area off the path where something large had been digging and foraging. "We chose the right direction. I think this is our guy."

"What was he doing?"

"Digging for a ground squirrel? I don't know. The thing is, he's in the area. Probably staying relatively close to last night's kill, but on the hunt for more."

"That's comforting," Lacy said warily.

"Don't sweat it. We just have to find him before he finds us. Simple."

She managed a smile.

The bear's path wandered back onto the game trail. But that trail ended at the park road. If they walked about a mile to the west they would be back at their trucks. So far their trail had led them in, essentially, a large loop.

"Maybe we should have just waited at the truck for him to come back to us," said Lacy.

"We could have had another cup of coffee at least," Steward added. He then crossed the road and tried to find the bear's course.

He finally stopped on the Storm Point trail. This short, two-mile trail was maintained by the Park Service. It started out near a small circular pond that was formed in a long-dead thermal crater. Then it entered the woods toward the shore of Yellowstone Lake. But Steward was not admiring the scenery. He was staring at a pile of poop in the middle of the trail. There are scientists who specialize in the study of animal droppings. Scatologists, they're called. Steward was no expert on dung, but he had worked in the park long enough to make a pretty good guess about which animal had done the work.

"Eva. He went this way."

She caught up to him, agreed with his findings, and looked around.

"Has it only been a few short months since we were out this way and the whole thing started?" she asked.

"Just about two miles there," he pointed to the east, "was Jenny Patrick's campground. And somewhere here," he pointed to the south, along the Storm Point trail, "we will end it."

One at a time he stretched his strong arms and then positioned his rifle for comfortable walking but quick firing. Without speaking, Lacy did the same. They walked toward the woods along a flat, easy and deadly quiet trail.

After a few moments of tense, careful, alert hiking, Steward stopped.

"Well, Eva. I don't know quite what to tell you." Steward was looking at her face trying to read her thoughts. She was looking past him at the place where the trail split in two.

He knew the trail did this. At the road it started as a single trail but after a while in the woods it turned into a loop. He had hoped it would be obvious which direction the bear went. He hoped they could stick together. But he could not tell which direction the bear had gone. And if they both went one way, the bear might continue around the circle and escape. Worse yet, it could sneak up behind them.

"I guess this is where we split up," she said quietly.

"I don't think we should both go down opposite sides of the loop. We might meet at the bear and end up shooting toward each other." He waited a moment, then added, "So, probably the best thing is for you to wait here. If he comes around the other way, you've got him. If he gets off the trail and starts crunching through the brush, you'll know it."

She looked around for a moment. "We can keep in contact by radio but we should have some kind of signal."

"Just try to nail the monster. If I hear a gunshot, I'll come running."

She grabbed his arm and pulled him to her. Their lips met. Nothing more was said.

He marched along the trail toward Storm Point.

***************

"At one time, this arch was erected as a showcase for Yellowstone," said Lester Crane to the group of reporters in front of him.

Pierce noted TV cameras representing the major

networks, including CNN. In addition he recognized Phil Grossman from AP and a few other newspaper reporters Crane had worked with over the years. He caught sight of Bernie Wilson lurking at the edges of the pack. A handful of strangers were on hand too, but he knew Crane was confident he had them all in the palm of his hand. It was his day. His story.

"Today, we are closing the gate under this arch to create an even more important showcase. Where once an open gate led reckless visitors to a national park, the closed gate will lead the world to a new era. The era of national wildlife protection. Finally, our treasures our safe," he continued.

"It took a long time but I am proud of the work of the People for the Environmental Way and the support of the American public. As Congress finally began to recognize that we have been right all these years, I felt like the entire country belonged to the PEW.

"This is a great moment for the People for the Environmental Way. It is a great moment for the wildlife. It is a great moment for Yellowstone."

With that, Crane looked around the gathering and smiled. He and Pierce had been talking about what would happen next. Some of the reporters would ask about certain points of strategy. One or two might ask which park was next on the agenda. Crane had already talked through clever answers to every possible question. Pierce was impressed, as usual, that his boss was so politically capable. But Pierce knew a few questions were coming for which Crane had not prepared.

"Les, you say the American people were on your

side," started Phil Grossman. "But do you think they were really aware of all your tactics?"

Crane had a funny look on his face. He had certainly not expected to be challenged, especially by his buddy Grossman.

"Our tactics were not secret. We taped rangers harassing bears. It was the rangers' tactics that appalled the public."

"But in your latest mailing you brag about planting food scraps in back-country campsites to entice bears into dangerous confrontations with humans," Grossman persisted. "And you boast about how much money your stunts and commercial brought into the PEW organization."

Pierce watched the color drain from Crane's face. Pierce always thought that was just a figure of speech, but he actually saw it happen. And that was saying something considering Crane's already pale complexion. Then he witnessed the wheels turning inside Crane's head, but this was truly just a figure of speech. Finally, he watched Crane turn toward him and felt his eyes bore into him. That is, for the most part, an expression, but Pierce could actually feel the rage directed toward him.

"Randy," Crane hissed. "Let me see the mailing."

*Bad move,* thought Pierce. *You know something is wrong. You shouldn't invite me up here to share your stage. I learned that from you.* Pierce walked up to the microphones and handed Crane the brochure he had created and mailed. But Pierce did not sit down.

Another reporter asked, "Is there some dissension in the ranks?"

Without hesitating, Pierce leaned toward the microphones while Crane studied the brochure. "There is no disagreement that we need to protect the environment. But we can't get people to love nature and want to protect it if we take it away from them. And it has come to my attention that People for the Environmental Way has gone too far to make that happen."

The buzz that swept through the reporters told Pierce he had just moved this story from late in the newscast to early on. From page 8 to the bottom of page 1. The angle would be quite a bit different from what Crane had planned. Only a couple of the reporters had read Pierce's brochure, even though Pierce had made sure they all had a copy before the news conference. Now the ones who hadn't read it were digging through their notes to find a copy.

Grossman, as usual, was on top of the situation. "Now, you're the PEW intern, right? What kind of proof do you have that PEW was behind the baiting of these campsites?"

"As I wrote in the brochure, Les and I talked about how the bear raids on campsites played into our hands. His tone and expression made me uneasy so I started to look into phone records and e-mails from some of the more militant PEW members. I have copies of all that because I had to keep a daily journal to get college credit for this internship." As he talked, Pierce could sense Crane shuffling. And he saw Bernie Wilson slip away from the crowd.

"Les?" asked Grossman expectantly.

"This evidence is very weak," said Crane. His voice was surprisingly strong. "PEW has done nothing but draw attention to a rotten situation created by the Park Service and the rangers."

"Mr. Pierce, what about Jenny Patrick's campsite? Was it baited?"

Everyone was silent. Everyone stared at Randy Pierce. Pierce said nothing for a moment, then quietly said, "I could not find any proof of that one."

*No, I don't have any definite proof,* thought Pierce. *But Lester Crane always taught me that sometimes a little PR effort rumbles forth with a force all its own. We'll see if it shakes anything loose.*

"You see," yelled Crane. "He is full of nonsense. He doesn't have any proof. He is no expert on bears. This is sabotage. This news conference is over."

It was too late. The reporters had been following the story of PEW and Yellowstone so long that it was getting stale. Even the fresh news of the park's likely closing was just an updated twist on old news. But this new angle ... dissension in the ranks ... an intern blowing the whistle on PEW on the eve of its greatest victory. Now *this* was fresh. Pierce knew it would happen. He now owned the news conference.

"But you don't believe PEW had anything to do with the demise of Old Faithful," Grossman asked.

"Not even Lester Crane can cause an earthquake. But I don't doubt for a minute that he would do it if it meant gaining a political edge."

Crane stepped in front of Pierce. "I said this news conference is *over!*"

With that, he shoved Pierce off the small stage. The former intern hit the ground hard and skidded across the crumbly dirt. He stared up at his old boss and smiled. This story was now going to be the lead story on TV and above-the-fold in the papers.

"Thanks," said Pierce.

Officially the news conference was, indeed, over. The reporters moved forward to witness any additional physical confrontation that might occur and to ask numerous questions.

"Mr. Crane, how do you explain the phone records?" "Doesn't this type of guerilla tactic match the PEW reputation?" "How will this affect the proposed closing of Yellowstone?"

As smoothly as possible Crane tried to reassure the press corps that the phone records were coincidental at best and that PEW would never endorse tactics that bring bears and people together. And, yes, the park would close according to schedule.

About five yards away Pierce was listening to Crane's response. But he also had to handle the questions directed toward him.

"Mr. Pierce, how confident are you in your findings?" "What is your next move?" "Are you going to work to keep Yellowstone open?" "Do you fear a lawsuit?"

Slowly and deliberately, Pierce explained the evidence listed in the PEW brochure he hijacked.

"The calls are from a couple public telephones here in Gardiner." He pointed to two numbers that appeared repeatedly in a column. "Now, notice these dates next to the phone numbers. I have compared the dates of the calls with the dates bears raided campsites. See? Les talked to somebody out here just before and just after each raid."

"Any idea who he was talking to?" asked Grossman.

*You bet I do,* Pierce thought. *But I don't want Lester Crane to have a scapegoat yet.*

He cleared his throat. "PEW has dedicated volunteers all over the country. I couldn't identify this particular contact," he lied.

Pierce continued to answer a few more questions. When he saw Crane in the corner of his eye moving toward. him, he discretely moved in another direction. Crane was probably just going to apologize in an effort to save face, but Pierce wasn't going to give him the chance.

Suddenly a hand clamped on his shoulder. A tall, strong ranger was standing next to him. The man leaned forward and spoke into his ear.

"That took guts. Do you have an escape plan? Are you stranded?" asked the ranger.

"Yeah," admitted Pierce. "This took so much planning that I really didn't prepare for the next step. I guess I don't really care."

The ranger shook his hand. "My name is Joe Lowry. Follow me."

# NINETEEN

Steward walked alone along the beach toward Storm Point, a rocky formation on the north shore of Yellowstone Lake. In the distance across the lake posed Mount Sheridan. It was part of a range, but stood mostly by itself. In a park full of lovely peaks, mountains can start to look alike. But a few mountains in Yellowstone were distinctive. Avalanche Peak and Top Notch on the east side of Yellowstone Lake were notable. But Mount Sheridan to the south seemed to find its way into more photos.

"That's a beautiful mountain," Steward said to the marmots. The groundhog-type creatures perched on large rocks, at what they deemed a safe distance, and eyed him suspiciously. He turned back to look at the snow-covered mountain again.

The wind picked up, making the water choppy. The usual blue was gradually turning green, as it did when the wind blew hard. He could see whitecaps forming farther from shore. As the small waves came up to his boots he could see bubbles where tiny steam vents broke through the sand and the icy water. The woods behind him hissed as pine needles combed the wind.

Since sunrise he had been completely focused on the bear, which he had been trailing but had not yet found. Now, on the shore of Yellowstone Lake, with mountains in the background, he had a hard time keeping up the intensity. The beautiful wonders of the park always brought peace to the soul.

"It will be a shame that more people can't experience this," he told the marmots. "And they are going to lose their chance because of one damned bear and an even more damned Lester Crane."

That was enough. Forget about this cursed bear. It's time to settle a score with Lester Crane once and for all.

"What do you think?" he asked the large rodents. "Should I leave the bear alone and start hunting that goon from Washington?"

He approached the path that led to the end of the rocky point and chuckled at the handful of marmots that stood on rocks to hold their ground.

"Pretty brave little guys, aren't you? I've got a gun after all," he said with a laugh. Marmots were not dangerous. No firearms would be needed. With a few more steps they would scurry into their dens.

Instead he stopped.

On his path lay the severed leg of a marmot and a bit of the animal's entrails.

He looked up and saw that all the marmots were gone, suddenly. The hair on the back of his neck stood in warning.

He whirled around in time to see a bear racing out of the woods toward him at full gallop. It was a grizzly. *The* grizzly. *His* grizzly.

The beast was 30 yards away and closing fast. Steward swung his shotgun into firing position. He pulled the trigger just after the bear arrived.

The gun was knocked skyward, sending the shot, and gun, into the air. Steward was knocked backward, sending his breath into the air.

He curled into a ball, making it even more difficult to regain his breath but hopefully protecting his vital organs and nerves from the charging animal. The bear pounced and sunk its teeth into the ranger's shoulder. Pain fired through his arm and side. He screamed as the monster began to drag him, tearing at muscle, tendon and bone.

Steward pulled a hunting knife with his good arm and tried to plunge it into the bear's neck. He felt the blade entering fatty tissue but knew he had not hit anything critical. The bear began to shake his head the way a dog shakes a rag toy and Steward twisted the knife and buried it farther.

Suddenly the animal released him. Steward rolled away and quickly scrambled to his feet. His arm was now numb and his legs were shaking.

"Bastard!" he screamed as he tried to back away. The bear stared at him a moment, then lunged. Steward could not get away and was knocked backward into the frigid lake. The bone-chilling water began to drain away his energy. Yet he could feel pin-sized burns where tiny steam vents hissed out of the sand.

Neither the deathly cold water nor the scattered hot spots deterred the bear. It bit Steward's leg and pulled.

Steward slammed his other boot into the animal's nose. It dropped his leg and roared while pouncing again.

This time the beast landed on Steward's chest, pinning the man underwater. Steward felt the monster's teeth sink into his scalp and grind against his skull, peeling back a sizable flap of skin.

Instinctively, Steward lashed out with his knife again. This time striking the bear in the ear. Again, the animal released him and backed off.

Steward raised his head out of the water and gulped air. With his good arm he tried to push himself into a sitting position.

The bear roared and then stood. Its size was impressive. No. Terrifying. Half again as tall as Steward himself and easily five times as heavy. Its paws were the size of chair cushions. Beneath the silver-tipped, brown fur, the bear's muscles rippled. Layers of protective fat made the movement even more dramatic. It roared again.

Steward's eyes narrowed. His body was numb to his injuries because of the icy water. But those same injuries and the same icy water kept him nearly immobile.

With utter rage Steward summoned the last of his strength and yelled, "This is for mankind!" as he hurled his knife at the bear.

It bounced harmlessly off the animal's chest.

The animal dropped back to the water to make its final approach toward Steward.

Then Steward heard a loud pop. And another.

This time the bear's roar had a different sound. The

monster turned and stood again.

Steward looked past the bear to the edge of the woods and saw Lacy taking aim.

One more shot sounded and Steward saw the exit wound on the bear's back. The animal teetered backward and Steward tried to crawl away. The massive beast toppled over and landed on him, driving the ranger's face back into the rocks and sand under two feet of unmercifully cold water.

The ranger was completely immobilized. He struggled against the limp weight of the massive beast. The harder he fought the more difficult it was to hold his breath. He could feel the cold from the water begin to overtake him.

He quit struggling and closed his eyes to the darkness that overtook him.

**************

"Dusty!" screamed Lacy as the bear fell on top of him.

She had seen the horrifying injuries of her friend. Tears burned their way out of her eyes as she ran toward the carnage.

The bear lay still. She was not certain she could move the huge beast off Steward. She dropped her rifle on the beach and ran through the water to reach the scene, only about 10 feet from shore. Instantly she felt the numbing cold soak through her clothes.

Beneath the bear she saw one arm and a mangled leg. She threw her full weight against the animal. It budged. So she did it again. And again. One more push and she had Steward's limp body free.

Steward's body was much smaller than the bear, but still much larger than she. She wrestled his frame to shore and began CPR. Nothing was happening.

"Dusty, come back to me," she sobbed. Exhausted, she stopped just to hug him.

Then she heard splashing.

The bear stood on three feet. The fourth, an obviously painful front leg, was kept from holding any weight. Lacy knew she had hit that leg with her first shot. The animal's head was hanging down but its eyes were locked on her.

She stumbled away from Steward to draw the bear's attention away from him. Then she looked for her rifle. Immediately, she realized her mistake. The rifle lay in the other direction, near Steward.

The bear limped between the two rangers. Fortunately, she thought, its attention was on her. She supposed the smart action would have been to abandon Steward to save herself. He was a goner anyway. *But I can't.*

Beginning to regain her strength she backed away faster. The bear tried to run after her, but fell. It waited a moment, growled, then went after her again.

Its speed surprised her. Before she had time to react, it was on her, smashing her into the ground. The animal bit into her side, cracking a rib. She dug her fist into the bullet wound that she had put in the monster's chest. It let out a low howl of pain.

Then she felt an odd ripple go through the animal.

It jumped off her and she saw blood pouring from a new wound in its rear hip. It roared at her but did not move.

She heard a loud pop and saw the bear's lower jaw explode. She tasted the spray of blood that washed across her. The animal fell over and lay motionless.

She looked to where the sound came from and saw Steward, standing and holding her rifle. He swayed in place. He lowered the gun and used it to help himself sit.

Lacy crawled to her feet, fully feeling the pain in her side for the first time, and moved toward him in a limping, lurching jog.

When she got there she tried to check his vital signs but he grabbed her hands. She looked into his eyes as he whispered, "Thanks." Then, "I love you."

She was crying. "I love you too."

Instinctively she reached to hug him and hit his bad shoulder.

"Ahh!"

"Oh, I'm so sorry, Dusty."

He reached out to pat her and let her know it was okay. But he hit her bad side by accident.

She winced. "Oof."

They looked at each other and started to laugh. But that hurt. So they started to cry. But that hurt worse. So they just lay on the ground laughing, crying and hurting.

Finally, Steward said, "Now what the hell do we do?"

\*\*\*\*\*\*\*\*\*\*\*\*\*\*

"Dad? It's Randy."

"Are you okay? Where are you? You sound funny."

"Don't worry. I'm fine."

"So what do you need?"

"I just want to let you know that you may be seeing me on the news."

The phone was silent so he continued. "I quit my job in kind of a glorious fashion. Um, I don't know what all the fallout will be, but just don't worry about me. Okay?"

"Randy," his dad's voice cracked. "You're not really making me relax."

"I'm in Yellowstone right now and I'm with a ranger, but I'm not in trouble. I may be here a while but I will be coming home soon."

"Oh, thank God." There was silence on the line. Randy knew his dad was gathering his wits.

"So, what happens next?" the man asked.

"I'm going back to school. I'm going to continue the environmental program I was in."

"Okay." The voice on the phone was strained. He was obviously not happy but trying not to let it show.

"But, Dad, this time it will be different. I still think companies are hurting the environment, but I think the better way to fix it is to work from the inside. Not as a guerilla, but, you know, actually help them. I'm not a big fan of protesting anymore."

For the younger Pierce, this was pretty close to saying sorry. As many arguments as he had with his dad about the environment, this was a type of concession.

He heard his dad exhale, in relief.

"That sounds good, Randy. I'll see you, when? Tomorrow?"

Pierce chuckled. "It's big country out here. Three days at least."

The two exchanged hesitant goodbyes.

When the phone was hung up, Lowry came back into his office.

"How'd it go?" he asked.

"Pretty well I guess," replied Pierce. "Thanks for letting me use your phone. And thanks for suggesting I contact my family."

Lowry shrugged. "Now I've got to get on my radio and try and contact some of my Yellowstone family."

**\*\*\*\*\*\*\*\*\*\*\*\*\*\***

Crane had lost the news conference, but his spirit was enlivened. He would not go down without salvaging what he could. Truth be told, he was probably better when he was fighting than when he was winning.

"Where is he now?" he rhetorically asked the remaining reporters. "He makes unfounded accusations, sabotages a crucial informational mailing and then literally vanishes into the wilderness."

"Les, do you think PEW will recover from this setback? Will Congress and the President still close this park?" asked a reporter.

"I can say this, the problems of man's encroachment on nature continue. Right now poachers are moving in to illegally hunt and kill the nation's elk and moose. Any roadblock Randy Pierce caused will be easily crossed when I provide video evidence of this poaching."

Two of the TV cameras and one reporter had already left, but the remaining press corps scribbled and recorded.

"You have heard about the most recent poaching last night. That guy was caught by a bear. The next poacher will be caught by me."

As the reporters left, Crane followed them with his eyes. His intern gone, Crane was left to clean up the news conference himself. He boxed up the remaining media kits and papers. And he cleaned up the discarded coffee cups. Then he picked up a copy of the brochure. How had he not seen this coming? What went wrong?

*You won this little battle, Randy. But I am not finished. I will triumph in the end.*

Crane started making plans. It had been a while since he had ventured into the back country. Now he had to. But first he needed supplies. What supplies did he need? Where should he start? Where should he find these poachers he promised to catch?

The environmental warrior stared into the park as he pulled a Green Saver out of his pocket. After a moment he spit out the candy and began to dig through his waist pack for some aspirin.

*I've got work to do.*

**\*\*\*\*\*\*\*\*\*\*\*\*\*\*\***

"Dusty, Eva, come in. Where are you guys?" Lowry asked the radio, again.

Pierce sat next to him in the ranger truck, a white sport-utility vehicle with a wide, green stripe. Unlike its suburban counterparts, the SUV made regular trips off-road. Currently, it was still on the pavement, zipping along as fast as the many curves and hills would allow. Already they had been driving over an hour and trying to contact Steward and Lacy every few minutes.

"Do you know where they are supposed to be?" Pierce asked timidly.

"They called me about three hours ago," Lowry said tersely. He was obviously concerned. "They said they were headed to Storm Point and that they thought they were on the grizzly's trail."

Pierce sat quietly. He watched the incredible scenery pass by. It stunned him how he could be so uptight and so peaceful at the same time. Maybe it was the release from having the courage to act once he discovered that PEW was not the righteous organization he once thought it was. But more likely it was the peace that came from the shapely mountains, winding brooks and grazing animals that decorated Yellowstone.

Lowry's words jolted him from his calm. "I can't think of one good reason we haven't heard from them. But I can think of a thousand bad reasons."

Finally the truck reached the intersection on the north

side of Yellowstone Lake. They skidded around the corner, raced over the Fishing Bridge, and into the campground. With no traffic or campers in the park they easily found the rangers' parked trucks. Rennison's truck was there too.

Lowry and Pierce jumped out of their truck and looked around.

"Oh, God. That smell," gagged Pierce.

Lowry ran around the scene, eyes darting in every direction. He stopped and peered in Rennison's truck.

"That's the smell of death," Lowry said quietly. "Steward put the poacher in the truck with his trophies."

Pierce steadied himself on Lowry's truck and looked away from the poacher's resting place. The knot of nausea in his throat made breathing difficult.

Lowry continued to trot around the camping area in a widening spiral. Finally, he came back to Pierce.

"No bodies besides the one in that truck. Let's go."

The men climbed back into their truck and quickly drove east toward the Storm Point trail head.

In less than five minutes, Pierce blurted, "What the hell is that?"

"Is it them?" asked Lowry, breaking hard as they neared the trail.

The truck jerked to a stop and the men jumped out in an instant.

Eva Lacy sat by the side of the road, slumped over. Steward's head lay in her lap and his body was stretched out, but at strange angles. Neither was moving.

"Eva, Dusty. Talk to me," shouted Lowry as he carefully probed his colleagues, trying to assess the damage.

Pierce felt queasy. He had not yet recovered from the smell of the poacher, and now this. The injured rangers looked horrible. Their pale skin glistened faintly as if cold and clammy. Steward's open wounds were horrifying. His loose scalp hung like the rawhide on an abused baseball.

Lacy stirred.

"Eva! Eva!" Lowry begged a response.

She managed to lift her head. "It's about time."

"It's okay, Eva. I'm here now." He looked at each ranger's radio. "You weren't supposed to go swimming with these damned things. They don't work very well underwater."

She smiled. Then looked down at Steward and the tears began to flow. "I don't think he'll make it."

"I'm not giving up yet. But you gotta tell me, are we going to have to get through a big bear to get you out of here?"

Pierce startled. He had forgotten that the bear might still be out here. He immediately looked around, expecting a grizzly to come charging at them from any direction.

Lacy managed a faint chuckle. "Don't worry, Randy. We took care of him." Then she looked at Lowry. "Joe, what's he doing here?"

"He was a real trooper. You would have been proud of him. Dusty would have been proud of him. But we've got to get you out of here now or we'll never be able to tell you the story."

Lowry threw his keys to Pierce. "Randy, open the truck. I'm going to ride in the back using every bit of medical training I can remember. You're going to drive like hell to the Lake Hospital."

Without pause Pierce moved, trying to ready the SUV. Then, following Lowry's directions he helped lift the injured rangers into position. Once he was behind the wheel and stepping on the gas he finally spoke.

"Is it far?"

Lowry finished wrapping a tight-fitting bandage to teeth marks on Steward's arm. Then he looked up.

"Less than five miles. Just head back over the Fishing Bridge. Turn left. Then left again and follow the signs."

Pierce focused on the road and pressed the accelerator. He concentrated as well as he could in light of the distracting noises of groans, curses and rattling equipment.

"Is he breathing?" Pierce asked.

"Just drive," Lowry scolded.

When they roared into the hospital drive, Pierce gasped. "Nobody's here."

"Of course not," barked Lowry. "This was closed weeks ago. But I've got a key that should work and hopefully they still have a good stock of supplies on hand."

Lowry and Pierce rushed to the door, leaving their injured cargo in the truck. The key worked, not that Lowry would have hesitated to kick down the door if needed.

"Now, Randy, you are going to help me carry Eva and Dusty in here. Then you are going to get on the phone and call headquarters and every hospital in the area until you can get a decent doctor here."

"Where's the closest one?" asked Pierce.

"At least an hour. Probably more."

**************

"Sir, I finally found a copy of this. They'll probably start landing in people's mailboxes tomorrow," said the young staffer, handing over a crumpled copy of the new PEW brochure.

Senator Patrick slowly took the pamphlet and started reading it. He did not get very far before he started shaking his head.

"And this has just gone out in the mail?" Patrick asked.

"Yes, sir. That one I got from the mail house. It was damaged by the sorting machine and thrown away."

"This is what that intern was talking about at that news conference out west?" Patrick was confirming the details he already knew.

"Yes, sir."

Patrick let the staffer stand while he continued to read the brochure.

On the cover, a family of typical tourists, complete with cameras and maps, stood in front of a beautiful mountain vista. But they faced toward the reader, oblivious to the view behind them. And even if they had turned to the mountains they would not have seen the peaks because their eyes were covered by bright orange PEW stickers.

Below this graphic large letters proclaimed, "Sorry. But we have gone too far."

Inside, under the headline "Baiting bears? Shame on us," the PEW intern detailed his suspicions of how Lester Crane had contacted PEW operatives in Yellowstone to leave food buried in campgrounds to attract bears. As evidence he listed phone logs and bits of conversations he had overheard from Crane's office. He tried to compare that with reported bear incidents in the park.

*Kind of weak evidence,* thought Patrick, *but effective enough to plant doubt about PEW tactics.* For that matter, it was not much of a stretch to believe the always-militant PEW would do such a thing. Unfortunately, a lot of the people on PEW's mailing list would probably applaud the bear baiting.

The people who might be disturbed by such a revelation are the moderate environmentalists, and the policymakers. This could make the powerful people hesitate before following the PEW line. *And it's working,* thought Patrick.

Throughout the remainder of the brochure, Randy Pierce – Patrick noted that he had been man enough to sign it at the end – questioned the wisdom of trying to keep people out of parks. Apparently Pierce decided the PEW line on Yellowstone was wrong and that the public was going to pay the price. And in fact the park would be better off if people continued to be a part of it. He sounded kind of like that ranger who had been on the Sunday TV show.

But if Pierce's arguments were sound, Patrick couldn't focus on them. As he tried to concentrate on the end of the brochure his mind continued to return to the early part.

*They baited campsites to attract bears?*

*Jenny?*

Finally, he placed the brochure on his desk and looked at his staffer.

"Please set up a meeting with the senators working on the Yellowstone appropriation," Patrick said quietly. "If they saw any of the coverage on that news conference, I think they will understand the urgency of this matter."

"Yes, sir," he said and walked briskly out the door.

As Patrick watched him leave, he felt the rage boiling from his gut to the top of his head. That subsided enough for sorrow to take over. The anguish that he had just recently begun to get a grip on, now was prevailing again. He looked at the photo of Jenny that sat on his desk.

A tap on the door shook him back to the present.

"What now?"

The staffer peered around the door. "Senator, I've got a call you may want to take. I've been trying to get rid of him, knowing you're busy and all, but … well … He says it's about Jenny and he sounds like he might know something."

Patrick stared at the phone. Information about his daughter usually ruined his day. Details of that horrible event absolutely crushed his spirit. He was about to tell his staffer to say he was gone, but he changed his mind and picked up the phone. The staffer backed out of the office, leaving Patrick, the phone and the memories of Jenny alone.

"This is Senator Patrick."

"Yes ... uh ... You don't know me. But I used to work at Yellowstone ... with your daughter. I knew Jenny pretty well." The voice was of a young man, probably in his twenties. It's amazing how accurately you can judge a person's age by the tone of his voice, the inflection of words, the phrases.

The caller continued. "I was camping with Jenny that night before ... You know."

"What's your name?"

"I'd rather not tell you that right now."

"Okay." Patrick would let him play that way if he felt more comfortable. The senator smiled lightly. He had read the accident report. If the caller was telling the truth, he was one of only two young men who camped that night. This could be verified easily enough.

"I should have said something earlier, but I'm a big supporter of the environment," the voice said.

"A lot of Jenny's friends were," Patrick said calmly. Keep the guy relaxed.

"I didn't want to interfere with other things that were happening. You know?"

"I understand." Patrick spoke more patiently than he felt.

"Then I heard on the news about that latest PEW brochure and it got me thinking. I mean, I never dreamed they would do something like that. I practically tithe PEW." The voice became more agitated. "And I never saw him do anything. But he lingered there longer than the rest of us. You know … before we hiked out. And … and …"

"Just relax, son. Who are you talking about?"

Patrick heard a deep breath. Then the voice said, "There was one other person camping with us that night. Somebody we didn't mention to the rangers."

# TWENTY

Lacy answered her urgent summons and limped into the Ranger station at Mammoth Hot Springs. A flurry of activity greeted her. Half a dozen rangers and some men in FBI jackets scrambled around the cramped office space.

"Eva, over here."

She turned to see Lowry in a corner with Randy Pierce. Two of the FBI agents scribbled on note pads. She joined the gang.

"Anything new on Dusty?"

She shook her head. Then, to Pierce, she said, "Thanks again for your help."

"He was just finishing a debriefing. Then he's going home," said Lowry as he slapped the former PEW intern on the back.

Pierce smiled but didn't say anything.

"What else is going on here," she asked the ranger. "Why do they need me?"

"Our guests here," he gestured to the FBI agents, "are looking for Bernie Wilson."

"What's up?" She noticed that Pierce suddenly sat up

straight and took notice.

"They want to ask him some questions about baiting campgrounds for bears. Those guys over there are organizing a manhunt strategy."

She saw agents and rangers pouring over topographical maps of Yellowstone. Some drew lines and pointed at each other, establishing a chain of command, perhaps.

"You didn't tell me they were looking for Bernie," said Pierce. "He ought to be easy to catch."

His voice must have carried farther than he anticipated. Everyone in the room stopped what they were doing and stared at him expectantly.

"Did you use your regular radio frequency to call all these people here?" He gestured to the group.

Lowry nodded.

"Did you say specifically who you were looking for?"

"No, Randy. We just called all rangers on duty to report here. And we called in a couple who were off duty." He pointed to Lacy. "We didn't give any details."

Pierce cleared his throat. "I guess I know as well as anybody how people like that think. Crane always praised Bernie for getting the fastest information about what was going on. To know what the rangers are up to, you listen to their radio frequencies and then follow the excitement. If this is where the action is, he's probably right outside."

Silence. Then, as if connected, all the heads turned toward the front window.

Pierce was the first to speak. "Isn't that him, across the street, with the binoculars?"

The ranger station door burst open like a fault in a levy, and out poured a reservoir of law enforcement.

**************

Crane mumbled to himself as he picked up a few supplies from the Gardiner grocery store. Some nuts and raisins for trail mix. An extra set of batteries for his flashlight. Several packages of Ramen noodles. And, of course, some toilet paper.

At the checkout he informed the manager, in a voice most displeased, that the store should carry toilet paper made out of recycled, unbleached paper.

"Considering what we do with this stuff, it's hardly worth cutting down new trees and running it through chemicals is it?"

"I understand, sir. But most of the people who shop in my store prefer the white, fluffy paper that they rub on cute baby faces on television," replied the store manager. It sounded polite enough, but it was obvious that he didn't really care what Crane thought.

Crane had dealt with enough of these people over the years. They failed to recognize the power of the environmental movement or the power of a great environmentalist. But he didn't have time to teach this guy a lesson. He paid for his collection, then slapped an orange PEW sticker on the door on his way out.

Once back to his rental car Crane evenly distributed the new acquisitions throughout his backpack. The pack would be his source of livelihood for the next few days. He would be carrying it everywhere he went and that would be miserable if the pack leaned one way or the other.

On the east side of Gardiner Crane parked the car, hoisted the pack onto his back, and started along the Black Canyon trail. Bernie Wilson had recommended the trail as a good spot to catch a poacher.

*Keep up the good work, Bernie.* Crane looked forward to Wilson joining him, after the younger environmental warrior found out what all the hubbub was about at the Mammoth Ranger station. *Just keep the info flowing, buddy. At least* you *did not betray me.*

He paused. *How could Randy do that to me? Or, more importantly, how did I not see it coming?* Crane hefted the pack on his shoulders one more time and began his march along the trail.

The path follows the Yellowstone River from Gardiner, through a small stand of trees, and along steep canyon walls. As hikers continue, the trail presents other, more varied views. Meadows, forest, rugged rocks, a quiet Yellowstone River, a raging Yellowstone River, bright blue ponds, flower-covered hillsides. It's as if at every turn the trail says, "Look what else I can do."

Try as it might the trail could not get Crane's attention. He was focused.

\*\*\*\*\*\*\*\*\*\*\*\*\*\*

"Boy, Eva. I've seen you look better," said Tom Rich, the Gardiner grocery store manager.

"Thanks, Tom." Eva Lacy smiled at him. Her bathroom mirror told the story. She had seen the purple, swollen eye. She had seen the bulky gauze bandage protruding from the top of her collar, protecting the one-inch-from-fatal laceration on her neck. The tape job securing her cracked ribs and the bandages and stitches covering bite wounds and scraps on her arms, legs and torso were not visible. But the pain constantly reminded her of their presence.

"Imagine how it feels," she added.

Lacy knew Rich since she started working at the park three years ago. Though millions of people visited the park each year, few people actually lived at the borders year-round. The park's perennial residents tended to know each other. There were only so many bars, restaurants and grocery stores. Lacy bought food, so she knew Tom Rich.

She noted that Rich's eyes drifted from her wounds to the two men in matching hiking outfits and the young, rumpled local who had come in with her. The strangers were wearing durable boots, black heavy nylon pants and jackets. The jackets sported large white letters reading FBI. She was sure he had noted them as soon as they came in but he acknowledged Lacy first out of local courtesy. He didn't even look at the other local, the young man.

She handled the introductions. "Tom, these are agents Clark and Williams from the FBI." She noted Rich's expression become even more serious. "They want to know if you've seen this guy." She handed him a photo of Lester Crane.

"Yeah, I saw him. Is this the guy in the paper?"

She nodded. On the way in the store she had noticed that the story about the PEW fiasco was above-the-fold in the *Billings Gazette*.

"He was in here early this morning," continued the Gardiner store manager. "He picked up food, batteries, matches. You know, the stuff to go into the back country for a couple nights."

He waited a moment and then added, "And I'm pretty sure I've seen him with Bernie Wilson there." He nodded toward the disheveled youth standing between the agents.

"You know Mr. Wilson?" asked agent Williams.

"He hangs around a lot," shrugged Rich.

"Do you have any idea where the man in the photo was going?" agent Williams inquired.

Lacy broke in. "Bernie has not been as helpful as he should be."

"It's hard to say where he might go, Eva. What was he after?"

"We think he might be trying to catch poachers on tape."

Rich thought for a moment. "Black Canyon is close by. He could follow a trail instead of bushwhacking."

"That was my guess too." She looked toward Bernie Wilson, who was avoiding eye contact.

The two FBI agents thanked Rich and led Wilson out to a waiting car.

Rich nodded. "Wish I could help you more."

Lacy turned to leave and winced in pain.

"Eva, what are you doing out here. Shouldn't you still be in the hospital?" asked Rich.

"Yeah, Tom. I probably should be. But I've got to see this through."

"Are you really going to go trudging along the trail? You're in no shape for that."

Tears welled up in her eyes. "I've got to get Lester Crane. I can't count on the FBI guys to do it without me."

Rich reached out and gingerly patted her shoulder. "How's Dusty?"

"Not good. But I just don't know."

"Good luck, Eva."

She took a deep breath to regain her composure and left the store.

Outside, Lacy conferred with the agents for a moment. She climbed back into her truck to lead them to the start of the Black Canyon Trail.

***************

"This year, they ain't gonna laugh at Matt Wise," Matt Wise told his horse.

Two hunting seasons in a row, no deer. Of the guys

with whom he hunted and drank -- these activities were not always done at the same time, but not always separately either -- everyone else had bagged at least one in his home state of Michigan. And several of the guys had gotten deer with shotgun *and* bow. But Wise had nothing to show for the cold mornings spent in a tree stand.

To make matters worse, last year he hit a deer with his car.

This brought much howling around pitchers of beer. "You couldn't shoot him so you run him down?" Screaming laughter, followed by "All this time I been hunting with Dale Ernhardt." And "Hey, can I turn in my gun for a steering wheel?" And "Gives a whole new meaning to 'riding shotgun' don't it?" Haw haw haw.

When he found a web site about hunting near Yellowstone, he figured he found his way to save face. He drove to Cody with a list of hunting guides, thinking he could convince at least one to do some "special" guiding. His first contact was a well-known guide named Pete Crummel. But Crummel said "no way," and Wise thought he might have wasted a long drive west. That night his phone rang. Bingo. A different guy, must have been a friend of Crummel, called and was willing to take him in the park.

Wise eagerly signed up for a hunting trip that was definitely illegal, but almost guaranteed to net him a big deer or elk. Ranger patrols were so few that the chances of getting caught were slim at best. It cost plenty. But he knew it would be worth it.

"Buttheads," he said to his horse but about his friends. "I'm going to bring back the biggest set of racks they ever seen and shove 'em up their asses."

His guide, Travis Raines, was back about a mile setting up camp as Wise rode around looking for a kill. Based on what the guide told him and the rough map in his pocket he knew he was near the northern park boundary, close to a pond where elk came to drink.

As he neared the trees he dismounted to tie his horse and continue on foot. The trees were too thick for riding. Besides, he needed to stretch his legs anyway. Removing his shotgun from its scabbard he walked toward where he thought the pond should be.

A rustling sound up ahead froze him. He slowly brought up his gun and continued toward the noise. He heard it again, about 120 yards ahead.

His guide had told him he didn't need to shoot at the first animal he saw. Elk are plentiful, he said. The patient hunter has the luxury of waiting for a closer shot, or a bigger bull, if he so chooses. But coming from his Midwest perspective of small hunting areas and limited seasons, he didn't believe it. Not enough to take a chance.

Wise was not hunting to gun down an elk. He was hunting to gun down his embarrassment. Two years without a deer? Not since he had first started hunting. And not this year dammit.

He steadied himself against a tree and aimed toward the rustling bush. And waited.

Suddenly, he saw the white flash of a deer's tail. The sign they give to run. Not this time. He adjusted his aim toward the white and squeezed the trigger.

He heard the thud of the animal falling. But something was wrong. A large deer, elk, moose or whatever should make a pretty loud thump. This didn't sound large at all. Did he get a fawn? God, the guys back home would give him hell about that.

Deciding to hide the evidence of a dead baby deer from his guide, who somehow might tell his friends, he trotted toward his kill.

At the scene the blood left his face and the strength left his legs. He dropped to his knees and worked on regaining his breath.

Before him lay a man with long hair and a beard, one of those tree-hugger types, but older than most. He lay chest down but with his head turned to the side. A bloody hole decorated the middle of his back, a clean shot scoring an instant kill. A video camera and backpack lay to one side. The man's pants were around his ankles and in his right hand was a wad of bleached, non-recycled toilet paper.

# TWENTY-ONE

"What the hell did you do!?" yelled Travis Raines. He was staring at the dead man lying in the bushes.

"I thought he was a deer," squeaked Matt Wise defensively.

"You just shoot at the first thing that moves? Thank God I didn't come riding up to check on you. I might be lying there instead of him."

"We gotta hide him."

Raines sadly shook his head. How did he get involved in this? He had always thought being a hunting guide would be easy. After all, he was a pretty good hunter himself. Tracking elk, moose and mule deer wasn't too tough. Then, all you have to do is take newcomers around to where the animals are. And those people pay you good money to do it. Certainly poaching would be even easier, especially when nobody would be around to catch them.

But from the start this had been a bad idea. Matt Wise, his very first client, was an idiot. First he talked endlessly about how great Michigan was. Then he complained about how bad his Michigan friends were. Who cares about any of it? *Just pay me the money and be quiet.*

Finally, after a long, cold journey, they reached a spot that Raines was sure would have some trophy elk. And Wise shoots at the first movement he sees and kills a person. Now he wants to hide the body.

"Matt, we're in it now." Raines was struggling to keep his voice nice and even. "We were breaking the law by being here in the first place. It was a bad idea and you just made it worse. But this isn't the kind of thing you can hide. You killed somebody."

"It was a damned accident." His tone was rising and his eyes looked wild. "My friends in Michigan will never let me live this down. Nobody can find out about this."

"Forget about your friends. Just look at this guy." Raines jabbed his finger toward the dead body. He was losing his controlled tone. "We gotta call the rangers or somebody. You screwed up and now you need to take it like a man."

"No way! You can just join that little pissant on the ground." Wise swung up his rifle and pointed it toward Raines' chest.

Raines had left his gun by his horse. He was trapped.

"Drop it!" came a yell from on top of a nearby hill.

Both men startled and looked to the sound. Two men in uniform-type hiking clothes and a woman in a ranger's outfit were pointing weapons at them.

Raines slowly and deliberately raised his hands. Wise hesitated, then set down his rifle and raised his own hands.

Raines saw the white FBI lettering on the men's jackets. He let out a breath of relief and gladly subjected himself to the handcuffs while he volunteered to offer any information he could. Then he stared darkly at Wise.

"Try that again sometime without the gun," he said. It must have sounded like the threat he intended because Wise shrunk back.

As they were being seated, apart from each other, Raines watched the agent and the ranger examine the body of the dead guy. He also noticed that even while they were studying the situation, they kept an eye on Wise and him. They stayed in position so they could react quickly if either capture tried to make a run for it. He hoped Wise would try. It would serve that jerk right to get shot trying to escape.

After a while, the ranger woman said something to one of the FBI agents about leaving to visit a friend in the hospital. The men thanked her and she rode away.

"Man, she looks like she's been roughed up pretty bad," he said to the nearest agent.

"That's not your concern," said the agent sternly. "Now, let's start with your name and your reason for being out here."

★★★★★★★★★★★★★★★

Dusty Steward opened his eyes. Lights. Tubes. Strange machines. He felt bandages wrapped around his head, arms, legs and various parts of his body. He tried to lift his head. Then he felt pain.

"Ugh."

Suddenly he saw the somewhat battered face of Eva Lacy, staring down at him. She was smiling.

"You staying with us this time?" she asked.

"It depends. Where am I?"

She chuckled. "Yesterday when you asked me that, I told you we were in the hospital in Jackson. Last night when you asked me, I told you the same thing. And now. Well, where would you like to be?"

"Um, in your arms?"

She smiled, but it left her face quickly. "Dusty, you have been going in and out of consciousness for two days now." She appeared very concerned and tears were forming in the corners of her eyes. "I've been so worried. I've told you that several times, too. So, are you staying with us this time?"

Steward grinned, as well as he could. "I almost remember talking to you before. I think I'm with you this time for sure." He looked around. It didn't hurt as much this time. He was obviously in a hospital room. But in Jackson?

Remarkably, he felt pretty good. Pretty alert.

"How did we get here?"

She was smiling at him but the tears were maturing rapidly. "Do you remember the bear?"

He grimaced and nodded.

"How about crawling from Storm Point to the road?"

He looked at his bandaged hands. Something had happened to them, but it was a fog. He shook his head.

"We were about to bleed out at the side of the road when Joe and that Randy Pierce kid drove up, out of nowhere," she prompted. "They were great. Joe got us to the Lake Hospital and held us together until an ambulance could get us down here."

"Randy Pierce? What the hell was he doing here?"

"Oh, Dusty. You wouldn't believe it." Her smile widened. "We won."

"Huh?"

She reached across his body and pushed the call button. A nurse responded quickly.

"Ranger Steward is ready," she told the small speaker. Then she kissed Steward on the cheek.

When her eyes moved to the doorway, Steward's followed. He gasped as Senator Patrick walked in.

"Ranger Steward, I'm so pleased to see you are doing better," said the senator, his strong, deep voice filling the small room. "I have to thank you for many things."

Steward stammered, "I don't really know what is going on right now and I have to–"

Patrick held up a hand. "Don't worry. I understand. Let me help bring you up to speed. Randy Pierce was impressed by you and Ranger Lacy. To the point that he started to question the PEW activities."

As Patrick described the brochure and the accusations within, Steward's eyes widened.

"So PEW was responsible for those campsite bear problems," said Steward. "I wondered, but I didn't think even PEW would go that far."

"I had been giving them the benefit of a doubt too,"

said Patrick. "The public was supporting PEW, local residents were supporting PEW. So Congress was supporting PEW. But they pushed their luck. When they had the momentum they couldn't help themselves."

Steward pondered that. Then, despite great pain, he sat up. "What about your daughter? Were they involved?"

Patrick turned to the window. Lacy lightly held Steward's hand.

"Do you know Bernie Wilson?" asked Lacy.

"That wormy guy who is always hanging around the ranger stations? The one who pushed in to that news conference at Old Faithful?"

She nodded. "He purposely left out food at Jenny Patrick's campsite."

"But we talked to the kids who camped with her the night before. They didn't say anything about Bernie Wilson."

"He convinced them that keeping quiet about him would be a great way to save the environment."

"But still–" Steward protested.

She held up her hand. "Dusty, those kids didn't know Bernie was leaving smelly food in the area. When Pierce's accusations were reported one of the other campers broke his pledge to Bernie."

Steward was puzzled. "I knew Bernie was a PEW supporter, but most of the young people working out here are PEW supporters. Was he really acting on Crane's behalf? What does Crane say about it?"

Lacy glanced over to Patrick, who was still staring out the window.

"Crane was killed yesterday. A poacher thought he was a deer and shot him."

Steward was shocked. "Wow. Lester Crane is dead." He could hardly believe it. The room was quiet as Steward considered the news. Then he added, "But Crane doesn't look much like a deer."

"It's a long story," she said. "Anyway, the FBI put some pressure on Bernie Wilson who has pretty much confessed to working with Crane to get this thing started. At first he was reluctant to talk, but now he's preaching as if he and Lester Crane are great martyrs for the environment."

"Now what?" asked Steward.

Patrick turned around, his eyes were red and moist. "Here is where I come in. As soon as I found out what PEW had been up to, I contacted my colleagues. Not one of them wanted to be associated with a PEW-led policy. They have decided to back off closing the park for at least another year. Probably longer."

Lacy smiled at Steward and kissed him on a small part of his forehead that was not bandaged.

"Starting in the spring, we're open for business again," she said.

Steward said nothing. He smiled at Lacy, once again admiring her beauty, even with a swollen eye and a couple bandages. Then he turned to Patrick.

"Thank you."

"Ranger Steward, most people will probably never know how important you were to this park. For a while you were the lone voice calling for us to protect the park by using it. Finally it is sinking in." Patrick paused.

"I had the chance to talk to Park Superintendent Lightfeather," Patrick continued. "He told me about your dedication. Then he also told me about your special assignment. One that you seem to have won by default. He said you are usually the person who calls the families of people who die in the park."

Steward nodded but didn't say anything.

"When Jenny was killed," Patrick choked and was quiet for a moment. "I'm sorry. I still have trouble saying that."

Steward and Lacy waited patiently.

"When that happened, I was notified by the Secretary of the Interior. I suppose it was a protocol kind of affair. But I wonder what you would have told me if you had called instead."

Steward looked steadily at the senator. He reached the adjustment button on the bed and slowly maneuvered into a more comfortable sitting position. Lacy poured him a cup of water and he took a sip.

"Senator, I'm not exactly sure how I ended up being the guy to call grieving families. I don't especially like it. But a couple of times the families I talked to reported back to the boss that I had made them feel better." He looked at the ceiling and shook his head. "I'm kind of grumpy by nature so I don't know how I could have been very reassuring. I don't have any magic words or anything like that."

He returned his gaze to Patrick. "If I had been the one to call you after finding Jenny's body I would have first told you how genuinely sorry I was. And that is more than just a line. I really think people are important."

Patrick looked at his feet. It was obvious he was still listening so Steward continued.

"Then I would have told you about where Jenny was when she died. She had been camping near Turbid Lake, not far from Yellowstone Lake. The air is crisp and clear. In the morning you are chilled, even in the summer. In the middle of the day, the sun is warm but never scorching hot. At night the skies reveal more stars than you could count in 10 lifetimes. If you're standing on the shore of Yellowstone Lake on a clear night you can see the white, shimmering reflection of the moon from the far shore all the way to your feet. If the moon isn't out, you can see the reflection of the Milky Way. Turbid Lake can display equally breathtaking sites.

"Near her campsite, she would have smelled the fragrance of pine. For years car air fresheners have tried to copy that scent, and she would have realized that they haven't even come close. When the wind shifted she could have caught the odor of sulfur. By itself, sulfur is not a pleasant smell. But with the understanding that the odor was coming from miraculous hot springs bubbling out of the earth and that she was in a rare spot in the world to be able to smell it, the scent of sulfur is exquisite."

Steward couldn't help but become animated. Thoughts of the park always gave him energy. He sat straighter and continued.

"Nearby, animals that most people only see in books graze on the grass, or fly through the air. Mountains that always wear decorations of snow stand in the background of nearly every view. It is impossible to step into Yellowstone and not be touched, deeply, by everything around you.

"So the passing of your daughter was tragic. But she was surrounded by beauty and was being enriched by it all, right up to the final moment. And just as important, the park was made better by her presence, by her being able to enjoy what it offered."

Steward let out a breath and looked at Patrick. The senator was smiling faintly and had a tear in the corner of one eye. Steward held out a bandaged hand.

"That's what I would have said."

Patrick took his offered hand and shook it gently. "And I would have appreciated it. Thanks."

The two men looked at each other a minute longer without talking. Patrick said he had to head back to Washington to finalize details and excused himself from the room. Steward looked over to Lacy, who also had tears in her eyes.

"What? What did I say? Why is everybody so weepy?" exclaimed Steward.

"Oh, Dusty. You're something else," and she hit him on the shoulder.

"Ow! Stop that."

She ignored him. "Do you realize you saved the park?"

He shrugged. "Whatever was done, we did it together. But the thing is, Eva, we still have a problem with the park."

"How could I forget?" She hit the edge of the bed.

"Old Faithful is still out of order."

"And people might be inclined to stay away from the park," he concluded. "The damage was done by Crane. I hope we can get people to come back."

# TWENTY-TWO

## EPILOGUE

Near the northeastern shore of Yellowstone Lake, still ice-covered until summer, lay a narrow, rutted road that leads visitors up a winding path to Lake Butte. Most tourists would drive by the road without ever noticing it was there, despite the small, wooden sign pointing the way.

But if they knew what they were looking for and traveled the short side trip they would discover a small parking area where generations of tourists and employees watched magnificent sunsets. If they had asked any park employee where to view a sunset in the park, they were always directed to Lake Butte.

But not today. In mid May there were few tourists to visit the lookout, and only a handful of employees to direct them there. The park's summer season was not yet underway. Besides, the road would normally still be snowed in. And on this day, despite the fact that the road had been uncharacteristically cleared with a snow plow, they would not have been admitted to the parking area without an invitation. Not just anyone was allowed to stand on the cliff to watch nature's paint show this evening.

Eva Lacy was there, dressed in a lovely white parka and veil. Dusty Steward was there, in a black parka and bow tie. And an assortment of rangers and locals filled out the rest of the guests.

As the sun dropped behind the Gallatin Range, the sky yellowed to the color of lemons. The few clouds in the sky were painted bright red on the bottom, as if they had been dipped into candy-apple syrup. These colors were reflected and refracted across the still-frozen lake surface until it appeared as if someone had sprinkled multicolored glitter over the ice and snow. Gradually, the sky turned more orange, then dark.

The gathered guests applauded, though it wasn't clear if they were cheering for the sunset or the presentation of Mr. and Mrs. Dusty Steward.

Given the excitement of the evening, and the vanishing light, the guests had to be forgiven for not wandering around in the nearby woods. But had they ventured into the trees, they might have discovered a short corrugated metal tube sticking out of the ground. The tube was covered by a locked lid bearing a sign. The sign, like the tube, was placed by the U.S. Geological Survey. It pleaded with explorers not to touch or bother the tube, which contained sensitive seismological equipment.

Inside the tube, after the sun had finished its production and moved on to entertain other parts of the world, and after the guests were preparing to entertain themselves at a nearby reception, the sensitive seismological equipment stirred. If the revelers felt anything, they attributed it to the excitement of the wedding.

Otherwise, the slight earth tremor had little effect.

Except on the other end of the park.

The Upper Geyser Basin was vacant of people until tomorrow, when the employees and rangers would continue getting it ready for visitors. But it was a favorite year-round feeding ground for park bison.

Heads down, not that they would have cared anyway, the bison didn't notice the increased steam and the small bursts of water coming from the world's most famous inactive geyser. Nor did they notice that the bursts of water increased in intensity and size until one of the spouts reached 175 feet.

They continued feeding as Old Faithful lay silent again.

Eighty-five minutes later, as the geyser belched out a 150-foot eruption, the bison took no notice.

Within the next 75 minutes, several bison had wandered off to find a warmer place to sleep, and Old Faithful erupted again, about 100 feet high.

The 100-foot mark was reached again 70 minutes later.

Following that regular interval, the geyser, the symbol of Yellowstone, erupted again. And again.

And again ...

## Acknowledgments

A special thanks is extended to all the employees who maintain Yellowstone as an outstanding place to visit. Above all, thanks to God for creating it in the first place.

Additional appreciation goes to Lee Whittlesey for setting me straight about ranger hierarchy. As the pre-eminent historian and archivist for the area he is a source for much great information. In addition, a true study of Yellowstone is not complete without both volumes of *The Yellowstone Story* by Aubrey L. Haines. *The Grizzly Bear* by Thomas McNamee is a good source for bear info.

Many thanks to the Michiana Writers Workshop for the helpful suggestions. And a huge thank you to the folks who hiked, climbed and forded with me in Yellowstone, including my wife, Shawn, who encouraged and supported this endeavor.

## About the Author

*Kyle Hannon worked as a front desk clerk in Yellowstone's Lake Lodge during his college years. His hiking exploits took him over hundreds of miles of trails in Yellowstone and the Tetons.*

*Hannon earned a political science degree from Ball State University and graduate degrees in public affairs from Indiana University. Out in the real world, he worked in government and politics in the Indiana State House.*

*In addition to* The Yellowstone Faithful, *Hannon is the author of* The Break Room *and pens a weekly column for* The Elkhart Truth *in Northern Indiana.*

*Yellowstone is still his favorite vacation spot.*